SUDDEN DEATH

Suffer and Grow Strong: The Life of Ella Gertrude Clanton Thomas, 1834–1907

SUDDEN DEATH

A Novel

Carolyn Newton Curry

MERCER UNIVERSITY PRESS
Macon, Georgia

MUP/ H1026

26 25 24 23 22   5 4 3 2 1

Books published by Mercer University Press are printed on acid-free
paper that meets the requirements of the American National
Standard for Information Sciences—Permanence of Paper for
Printed Library Materials.

Printed and bound in Canada.

This book is set in Adobe Caslon Pro

Cover/jacket design by Burt&Burt.

ISBN   Print   978-0-88146-850-2
ISBN   eBook   978-0-88146-851-9
Cataloging-in-Publication Data is available from the Library of Congress

Sudden Death is a work of fiction. All incidents and dialogue, and all
characters with the exception of some well-known historical figures, are
products of the author's imagination and are not to be construed as
real. Where real-life historical persons appear, the situations, incidents,
and dialogues concerning those persons are entirely fictional and are not
intended to depict actual events or to change the entirely fictional nature
of the work. In all other respects, any resemblance to persons living or
dead is entirely coincidental.

To my husband Bill, who is very much alive and well,

all my love and gratitude

MERCER UNIVERSITY PRESS

Endowed by

TOM WATSON BROWN
and
THE WATSON-BROWN FOUNDATION, INC.

Weeping may linger for the night,
But joy comes with the morning.

Psalm 30:5

A Note to the Reader

I was in Hawaii twenty years ago with my husband Bill, where he had the job of broadcasting the college all-star game called the Hula Bowl with ESPN. It was "tough duty" for him, and I felt that I should accompany him. While he worked, I had a lot of leisure time. I picked up a yellow legal pad and started writing a novel. I was a historian, had never written a novel, and knew nothing about the craft. I did have a lot of life experiences being the wife of a football player who went from pro football into coaching and stayed in the profession for twenty-seven years. I knew about the joy and excitement but also the stress and anxiety. I also had the experience of trying to balance going to graduate school, raising two children, and moving frequently. The story just poured out onto the paper. I ended up filling two legal pads front and back. I enjoyed it.

When I came home, the two legal pads were filed away, and I didn't pick them up until I was cleaning out a closet at the beginning of the pandemic in 2020. I decided to put what I had written into a Word document. After I copied the two pads, I kept writing and didn't stop for months. I have often said this book was a godsend during the months of lockdown. It got my mind off the trouble in the world and kept me busy. I have referred to it as my COVID-19 novel.

I want everyone to know that this book is a work of fiction. All the characters are taken from my imagination. Any resemblance to any individual is purely coincidental. I tried to get as far away from reality as possible. Thankfully, my husband Bill was not shot on the football field. But he did receive death threats at three different universities, and I received a death threat at one. Other coaches' wives have told me of threats to their families. Coaches we know have been hung in effigy and had their dogs shot. Unfortunately, we have had presidents and entertainers assassinated in this country. One of our players at Kentucky, who was sitting on his porch visiting with friends on his twenty-first birthday, was shot and killed by another student who was hiding in bushes across the street. Is it possible that a coach could be shot? I hope that never happens, but I did decide to explore the question in this book.

I write about more than simply football. One issue of particular interest is the epidemic of spouse abuse in our country. I also talk about problems with addiction to gambling and alcohol, as well as the proliferation of guns.

As a historian, I have always been drawn to strong women who overcome great difficulty. It is only natural that I would want to create fictional females with similar characteristics. Also, I want to tell the stories of brave men and women who try to do the right thing and make a difference in this world. Yes, it is a love story, too.

My husband was the head football coach at four universities in the South—Georgia Tech, Alabama, Kentucky, and Georgia State University. I purposely created a fictitious university and town as the setting for this story. It is simply a university in the South where football is of paramount importance. That would apply to any number of schools in any part of our country.

I hope men and women both enjoy my story and, hopefully, learn something, too.

One more thing: The NCAA first passed the tie-breaker rule in February 1996. A college football game could no longer end in a tie. Starting on the twenty-five-yard line, each team would be given an opportunity to score. If one team scores a touchdown and the extra point, and the other team scores and attempts a two-point conversion and fails, they lose. It is sudden death. Fans are accustomed to it now, but that year it was a new phenomenon. I wanted to point this out because of its central importance to the book.

PROLOGUE

November 1996

Chapter 1

As she inched into the lot toward the VIP section, Kendall noted that parking was slower than usual. She almost rear-ended a fan's car but slammed on the brakes just in time. She was exhausted when she finally reached her parking spot. Walking through the lot, she had to go past the tailgaters cooking hamburgers, holding up wings dripping in barbeque sauce, and waving beers in her face. She nodded, gave a weak smile, and said, "No, thank you." The thought of eating made her nauseous. She was always nervous before a game, but it was worse today. When she reached the elevator to go up to the skyboxes, she didn't have to wait. Most of the bigwigs connected to Mason Benton University were already upstairs hobnobbing, eating, and drinking—having fun. She always marveled at how these championship games were fun to so many people. They were never fun to her.

When she left the elevator, she kept her head down as she dashed to her box, hoping no one would notice her. But, of course, they saw her and started making comments immediately. "Good luck, Mrs. Astin." "We're with you and Coach." "Going be a great win." One of the wives of a big booster looked her square in the eye and said flatly, "Your husband had better win today." Well, thanks for that positive comment, Kendall thought. What's going to happen if he doesn't win? What had Coach Lombardi said? "Winning is not the most important thing, it's the only thing"? But some coaching friend had told her that, late in life, Lombardi regretted saying it. Too bad, Coach. It sure has stuck, especially around here.

When she finally swung open the door to her box, she breathed a sigh of relief. She had made it. Now she just had to live through the game. Her hands were sweaty—in fact, she was sweating all over. That was another thing. Why was it always so warm in the South? It was November, but it was hot. This was not football weather. It would be better for them all, especially the players, if it were cooler. How much did Duke say the equipment weighed? Ten or fifteen pounds? She was getting too analytical. She had to calm down. Not much chance of that, but she would try.

David and Vickie Flynn were already in the box when she arrived. They always went to the games and sat in the skybox with her. They were her effort at sanity. David was Duke's attorney and agent, but more than that, they were all best friends. David was a brilliant attorney with an easygoing, relaxed approach. Vickie was a petite brunette with an eager smile and the ability to laugh things off. They were both great company at the games, interested in other things, making small talk and telling funny stories—anything to keep the game from being a life-and-death matter the way it was to the other eighty thousand people in the stadium.

Simply exchanging warm hugs with David and Vickie made Kendall feel better. Taking off the jacket she habitually wore to look proper and professional, she sat down and made her best effort to relax. Closing her eyes, she took several deep breaths. Slowly it began to work. She would make it through this game; she had made it through all the others.

The game was tight, but the fans were loving it, cheering wildly on every play and booing if they thought the ref made a bad call. The lead went back and forth with one team scoring and then the other team following with their own touchdown or field goal. All the players on both sides were giving everything they had. It was what the media called a great TV game. She tried to get into the plays and watch the "chess match," as Duke had tried to teach her. But she kept losing her concentration. She just wanted the game to be over. She watched the clock, willing the game to end with Duke's team ahead. But no such luck. When the clock wound down to zero, the game ended in a tie. Oh, no. A new rule stated that if a game ended in a tie, the teams had to continue play and break the tie in overtime. She hated the new rule—talk about stressful.

In overtime, each team would have a chance to score starting on the twenty-five-yard line. The coin was tossed, and Duke's team won. Good sign. He chose to go on defense first. The other team scored a touchdown and kicked the extra point. Now what plays would Duke call? Kendall crossed her fingers. After a couple runs, one of the running backs ran the ball in for six points. Suddenly, Duke signaled for the offense to stay on the field. He was going to have the team go for two points. If successful, they'd win the game. If not, they'd lose. It was called sudden death.

"Relax, Kendall. It's only a football game." David laughed as he tried to make light of the desperate situation. It didn't work. Tension hung in the air; everyone froze as the quarterback took the snap from center. Eighty thousand people, with half of them yelling for the quarterback to succeed and the other half yelling for him to fail. Kendall buried her head in her hands and closed her eyes. She couldn't bear to watch. Then she heard the deafening roar. She looked up and saw the ref signaling "no good." The quarterback had thrown a pass and the receiver dropped it. Her heart sank. Duke's team had lost. She immediately started looking for him. She knew how disappointed he would be.

Duke always stood so tall and erect—the field general, the head coach, calm no matter what happened, instilling confidence in everyone. But just as she spotted him, Duke fell to the ground. At first, she wondered if an angry fan had thrown something at him from the stands. Or maybe he'd fainted or gotten sick. He didn't move. She knew something was bad wrong. She grabbed the binoculars, fumbled with them, focused with shaking hands, and then saw the pool of blood.

"He's been shot!" She could hear her own voice as if it were someone else screaming. David and Vickie tried to calm her. She could hardly breathe, and she felt a sharp pain as if the bullet had passed through her. Her knees went weak, and she fell back into her chair. She didn't think she could move. But she had to go take care of Duke.

"I've got to get down there. Get me out of here!" she screamed.

But David was holding her. "Wait, we don't know what's happened. An ambulance is already on the field. You can't get down there before they leave. Calm down, Kendall."

"No. I can't calm down. I know what's happened: someone shot him. One of those horrible people who made death threats finally did it." She could feel David and Vickie hugging her and telling her to wait and not jump to conclusions. But she knew immediately. She knew her husband would not survive.

She sat traumatized, staring at the orange-gray sky. Shivering, she wrapped her arms around herself. Vickie put the jacket over her shoulders, but Kendall still felt cool air blowing in the window. Looking at the sky as the sun went down, she knew it would be a dark, cold night without Duke to keep her warm.

Chapter 2

Kendall was dressed appropriately, in all black from head to toe. David stood on one side, and her brother Randy stood on the other, making sure she didn't stumble after her complaint of feeling light-headed. The front row of seats in the middle of the court seemed far away.

Stay upright. Stay dignified. Take one step, breathe, take another step, breathe. This is for Duke. She had to keep reminding herself.

Everything must be perfect. The basketball coliseum at the university was the only place in town large enough for the students to attend Duke's memorial service, and she knew they should be included. A podium for speakers was set up in the middle of the court, with folding chairs placed in front of it. There was a giant flower arrangement with glorious flowers from Hawaii—pink king protea, purple Mokara orchids, white phalaenopsis orchids, red ginger, and yellow plumeria. On the left facing the podium sat the university president, deans, the mayor, senators, and other dignitaries. Behind them was the entire football team. Kendall's family was there from Atlanta and Duke's from Hawaii. They all sat on the right, with Duke's college and pro teammates behind them. Fanning up into the stands were former players and coaches from around the country, parents of players, old friends from school, and, of course, hundreds of students.

The crowd was huge, but Kendall didn't make eye contact with anyone. She was in a trance-like state throughout the service. Donny Jamison, one of their friends from college, sang "Amazing Grace" in his soothing baritone voice. The entire coliseum seemed to vibrate when the congregation sang "How Great Thou Art." Duke's best friend from childhood in Hawaii, Sonny Lum, and one of the current players, Elijah Ray Johnson, gave loving testimonials while fighting back tears. Bartlett Evans, the minister who had married Duke and Kendall and was now a bishop in the Methodist Church, gave a brilliant eulogy about love and forgiveness. Kendall had wanted the service to be a celebration of Duke's life. This was her planning, and it was the best she could do.

She didn't shed a tear. Her outward appearance resembled calm, but rage filled her tight chest. Her breath caught in her lungs. Complete exhaustion soaked through her bones. She noticed all the comments about how calm and dignified she was. Little did anyone know that she was doing well just to put one foot in front of the other and get through the day.

Who could have done this to her husband? And why? Duke had had so many more years to live and give to others. Respected, loved, and admired by players, friends, and family, he always worked to help them any way he could. Duke wasn't perfect, but he was an honorable man. Maybe that was the problem. He thought he should play by the rules. But there were some who didn't agree. To them, it was most important to do whatever was necessary to get all the great players and win all the games, no matter the cost. Winning came before religion, family, and even life itself. But Duke's team had won all the games until this last one. Surely there was more to his murder than losing one game.

Leaving the service and looking into all the sorrowful faces, Kendall searched for the killer. This was like a movie; it was not happening to her. She was just playing detective. After all, she had a law degree, she had taught law, she wasn't dumb. If she could figure out who killed Duke, maybe that would help her find some resolution—something to help the pain go away. She was a long way from feeling the love and forgiveness Dr. Evans had just preached about. How could she get rid of the anger? And how could she possibly live the rest of her life without Duke?

Chapter 3

David insisted on driving Kendall's BMW home after the service. Vickie sat beside him in the front passenger seat since Kendall had insisted on being alone in the back. Kendall's father and mother were elderly, and her father was not feeling well. Her brother Randy was driving them back to Atlanta. Kendall was also concerned about Duke's parents, who had lost their only son. They were going back to Atlanta to catch a flight to Hawaii. Things would finally be quiet, but she didn't know if she could get any rest. David and Vickie planned to stay with her. Kendall had known Vickie since childhood, and Duke and Kendall met David in college. Vickie and David met at Duke and Kendall's wedding and married not long afterwards. They all had careers and had put off having children. They loved to travel together, preferably driving all over the United States. Even when they went out of the country, they managed road trips. The foursome had ridden all over England, Ireland, and Scotland, singing, laughing, and having Duke do all the driving on the wrong side of the road. After all, he was the daredevil. It felt natural for them to be together, but now one person was missing.

Kendall decided to be honest with her friends. "If you two are going to be with me, you have to know that I'm so angry I can hardly breathe. Why would someone do something like this to Duke? He was such a good person. He was always trying to do the right thing. He didn't hate anybody. How could a bullet just fly through the air from some place high in the stadium and nobody see anything?"

David slowed at a red light but said nothing. Vickie turned to glance at Kendall with a sympathetic expression. She took a breath as if to speak, but Kendall wasn't finished.

"But I don't know why we're all so surprised. From the moment we first arrived here, we got death threats. Duke never believed them, but he should have. There was some heroic side of his nature that said these people were bluffing. When the FBI said people usually don't follow through with their threats, that was all he needed. That's where he went wrong. He should have taken them seriously, and maybe he would still be alive."

"Would Duke have quit coaching?" David asked calmly, turning toward the lake where Kendall and Duke had lived in a condo for the last year. "Knowing him, he would have said, 'I'm not going to give in to the crazy people. They can't make me quit doing what I love to do. I'm not going to pay any attention to them.'"

"Yes, that's exactly what he said. We had some heated arguments about how nonchalant he was about the threats. You know his nature. He could throw things off. I was the worrier in our family. He had to concentrate on all-important football! Sometimes that was all he could think about. Don't let anything interfere with the game—even if they don't want you to be their coach and are trying to kill you! Isn't that crazy?"

"Kendall, no one knows anything yet. Please try to calm down. You're going to drive yourself insane with all this speculating."

"Now you're talking to me like a lawyer. Yes, my mind is going ninety miles an hour. I can't calm down. I keep thinking about all those death threats we both got. Isn't that ridiculous—death threats just for being asked to interview for a job, getting it, and being great at it! I can't help but think about the people who picked up a phone and made those awful calls. Who would do that?"

"What did they say?" Vickie asked. "Did you ever hear any of the messages?"

"Heavens no, Duke would never let me hear them. He wanted to protect me. Guess he thought it would upset me. Ha. I could have handled 'em. When the wackos called the house, I would just hang up on them. Wish I had saved some of the ones on the answering machine. But you know what? I bet the calls made to the newspaper and the university were saved. Maybe I could listen to those."

"I'm sure the FBI and the police will listen to them. You don't need to torture yourself," David said.

"What else can I do? Maybe one of them left a clue or made a mistake. It would give me something to do—something to keep me from going insane," Kendall said, tears of rage filling her eyes.

"I tell you what I'll do. I don't want you putting yourself through any of that. I'm a criminal attorney. Let me help you. Let me represent you. That is, if you trust me."

"Of course, I trust you. You're one of the few people I trust right now. This is all so surreal." Kendall heard the desperation creep into her voice. "Tell me this isn't happening. Tell me it's a dream."

David had finally reached the condo and pulled into the driveway. He put the car in park and turned to look back at Kendall. "You have my word that I'll be your eyes and ears, doing everything that I can to find out what happened. Please promise me that you'll let me do that for you. You know Vickie and I love you, and we'll be right by your side throughout this ordeal. We will find who killed Duke, I promise. But I can't tell you this is a dream. No, this is our reality now."

PART 1

THE EARLY YEARS

Chapter 4

1966

Kendall had had no idea where her life would lead her when she took off for UCLA in the fall of 1966. But Kendall Elaine Harris was headstrong and determined to leave the South. She wanted to go away to school—a long way off where things were different. Her parents, William and Martha Ann Harris, had always been great believers in the importance of education. She remembered well how she had begged, "Daddy, you always said if I made good grades, I could go wherever I wanted to go, and I want to go to California."

"I was thinking you might want to go to North Carolina or Virginia. Do you know how far California is from Georgia? You won't be able to come home very often. It will be too expensive," her father had said. "Just think about how you'll miss us and your friends."

"Daddy, you promised, and I did what you asked. You and Mama always told me I could do anything I wanted. You taught me to question and aim high, change the world. You've always talked about civil rights and how so much is wrong in the South."

"You'll find inequities wherever you go. Don't think California will be that different," her father responded.

"I know, I know. I just want to go and see for myself. And you never should have taken me to Disneyland in sixth grade. It's your fault I love California so much," Kendall said with a grin.

"Okay, okay. I give up, but you better not call us crying to come home. You are so stubborn once you make up your mind to something. I pity the poor man who becomes your husband someday." Her father laughed as he gave her a hug.

Now here she was on her first day of classes, feeling homesick, but she would never let her parents know. She was determined to make a good start. She got up early, showered, fixed her long, blonde hair perfectly, put on her white miniskirt with a pink silk blouse and her white leather boots. At five feet nine with long legs, she figured she could hold her own with all the beautiful, suntanned "California girls," but it took some work. She managed to leave the dorm early to make sure she could find the building for her History 101 class, which was to be taught by Dr. Anthony Barnett. Entering the huge classroom with tiered rows of seats, she marched down to the first row and immediately started getting organized. Opening her notebook, putting her purse on the floor, she was soon ready to take notes. She could hear other students filing into the room and taking seats behind her, but she didn't turn around. She was too nervous.

Even though she tried hard to speak differently, her Southern accent would not go away. She was afraid it might stigmatize her somehow. But maybe, as long as she made good grades in her classes, she could overcome her accent and not be thought of as empty-headed or "a dumb blonde." That was her greatest fear.

In high school, senior cheerleader Jenny Johnson had told Kendall confidentially, "I know you're a good student, and you want to be popular. But you should never make above a C because boys don't like smart girls." Dumbfounded, Kendall had not answered. But she didn't have to think about it. There was nothing wrong with girls being intelligent and making good grades. From that day onward, she made a promise to herself: she would work to prove that she could be smart and popular, too. Some of the folks back home may have thought she couldn't pull it off, but she would show them.

She was lost in thought in her usual competitive mode when the young-looking Professor Barnett walked in the room. He welcomed everyone and immediately opened with a question: "We are going to study how our country was formed. Who can tell me what kind of government we have in this country?"

Kendall shot her hand up, and he nodded for her to answer. "Well, Dr. Barnett, most people will say it's a democracy, but we live in a republic. Instead of a direct democracy, like in ancient Greece when citizens voted individually, we elect representatives who speak for the citizens."

When she finished, the instructor smiled and said, "You are correct, and I appreciate the promotion, but I'm only Dr. Barnett's graduate assistant. But coming from such a pretty young woman, let me say thank you."

Kendall immediately thought his response was inappropriate. Why hadn't he told the class he was the graduate assistant? She heard students snickering, and a male voice a few rows back said, "Honey, with an accent like that, where did you come from? Must be a Beverly Hillbilly?" She stiffened and wanted to bury her head, but she made herself look straight ahead. This was exactly what she had feared. She was mortified and wanted to disappear. Then she heard a calm voice behind her whisper, "He's a jerk. Pay no attention. I like your accent."

"Thank you," she mumbled, but she didn't turn around. At least she felt better.

Kendall did not say another word in class that day. When the class finally ended, she gathered her things, turned to go, and looked up. There stood the best-looking man she had ever seen. He was tall, she guessed about six feet four inches. He had dark wavy hair, brown eyes, a great tan, and the most beautiful smile. And it was his reassuring voice that had calmed her. She smiled back at him but could barely speak, her heart was beating so fast. He was saying nice things now, but she was flustered as they began to walk out of the room together.

They were both free the next hour, so they sat on a bench and talked. Kendall spoke first. "I'm Kendall Harris, and I'm from Georgia on the other side of the United States. That explains my Southern accent. I'm a long way from home. Where are you from?"

"Oh, I think your accent is charming. It's not bad, I assure you. I'm from Hawaii. I guess Hawaii is about as far west from here as Georgia is east. We grew up half a world away from each other."

"I've never been to Hawaii, but I know it's beautiful. Do you love it there?"

"Yes, you'll have to see it someday. It's beautiful and the people are friendly. My father was an officer in the U.S. Navy and was stationed on Oahu during WWII, where he met my beautiful Polynesian mother. I'm half Hawaiian. I went to Punahou in Honolulu and loved sports—played baseball, basketball, and football. Naturally, being raised in Hawaii, I love the ocean and I love to surf. My childhood hero was the great surfer Duke Kahanamoku. My full name is Jonathan Wayne Astin, but somewhere along the way my friends started calling me Duke, and I like that. Just call me Duke."

Kendall loved hearing his voice. Was that a Hawaiian accent or just the way he talked? Whatever it was, it was wonderful. She was thinking about how she could listen to him all day when she realized he was asking her a question.

"How did you end up at UCLA?"

"I had to beg my parents to let me come this far. My father is a professor at Georgia State University, and my mother is a high school English teacher. They always stressed the importance of education. They said if I made good grades, I could go to college anywhere I wanted. I wanted to get away from the South. Maybe I just wanted an adventure. I know I want to graduate and do something special. Many of my girlfriends back home aren't going to college. If they do go, it's just to find a husband and get a M.R.S. degree or whatever they call it," Kendall said with a grin.

"I understand that. I'm here on a football scholarship. I play quarterback. I got recruited by universities around the country. Many of my friends are staying in Hawaii and going to our state university, but I was drawn to California the same way you were. Maybe this was meant to be. We were both supposed to come here and meet each other," Duke said with a sheepish grin.

Kendall knew she was blushing. She liked what he was saying but could only manage to smile and reply, "Maybe." Then she quickly changed the subject. "My brother Randy was a wide receiver in high school, and I was a cheerleader, so I like football, too."

"That's great. Our first game is this Saturday. Would you like to go, and we could get something to eat afterward?" Duke asked.

"I would love that," Kendall said as they got up to go to their next class. As she walked across campus, she realized she hadn't even noticed what a glorious, sunny day it was. Also, she realized she wasn't homesick anymore.

Looking back many years later, Kendall knew that if there is such a thing as love at first sight, she fell in love with Duke Astin that day and loved him to the very last day of his life.

Chapter 5

1966–1970

Kendall had a wonderful time at the football game and especially afterwards, on their first date, talking for a couple hours. She and Duke began to spend most of their free time together. Fortunately, they had two of the same classes—History and English. The more Kendall got to know Duke, the more she marveled at how different he was from the football players she grew up with.

"You know," she told him a few weeks into their relationship, "the football players back home weren't the brightest bulbs in the chandelier. All they cared about was football. But you are bright, love to read, and can talk intelligently about current events."

"I've never heard the 'brightest bulb in the chandelier thing. Is that Southern? But I'm glad you think I'm smart because I can see that you're intelligent, and I love that about you," Duke assured her.

Kendall laughed. "No, the chandelier thing isn't Southern. I don't know where it came from. But back home, smart girls weren't always appreciated. It's different with you. And you aren't afraid to be enthusiastic about something some folks might think feminine. I saw the way you enjoyed *Jane Eyre* in our English class, and you weren't afraid to admit it. Some men think they have to be macho all the time and only care about sports. You're not that way. You're not afraid to show your gentle, caring side—and I love that about you."

"Thanks, but I don't want you to get the wrong idea about me. I have a tough side that comes out when I play football. But I think that's the good thing about sports. It gives us an outlet," Duke said with a smile. "I think we're good for each other. You're hard-driving and headstrong; I'm more relaxed and easygoing. Opposites attract. I love our lively conversations, when sometimes we agree and sometimes we disagree."

"Oh, yes, I love that, too. Everyone gets to see you on the football field. It's so much fun to go to your games and know that you're my boyfriend. Every girl in this university is jealous of me. But to me, that's not the most important thing about you. I love your gentler side," Kendall said as she gave him a hug.

She didn't know exactly what had drawn Duke to her, but she was happier than she'd ever been, because she already loved him. They had a great partnership, a mutual love and respect for each other that grew as they spent more time together.

He was a steady presence in spite of everything happening in the world around them. If she'd thought she would get away from civil strife by going to California, she was terribly wrong. Their college years from 1966 to 1970 were tumultuous—race riots, Vietnam War protests, and assassinations. But the national unrest made classes much more interesting.

Kendall and Duke both majored in History and spent hours talking about civil rights, demonstrating for causes they believed in, and trying to decide what they wanted to do with their lives. Duke seemed to go with the flow of classes and football. Kendall was the one who called the shots and decided where they would go and what they would do.

On a beautiful spring day of their sophomore year a couple weeks before final exams, Kendall had an idea. "Duke, I want to go hear Dolores Huerta speak this weekend at a rally. She's been fighting to improve the lives of farm workers for years. She's an unbelievable force, standing up particularly for women. You remember our professor in Labor History was talking about her."

"I remember something about her but not much. If you want to go, I'll drive you in my used Mercury Dad just purchased for me. Can't believe I have wheels now." Duke paused and studied her. "Where do you get these inspirations? Sometimes it's all I can do to keep up with football and classwork."

"Oh, I don't know. I hear about someone special, and if I can go see them, I want to go. I heard she's a powerful speaker and won't be too far away this weekend. We may have to drive two hours or so to get to Delano, but it'll be worth it. It's in the San Joaquin Valley. We'll have to start early to make it by noon. And the weather is supposed to be great. It'll be fun."

Duke laughed. "My stars, I thought you were talking about something around here. But I guess it will be good to see more of California than we usually see."

Standing in a large field outside a grape vineyard, Delores Huerta finished her talk. Hundreds of people, mostly farm workers, went wild, cheering and clapping. Duke was laughing. "I can't believe it was all in Spanish! Did you understand anything she said, Kendall? I sure didn't."

"I'm sorry, Duke. She said a few things in English. I did take Spanish in high school, but I'm not good at it," Kendall said. "I did try to talk to that young girl we were standing with. I don't think she understood much of what I was saying."

"She's probably never heard Spanish with a Southern accent. I bet that was hilarious."

Kendall laughed along with him. "I imagine it was pretty bad. I could understand some things. Huerta has worked to get better wages and working conditions, and to protect women from abuse. She says every minute is a chance to change the world. She was the originator of the phrase '*Si, se puede,*' which means, 'Yes, we can.' Here is this tiny woman—probably not five feet tall—standing up to power. She co-founded the National Farm Workers with Cesar Chavez. It meant a lot to me just to see the looks on the people's faces. She's making life better for them and giving them hope. That's what I want to do, make a difference, change the world."

"Well, there's no doubt that you'll do something big someday, helping women probably."

"I know I get carried away sometimes. Thanks for putting up with me. I promise I'll never make you drive all day to hear a speech in Spanish again. But I'll remember this day always."

"Glad I can be of service. Now, don't you think we better get started on our long drive back?" Duke took her hand and led her toward the car.

"Oh, let's leave the windows down and enjoy the day. Isn't it glorious? Sunny but not too hot. Let's feel the wind in our hair." Kendall grinned and switched on the radio. Otis Redding was singing, "Sittin' on the Dock of the Bay," and they both sat quietly and listened.

I left my home in Georgia
Headed for the Frisco Bay
'Cause I've had nothing to live for
And look like nothing's gonna come my way
So I'm gonna sit on the dock of the bay
Watching the tide roll away

"Oh, Duke, what a sad song. It always moves me because he came from Georgia to California, too. Just like I did, but he died in that horrible plane crash before he got to live his life."

"I always feel it, too. Do you hear the waves in the background? It makes me think of Hawaii, the ocean, and happy days I've spent there. But it's a sad song. He has given up."

"Those lyrics when he says, 'I've had nothing to live for, Looks like nothing's gonna come my way,' are not true for us. We're so fortunate, and we're going to be a part of the change," Kendall insisted. "I want you to keep thinking about law school with me. That's a good way to make change."

Duke laughed. "You never let up, do you? How in the world did you start dreaming of frigging law school for me?"

"Because I'm going, and I want you to do it with me. You know me. I get something in my head, and I won't let go of it."

Kendall sat quietly for a few minutes and began to yawn. "It's horrible for me to miss anything on this wonderful day, but I think I'm going to take a short nap. Do you mind?" She lay down on the seat, put her head in Duke's lap and fell asleep.

Never had he seen anyone fall asleep so fast. He smiled, but only to himself. He would never want her to think he was laughing at her. For that matter, he had never felt as protective of anyone. She has no idea of the impact she has on me, he thought. She's more than just a beautiful woman; she has the capacity to be happy, and it's contagious. Maybe this is what real love is.

In high school and now in college, girls were always giving out signals that he could have his way with them. But Kendall was different. Every time he took her in his arms and kissed her, he thought he would go crazy with the raging feelings he had. Sex with her would be amazing, but it was out of the question. Plenty of girls were doing it these days, but Kendall had her standards. She had made it clear that they would have to wait. God, it was going to be hard, but he would do it for her. They would just have to find a way to get married as soon as possible.

Driving through mile after mile of flat farmland, Duke had a rare chance to think quietly. What could he say to her about this law school stuff? Law school had never entered his mind. He was a jock. Sports came first with him. In high school it was football in the fall, basketball in the winter, and baseball in the spring. There was never a day without a game or practice. Then the summer was full of surfing. He'd made good grades to please his parents. Dad was a hard ass, and he wouldn't let Duke get away with goofing off in school. And of course, he had to do well in classes to stay eligible for sports. He knew Dad would jerk him off the team in a heartbeat. Sports were all he ever wanted to do. So far it had paid off and gotten him a scholarship to a great school. Now this girl wanted him to go to law school. She thinks I'm so smart. I guess I'm smart enough, but I don't know if I'm smart enough for law school or if I even want to do it.

The freeway wasn't too busy as they neared campus. Kendall was catching some Z's this afternoon. It was no wonder, since she went like a house afire all the time. And she was asking Duke to go along for the ride. If it weren't for her, he probably wouldn't do any of the things she asked him to do—concerts, lectures, rallies. She was good for him, enriched his life, and kept him from being too one sided. She made him laugh and he was happy with her. He knew he'd never give up football, but he could go along with law school. He loved Kendall and wasn't about to disappoint her. No matter what she asked him to do, as long as it wasn't illegal and didn't hurt anyone, he would do it for her just to stay close and marry her as soon as possible. It might be a little deceptive, but he wouldn't be lying to her. It sounded like a good plan to him.

A couple miles from their dorms, Kendall popped her head up. "Oh, no, I slept all the way back. What did I miss?"

"Nothing much. I was thinking about our future together and what you might get me to do next. Do you have anything in mind now?"

"As a matter of fact, I do," Kendall said, grinning. "How did you know?"

"Kendall, I still can't believe you got me and the guys to get up early to come to a shopping center and give out flyers for Bobby Kennedy's campaign," Duke said through a yawn.

"But you did, and that's what matters," Kendall assured him.

"Well, for whatever reason, here we are. I told the guys to wear a UCLA football jersey with their numbers on them, just like you instructed." Duke picked up a stack of flyers. "I also told 'em to behave themselves. No smart remarks to Southern Cal fans, either."

Kendall handed each player a stack and said with enthusiasm, "Thank you so much. I appreciate you getting up early on a Saturday morning, especially right after exams. It will really help the campaign."

One of the big offensive linemen, Barry Simmons, came up close, smiled, and said, "I'm happy to help such a beautiful woman."

Duke suddenly chimed in, "Okay, guys, she's my girl. She's already spoken for. Now get out there, smile, be nice, and give out these flyers."

Kendall stood at the display table greeting everyone. She was able to watch as Duke began to meet people. He was so handsome and friendly. As soon as people saw him, they hurried over to get a flyer, along with an autograph. Polite and gentlemanly, he could make small talk with anyone. She heard someone say, "You ought to run for office someday." Kendall had to laugh. She walked over and put her hand on his arm. "Duke, you charmer. You have such a way with people. You draw people like flies to honey."

"There you go again with your Southern charm," Duke said with a grin. "What else do you want me to do for you?"

"Glad you asked. Now that you're into the campaign, I want you to take me to the Ambassador Hotel to hear the results of the primary and see Bobby Kennedy. I feel sure he is going to win. It'll be fun. It's on June 5th."

"There you go again. Do you ever slow down? But sure, you know I'll be happy to do anything for you that I can. Who all will be there?"

"I don't know, but I'm sure it will be fun," Kendall assured Duke. "No telling who you might see at a Kennedy event. They have so many friends in sports and Hollywood. Trust me. It'll be wonderful."

When they entered the lobby of the grand hotel on Wilshire Boulevard, Duke was so excited looking around for celebrities that Kendall had to lead him by the hand. The old sprawling hotel of Mediterranean architecture was packed. They were squeezing their way through the crowd when they heard a Mariachi band, followed by about two hundred Mexican Americans. Leading this jubilant brigade was Cezar Chavez.

"Look, Duke, there's Cezar Chavez. He's been working with Huerta to help farm workers," Kendall said.

"Maybe this is going to be in Spanish, too," Duke said, laughing. But when he saw the look on Kendall's face, he said he was just kidding.

Everyone seemed animated in this festive, ethnic mix of California—blacks, whites, old, young, the famous and not famous. Suddenly Duke spotted someone. "Look over there; it's Rosey Grier, who played pro football for the L.A. Rams. And that's George Plimpton with him. He's what they call a participatory journalist, who played football with the Detroit Lions and wrote a book about it called *Paper Lion*. It was a best seller and I loved it."

"See, I told you. I knew you'd enjoy this. But come on, it seems like there's such a big crowd, we better get in the ballroom quickly and get up close to the platform. Aren't you glad we did this?" Kendall grabbed Duke's hand and pulled him toward the ballroom.

They managed to get to the second row of folks standing in front of the podium. People were pushing from behind and it was getting tight—too tight. Some guy got mad and shoved the person in front of him. Duke, who towered over the guy, turned and said firmly, "Hold it down." Recognizing Duke, the man immediately apologized.

"Be cool, dude, we tight tonight!" Duke quipped as everyone laughed. Thankfully, they were not there long when a side door opened and out came Bobby Kennedy with an entourage.

"Look, Duke, here he comes. See his wife Ethel and family members. But look who's right beside him: Delores Huerta. Can you believe it? We just saw her a couple of weeks ago."

"There's Rafer Johnson. He won the Decathlon in the 1960 Olympics. The winner is called the world's greatest athlete," Duke said. "No, I can't believe this. It's exciting!"

But Kendall didn't respond. Lost in thought, she started remembering how she had loved President Kennedy when she was in high school and how heartbroken she'd been when he was assassinated. His words in his inaugural address, "Ask not what your country can do for you—ask what you can do for your country," were running through her mind when Bobby stepped up to the podium. Tears of joy filled her eyes as Bobby started thanking everyone who had helped him win the California primary. Even if her part was small, Kendall felt she had done something meaningful.

Kennedy talked about the problems and divisions in the country and how everyone had to work together to overcome them. When he finished, the crowd cheered. Kendall and Duke were gleeful, hugging each other, acting like excited kids, as were so many others around them.

"I'm so glad you got me to come down here tonight. Did you hear him mention that Don Drysdale pitched his sixth shutout in a row for the Dodgers today? What a clever way to connect with these folks. At any rate, it's been fun. We might as well stand right here. We can't get through this mob until it clears a little." Duke barely got the words out of his mouth when they heard gunshots coming from the direction where Kennedy had exited.

A tall man dressed in a dark suit, part of security, appeared at the exit door. He was saying something. "Quiet, quiet," people were shouting. Then they heard his words. "Kennedy has been shot. Is there a doctor in the crowd?" Immediately, hysteria broke out. People were crying, cursing, and yelling. Some people were shoving to get out, thinking there was a gunman in the house. Some stood stark still, staring at nothing. Kendall looked at Duke. "This can't be happening. Who would do such a thing? We were so close to him just a few minutes ago." Tears spilled down her cheeks as Duke held her in his arms.

The next afternoon, they were sitting on the sofa in Kendall's apartment. Duke had the latest copy of *Sports Illustrated* and Kendall had a copy of *Glamour*, both reading something frivolous to keep their minds off what had happened. Finally giving up, Kendall turned on the small TV she kept mainly so they could watch the Saturday night movies. The news was beginning, and the broadcaster was about to make an important announcement. They sat holding their breath as he began to speak.

"Robert Kennedy died in the hospital today. He was shot by a man named Sirhan Sirhan, who was held down afterwards by Rafer Johnson, Rosey Grier, and George Plimpton."

They both sat quietly for a few moments, and then Duke said, "How awful it must have been to be right there and hold that man down with Bobby lying a few feet away. Those men will never forget that."

"I'll never forget it either," Kendall said. "President Kennedy was assassinated a few years back and Martin Luther King Jr. only in April this year. How can all these deaths be happening? Now Bobby's dead? What's wrong with this country?" She couldn't hold back the anger in her voice.

"I don't have an answer for that. But I know one thing. The world seems to be divided between good and evil. Kendall, you and I are going to devote our lives to doing all we can to make the world better, not worse. Just keep that on your mind. That's what you've always said, and we must not forget it."

"I know you're right. But this is hard. I seem to have lost my optimism about everything. I'll have to work to get it back." She paused for a moment to gather herself. "Yes, I've always said I wanted to change the world. I just didn't know it would be this hard."

Chapter 6

1970

Kendall wasn't the same naïve person she had been before Bobby Kennedy's assassination, but she was able to throw herself into her schoolwork, and time helped to put the tragedy in the back of her mind. Duke continued to excel in football so that by senior year they were both enjoying the season.

"I can't believe it's the last game," Kendall said to her friend Cynthia, who sat by her in the stands at the Southern Cal game.

"This year has flown by, but it's been so fun to cheer on our guys," Cynthia said, referring to her boyfriend Barry Simmons, the center on the offensive line.

Barry's father was sitting behind them and joined in the conversation. "I enjoy watching this team more than any I've ever watched. I know my son is on the team, but it's more than that. It's just fun to watch this team. You never know what to expect on any play."

Duke had already thrown for two touchdowns in the game and was now leading his team down the field in the fourth quarter with only a three-point lead. They were on the twenty-yard line. Duke did a pump fake to the left and drew the defense off. Then he surprised everyone and started running to the right, dodging, swerving, outrunning defenders, and charging into the endzone for six points. As the stands erupted with a roar of approval, Kendall and Cynthia hugged each other and jumped up and down. Kendall turned to Mr. Simmons. "Is that what you mean?"

"Yes, exactly. Duke is an exciting player," he yelled over the crowd. "He has everything it takes to be a great quarterback—height, speed, agility, arm strength, and leadership ability. On that touchdown run, he sensed he had an opening, and he took it. He trusts the team to protect him. He loves the team, and they love him, too. Young lady, Duke is going to be playing on Sundays for a long time."

Kendall grinned. She was proud of Duke and the team. Maybe this was why Duke loved the game so much.

At the end of the season, Duke won All-American honors. One night in the spring, he got a call from the sports information director, Bronco Nelson. "Duke, have you heard the news?" Bronco asked. "This is great!"

"No, I have a big history test tomorrow. I'm studying. What's happened?"

"Just like you, Duke. Don't you know the NFL draft is today?" Bronco was laughing. "You've just been drafted number one by the Los Angeles Rams!"

"Are you sure? Man, that's cool! I haven't been paying much attention to the draft. My girlfriend and I are planning on going to law school," Duke said. "But playing at the next level for a few years would be awesome. It would be nice to earn some money, too."

"Sure, this is great. So happy for you. Now go tell that girlfriend of yours that you're going to take a little longer to go to law school. You'll have to take your classes in the off season. But you can do both. This is a great opportunity."

Duke found Kendall studying in the library. "You're not going to believe my news. I just got drafted number one by the L.A. Rams. Folks have been talking about it and I've gotten some calls from agents, but I wasn't paying much attention to it. I know we want to go to law school."

"Congratulations, I guess. But you know law school should be our first priority," Kendall said immediately.

"But I can make some money doing this. Good money. We can buy a new car; you know my old used one needs to be replaced. Bronco was saying I can go to law school and play. I'll just have to take classes in the off season. We can get married quickly now. The money will pay our way to law school. Don't you see? This is really good. And I do want to see if I can play in the big league."

"Well, this is a lot to think about all at once. But the thought of us being able to be on our own and pay our way appeals to me. And I would love to get married sooner. Let's surprise our families at graduation. Won't that be fun?" They both had to stifle a laugh as someone shushed them.

In late May, graduation day was beautiful. Kendall and Duke were able to find each other in the crowd after the ceremony and congratulate each other. They had both graduated cum laude, and as Kendall jumped into Duke's arms her mortar board hit him in the eye. "Oh, I'm so sorry, are you okay? I just get flustered when I'm excited."

Duke was laughing. "Sure, I'm fine. I can play football with one eye. Seriously, you didn't hurt me. I'm excited, too. Let's find our folks."

"I can't wait for you to meet my parents. They're going to love you. Isn't it wonderful that both our parents can be here today? You'll love my brother Randy, too."

At that moment, she spotted her parents and started waving as she ran toward them. "Oh, Mama and Daddy, I'm so happy. I want you to meet Duke. I've told you so much about him, you probably feel like you know him already."

"We certainly do, and we are pleased to meet you, Duke. I'm William and this is Martha," Dr. Harris said as he reached out to shake Duke's hand.

"Not so formal. Let's all hug," Duke said, opening his arms wide. "And this must be Randy. I understand we have a lot in common." Immediately, everyone was laughing and hugging each other. They made small talk as Duke's mother and father appeared nearby.

"Mom and Dad, over here," Duke said as he proudly introduced his parents, John and Maya.

Kendall stood to the side and watched. It had gone through her mind once or twice that her mother might be disappointed that she didn't fall in love with someone from back home. She knew Randy would be fascinated with Duke because of football. And her father had grown used to her unconventional behavior. But her mother had mentioned once or twice that she hoped Kendall wouldn't marry someone and live far away. Now she saw her mother holding Duke's hand and looking up into his eyes. She was instantly taken with him, just like every other woman when Duke turned on his charm. Nothing to be concerned about—her mother was a goner, too. Everyone was hitting it off. Kendall could not be happier.

She had made reservations months earlier at a little French restaurant with private rooms in the back. The white tablecloths and flowers on the tables created a perfect family atmosphere.

"Wasn't that grilled salmon divine?" Kendall asked. "How about your beef tenderloin, Daddy?"

"Wonderful—couldn't have been better. You outdid yourself with this choice. Great restaurant. Thanks to you and Duke for footing the bill," her father said.

"One advantage of Duke playing football. He got a signing bonus. We have some money now. Isn't that great!"

"Mighty nice. Thank you both. We are certainly enjoying this evening."

"Daddy, remember when you didn't want me to come to California for college? Aren't you glad now that I did?" Kendall asked.

"I had no choice. There would be no peace until I said yes. Duke, do you know how strong-willed Kendall is? She will drive you crazy until she gets her way."

"You don't have to tell me how tough she can be," Duke said, squeezing Kendall's shoulders. "But I love that about her. As a matter of fact"—he raised his voice to get everyone's attention—"Kendall and I would like to make an announcement tonight. We have decided to get married as soon as possible. She kept asking me and would give me no peace until I said yes."

"Don't believe a word he says. He asked *me*. You know I would never be pushy," Kendall said with a grin. "But we also have another announcement: Duke and I have decided to go to law school together. Duke will take longer because he can only go to classes in the off season. But eventually we'll work together and solve the problems of the world. Maybe there will be a little law firm somewhere—Astin and Astin. Doesn't that sound great?"

Everyone approved. Duke's father said, "I've been worried because I know you can't play football all your life. But now you'll have a real profession, too. Thanks, Kendall, for steering him in that direction."

"Oh, he'll be a great lawyer. Just as good as he is at football. He has what it takes, I'm sure," Kendall said with conviction.

As everyone finished their coffee and prepared to leave, Kendall suddenly spoke up again. "Oh, Daddy and Mama, I have another surprise for you. Duke and I would like to have a small wedding in Atlanta in three or four weeks. Don't panic. I have it all figured out. I'll wear Mama's wedding dress, and we'll have the reception at home. Daddy, look at all the money I'm saving you! You'll recoup some of the money you've spent flying me to California for school."

Her parents could only shake their heads and smile. Walking out of the restaurant, Dr. Harris asked, "I wonder if our daughter has any more surprises this evening?"

"Nope. That's about it for tonight." Kendall laughed as she put her arms around her father. The night had been magical, and she was overjoyed. She was sure everything would work out fine.

Chapter 7

June and July 1970

On a beautiful Saturday afternoon in late June, Duke and Kendall walked out of the chapel at Peachtree Road Methodist Church in Atlanta as Mr. and Mrs. Jonathan Wayne Astin. "Duke," Kendall said, "now you're a married man and stuck with me forever."

"Are you kidding me? I'm the luckiest man alive with the most beautiful wife in the world," Duke said, leaning down to give Kendall another kiss.

Family and friends began to file out of the chapel, offering their congratulations. Kendall's mother put her arms around her and said quietly, "Darling, it was perfect. We love Duke and his family. And you have made me happy, too. I'm so glad you wore my dress. I had always hoped you would, but I was afraid you would want a new wedding gown. And all we had to do was let out the hem a little."

"I love wearing it. I couldn't have found a lovelier dress. Silk with pearls and applique embroidery hand sown by your mother—it's true vintage. Thank you for taking such good care of it for me." They squeezed each other's hands as Duke's mother and father walked up to hug her. How fortunate she and Duke were to have parents who were still vibrant, active people who enjoyed each other's company so much.

Kendall's father was soon encouraging everyone to get in their cars and join the family at their home for the reception. Their old two-story colonial home, built by Dr. Harris's father in the 1920s, was nearby on Peachtree Battle Avenue. Kendall's father was an only child and inherited the house when his parents passed away. Surrounded by huge live oaks and magnolias, Kendall and her brother had enjoyed a happy childhood there. In the spring it was glorious with dogwoods and azaleas everywhere. It had a sense of history, with keepsakes and family pictures in all the rooms. Beautiful old heart pine floors and ten-foot-high ceilings added to its grandeur. With a warmth and charm that was always inviting, it made the perfect place for the wedding reception. Filled with pale pink and white roses, it was a beautiful setting.

One of her mother's best friends, Patti Shaw, had a catering service and had covered the dining room table with what she called a "Southern Summer Supper" for all the wedding guests. Wanting Duke and his family to taste true Southern cooking, she included shrimp and grits, ham biscuits, fried chicken, bowls of fried okra, lady peas, and, of course, fried green tomatoes. In addition to a lovely wedding cake, she'd also made her specialty of Georgia peach cobbler with ice cream. Everyone praised Patti's expertise, sampling each item and enjoying the delectable food. After the meal, to Patti's delight, Duke raised a glass and said, "Thank you, thank you, Mrs. Shaw. You have given us a taste of Atlanta. It has been simply great—a wedding feast to remember always."

When Kendall went upstairs to change, she invited her girlfriends to gather around the staircase. She had a sizable group of anxious brides-to-be. Kendall's closest friends from high school were there, along with a few friends from college. Randy's girlfriend Sue Dean was among them, as was Vickie Anderson, Kendall's best friend since childhood. Vickie had struck up a serious friendship with David Flynn, a friend from UCLA who had come to the wedding and planned to go to law school, too.

When Kendall climbed a few steps and turned to toss her bouquet, she couldn't help but deliberately throw it toward Vickie, who excitedly jumped to catch it. She immediately gave David a shy smile, and he returned it. Kendall was delighted and threw them both a kiss. Wouldn't they make a great foursome in the future and have lots of fun double dates together?

After carefully hanging the wedding dress, Kendall came down the stairs in a pale blue pantsuit that would be comfortable on the long trip to Hawaii. Getting in the limo, she turned to look at the faces of the people she loved most in the world. She was so happy they were there to share this special day. She felt a great sense of gratitude to them all.

They had helped to make this the happiest day of her life. The wedding was a dream come true.

Kendall and Duke flew to L.A. and had a two hour layover. As they boarded their flight to Honolulu, Kendall could stand it no longer. "Duke, I'm so excited about going to Hawaii. And you have planned it all. You know I'm used to organizing everything. Can't you tell me anything?"

"No way. Everything is going to be a surprise. I know it drives you crazy not being in charge." Duke laughed. "But I'm not telling you anything—only that you're going to love it."

"Okay I give up. I'll just have to wait," Kendall said as she settled into her seat. "If you aren't going to tell me, I'll just take a little nap." She put her head on Duke's shoulder and fell fast asleep, remembering their happy wedding day.

When they arrived at the airport in Honolulu, they heard ukulele music as a handsome, exuberant young man came running up to them. He was dressed in a flowered silk shirt, shorts, and flip-flops. His arms were covered with orchid leis as he began hugging them both.

"Duke, congratulations. You said she was beautiful, but she's a knockout. You're a lucky man."

"Kendall, this is Sonny Lum, my best friend from childhood," Duke said.

Sonny grinned as he piled leis around their necks. "Aloha, welcome to Hawaii."

"Thank you, Sonny. I've been looking forward to meeting you. I've heard so many things about you," Kendall said as she gave him a hug.

"I hope Duke told you good stuff," Sonny said, with a questioning look at Duke.

"You know I did, bruddah, and thanks for picking us up." Duke lifted Sonny off the ground and gave him a big bear hug. "And I'm glad you're already married to Anna, or you would be hitting on Kendall."

"Man, you know I'd never do that," Sonny said with a laugh as he began picking up their carry-on bags. Directing them to baggage claim, he was talking a mile a minute. "Everything is ready. Just like you told me to do. Now follow me to paradise."

They soon piled into Sonny's convertible and started the drive into Honolulu. It was a glorious, sunny day with a slight breeze. "Thank you, my friend," Duke said. "Now please drive us to the Hilton Hawaiian Village on Waikiki." He sat with Sonny in the front seat and chatted with him about the old days. Kendall sat in the rear, laid her head back, and looked at the beautiful sky. She noticed trees she could not identify and saw quaint buildings. Yes, she was thinking, this is paradise.

In no time at all, they were pulling into a beautiful hotel. A valet appeared, took their bags, and put them on a golf cart. "No need to go check in," he said. "Mr. Lum has taken care of everything."

"I didn't pay. I just checked you in," Sonny informed them with a laugh. "I knew you would be tired and want to go directly to your room. You are on your honeymoon, after all."

"Get out of here. Sonny, you've done enough," Duke said. "Yes, we are tired." He waved good-bye to Sonny, and he and Kendall climbed onto the golf cart. The valet drove them toward Duke's surprise. It was the most charming place Kendall could have imagined—a thatched-roof cottage right on the beach.

"Duke, it's so wonderful. I love it. Hawaii is already special, and it just gets better and better," Kendall said as she threw her arms around Duke's neck.

"I want the best for our honeymoon. How better to spend some of my NFL bonus? I want us to relax and soak up all the beauty here. I love Hawaii, and I want you to love it, too," Duke said.

He put his strong arms around her and pulled her to his chest. Kendall felt a warmth all over her body as she relaxed into his embrace. How could she feel so protected and safe? She was going to spend the rest of her life with this handsome, loving man—a man to whom she could give her whole being. She was as happy as she had ever been. Nothing could spoil her joy.

Upon their return from the honeymoon, they rented an apartment not far from the Rams' practice facilities. "Duke, isn't it wonderful? This apartment is going to be our first home. Someday we'll build a real house, but I think we'll be happy here. Football practice will start soon. I will have a few more weeks before my law classes start. You won't believe the changes I'll make to brighten up this place." Kendall was walking from room to room, Duke following along behind her. "Bright-colored pillows and flowers will really help. There are two bedrooms. I'll fix up one to be an office that we can both share when we study."

"I have no doubt you will work wonders. I'm not worried about that," Duke said.

"With the money you make in football, we can buy some furniture and pay for law school. I may make a little at the law firm, maybe doing some part-time things. We'll be here awhile," Kendall said.

"Remember, I can't start law classes until after football season. I won't have time."

"I know. I didn't understand that quarterbacks had to study so much, but now I get it," Kendall assured him.

"Yeah, I'll have to really work hard to learn the offense. The quarterback calls all the plays. He has to know how to change them if he sees something unexpected in the defense—those changes are called audibles. I think of the game as a big chess match. I'll teach you all about it," Duke said as they left the office/bedroom. "One of us may have to work in another room at times. You're a distraction to me sometimes, you know."

Kendall laughed. "I'll try not to distract you too much. You know I have studying to do, too. You're so smart. I'm sure you can keep your mind on football even with me around."

"I don't know, Kendall. You may have to stay in another room at all times when we study."

"Duke, you know we're going to be busy with law classes and football. You must behave yourself. You know we've decided to wait and have children after law school. If you can't behave yourself, I'll lock myself in the office where you can't get to me."

Kendall was loving the banter. Everything was working out so well. She felt like they were part of a storybook. They were going to have a great marriage, and this was just the beginning. Nothing would ever keep them from being happy.

The Rams players and their wives lived in various parts of the Los Angeles sprawl, so social times together were not easy. But they would gather after most of the games for tailgate parties at the L.A. Coliseum where they played their home games. Sometimes six or eight couples would go to a restaurant. Because of its Polynesian-inspired décor, Trader Vic's at the Beverly Hills Hilton was Duke's favorite by far.

Kendall loved to see Duke get up and entertain the group. After the games, he would change into a silk Hawaiian shirt with white slacks. He looked so handsome to her as he began to charm the group.

"My friends, I've invited you to my tiki house tonight. This feels like Hawaii—relaxed and beautiful. You women enjoy your Mai Tais while the guys have some beer. Great game today. A real team effort. I couldn't have thrown those passes without you big men on the offensive line," Duke said with a smile.

"Duke, you're killing us—you are so slow. Why don't you move your ass faster?" yelled Big Joe Watkins, the offensive center.

"You're full of it, Joe. But I tell you what—all the drinks are on me tonight. I really appreciate you guys," Duke said as the men cheered.

Kendall laughed with everyone, thinking they would enjoy it all while it lasted. Because they would leave it when law school was over to enter the real world.

Chapter 8

1980

The problem was that, year after year, Duke would decide he wanted to play another season. Kendall really couldn't object—he was just so darn good at the game. Everybody loved him. Of course, his law classes took longer than expected. Kendall thought he deliberately delayed some of them so he could justify playing football longer. Before they knew it, he had played for ten years.

Kendall was happy when she finally finished law school and decided to quit playing. Shortly after this decision, Duke said he wanted to talk about some things and invited her out to dinner at Trader Vic's. They had a quiet booth in the corner where they could talk and not be noticed.

"This is a celebration," Kendall said "I'm so excited. Isn't it wonderful to be back at Trader Vic's? It hasn't changed in all these years. And here's our favorite waiter bringing us drinks. Thanks, Manuel."

"Always great to have you both here. We goin' to miss seeing you play ball. Nobody is as much fun to watch as you, Duke," he said as he put down two beers.

"Thanks, Manuel. I'm really going to miss it, too. Probably more than I realize now," Duke said, shaking Manuel's hand.

"I'm goin' to miss that gang of players that used to come in with you. What a fun group."

"Yes, they were great guys. Sadly, they can't be replaced." Without even glancing at the menu, Duke ordered the seafood special for them both, and Manual moved on to another table.

Kendall took a sip of her beer. "I know you'll miss the camaraderie of the team. But you'll find that same friendship and mutual trust with other friends." She paused as Duke shook his head in disagreement.

"Honey, what's wrong? This is a happy night. You've had a great career, and you managed to work your way through law school at the same time. Not many men would have been so dedicated. I am so proud of you." She took his hand and squeezed it.

"Kendall, you know I love you. And I want to tell you something I've been thinking about a lot. I haven't arrived at this suddenly. I know it's the right thing for me to do, but I'm afraid you won't agree." Duke took a deep breath. Finally, he managed to say, "I have decided I want to coach football."

Kendall immediately blurted, "But why? You've worked so hard in law school. You'll make a great lawyer. Football is a child's game. You have played it all these years. I thought we would settle down in one place. I've always wanted to build a house. We've been delaying children until after law school and your time with the NFL. Now you want to go into coaching? Why?"

"Kendall, calm down and listen to me. I just feel like I have to do it. I guess it's in my blood. I can't put it off. And I do love the camaraderie. I enjoy being with the players—the team. I guess it's hard for you to understand what the team means to an individual player."

"Duke, that's selfish. You've played four years in college and ten in the NFL, and now you want to spend more years in football. No, I don't understand. I thought you wanted to change the world. Use your law degree to do good things." Kendall felt tears in her eyes.

"But I can do good things in football. I can teach life lessons, responsibility, and leadership. It isn't just a child's game; it's much bigger than that." Duke was pleading for her to understand. "Besides, I enjoy the X's and O's of the game, too. It is not simple: it's a big chess match. I'm good at it. And no, I can't find that camaraderie anywhere else."

"Oh, Duke, coaches never stay in one place very long. What do they say? 'Coaches are hired to be fired'? Moving from one place to another isn't the way I want to live. I don't think that's the best way to raise children either. Taking them in and out of schools would be difficult for them," Kendall said.

"If we do move around the country, why can't we go ahead and have children anyway? Kids are resilient. It will be a learning experience for them—meeting new people all the time. They'll do fine," Duke assured her.

"You always oversimplify things. You don't seriously believe that, do you? Come on, now. The coaching life is not an easy life for us or for children. It will be stressful, and I don't handle stress very well. I can work hard in a law class or on a case, but I have no control over your games. I just sit and wring my hands. It's not fun for me." Kendall paused and took a long sip of her beer. "Who knows how our children would respond to being moved from pillar to post, from state to state and school to school? No, we won't have children as long as you are in coaching."

"Kendall, do you hear what you just said? You said you would have 'no control.' You are so strong-willed; you have to always have your way. You got your way with your father and then with me. I've always loved your enthusiasm and determination. But not now. This is wrong. What if I told you that you couldn't do what you love—work with women or practice law? And doesn't having children have something to do with your career as a lawyer? Be honest."

Manuel appeared with their meals, and Kendall turned away so he wouldn't see the tears rolling down her face. They ate in silence. Duke had never talked to her like this. She couldn't eat much and picked at her food silently. She finally said, "I don't think you can compare the two."

"Oh, yes, I can. Just think about it for a while. Haven't you always gotten your way your whole life?"

For once, Kendall was speechless. She had to think about this. She loved Duke and she knew he loved her. She didn't want to destroy what they had built together. Finally, she said, "Duke, let's be careful what we say. I can see we're not going to agree on this tonight. I suggest we think about a truce. Maybe you could try coaching for a while. You might not like it as much as you think you will. I'm sure it's not the same as playing." Kendall was hoping her suggestion would end their evening on a positive note.

"I appreciate you suggesting that. I do feel I have to try it," Duke said without his usual smile.

The two of them had disagreed before, but this was their first big fight. They didn't really settle anything that night. For the next several days, they didn't talk to each other much. Kendall kept thinking. In her heart of hearts, she knew time might be running out for her to have children.

Even so, after a few more days they did agree on the truce. He would give coaching a trial run. She just hoped that once he got coaching out of his system, he would return to practice law. She had to admit that she hadn't been thinking about her law career when she said they had to delay children. Had she made a mistake?

Chapter 9

1980–1988

Walking into the law firm of Jamison and Edwards in her navy blue skirt suit with a white blouse, Kendall felt that she looked like a real lawyer. No more miniskirts for her—only mid-knee length now. She had learned that the cardinal sin of a lawyer, especially a female lawyer, was to attract attention to yourself. With no bright colors or expensive jewelry, she had become a true professional.

"Good morning, Kendall," said Andrew Jamison, one of the partners. With gray hair and a kind smile, he reminded her of her father. "Now you're lookin' the part. No more college intern rushing in after classes."

"Thank you," Kendall said with a smile. "At least one of us is using our law degree. Since Duke has decided he wants to coach, I keep thinking about how he's wasting his degree. I hope he'll get it out of his system quickly and come back to practice law."

"Kendall, Duke is just too good at football, and I can see how he loves it so much. Sometimes I wish I were a football coach," Andrew admitted, laughing.

"Please don't say that. You will be encouraging Duke," Kendall said as she set her coffee mug on the desk.

"Let him take his time and figure it out. He's still young enough. What I want to talk about is you. Kendall, you have a special interest in women's issues. You've taught me quite a bit. I think many of us old guys have a lot to learn. You know we're having more women than ever coming into the office seeking help. Sometimes I don't think I have the best rapport with them."

"I think all the talk about women's rights is empowering women to speak up and ask for more," Kendall said. "I feel passionately about women and how they have been shortchanged. Duke says I can be over-bearing at times. I know I might have overdone it a bit when I brought refreshments and pink balloons to the office when President Reagan appointed Sandra Day O'Conner to the Supreme Court." She laughed. "I was just excited and thought it was about time."

"No, we all had fun that day. It was a wise appointment. Come in my office. I have an idea that I want to talk to you about," Andrew said as he motioned her toward his door.

When Duke came into their apartment that day after practice, Kendall greeted him with the good news. "You're not going to believe what has happened. Andrew Jamison and I had a long talk today."

"I told you. You looked too good in that new 'lawyer suit.' No wonder he wanted to have a lengthy talk today," Duke said as he gave her a hug. "You looked mighty good when you left this morning."

Kendall was thankful that they were able to get back to their play-ful banter after the big fight. It had taken a while, but they were both working at being supportive of the other.

"Duke, I'm being serious. I can't attract attention with my looks. I must be professional."

"Honey, you can't help but attract attention, but it's in good taste. Now go on—what are you excited about?" Duke said as he opened the refrigerator looking for something to drink.

"I've told you how the other lawyers get annoyed with all the women coming in the firm asking for help. There's been a real increase. Women are asking for divorces from controlling husbands. They have to fight for alimony, custody of children, and equal share of property. Some of the attorneys get so frustrated with the women, they bring them to me," Kendall said enthusiastically.

"All those husbands better watch out!" Duke teased. "Here comes Kendall to make them do the right thing. Your stubbornness will pay off for those women. They're lucky to have you on their side."

"But the most upsetting cases are the ones where the women are abused," Kendall said, growing serious. "It's awful. You won't believe the number of women who are beaten, sometimes within an inch of their lives. They're fighting for their children, too. Did you know domestic violence is an epidemic in our country? I sure didn't. It happens to women of all classes. Obviously, I'm seeing the ones who can afford to seek help. Think of all the poor women who are trapped with abusers."

"No, I had no idea. It's wonderful if you can help some of them," Duke said.

"I'm excited about it. The other lawyers call them the 'hysterical women' when they bring them to me. But I love the women and really want to help them. Andrew says I can specialize in this work. He says I have the potential to make partner someday. Can you believe it?"

"Yes, I can believe it. This is what you love, and you're good at it. You will get better and better."

"It helps me understand your love of football a little bit. I mean, doing something you love is important. This work will help my career but also help women. I've found my passion. I want to specialize in Domestic Relations Law. I think that's what they call it. Well, that's my news! Isn't that great? Your passion is football—at least for now—and my passion is to help women. I always want to do this work," Kendall said with conviction.

"You will be so good at this. You can make a difference like you've always said. I'm really happy for you."

"I'll do all I can for as long as I can. Maybe I can help a lot of women survive," Kendall added.

"Oh, I have no doubt. With your drive and determination, I know you will succeed," Duke said, wrapping his arms around her again "Get something to drink, and come over here and sit on the sofa with me."

Kendall opened the refrigerator and poured a glass of wine. She sat down on the sofa. "It's your turn now. What do you want to tell me?"

"I have news for you, too. I've decided that I want to always coach at the college level. Pro football is a business, and the men are grown and set on their paths. But at the college level, the coach can still have an impact on young men's lives. You know I love the game, but I love the young men, too. I want them to get meaningful degrees that will help them live successful lives after football. You might say we've both found our passions, and maybe we can do some things that matter."

"I'm sure you'll do some good as a coach. Who knows what you'll do afterwards? I'm not giving up on you going into law. But for now, that's a good way to look at football," Kendall said, picking her words carefully. She figured they could put their differences aside for the time being and stay busy doing what they loved.

Kendall buried herself in her law work with women while Duke started coaching quarterbacks at UCLA. The practice field was on her way home in the afternoon, so occasionally she stopped by to watch practice. She could see Duke's natural rapport with the athletes and how they were always high-fiving after a good play. Duke just had a gift. She wasn't the only one to see it. After three years, he became an offensive coordinator. He was soon being discussed as a possible head coach. But he was happy where he was and continually refused those offers.

Kendall thought of the old cliché that when you're doing what you love, you lose track of time. She knew now that it was true. She and Duke had gotten to a comfortable place with him coaching at UCLA and her working with women. Before they knew it, eight years passed. But things hadn't gone the way Kendall had hoped. The longer Duke coached, the more he loved it. And he kept getting better and better at his job. Kendall knew he was refusing head coaching offers because of her. He had sacrificed for her; it would be her time to sacrifice soon. Even though she knew the time would come to move on, it caught her by surprise.

"Duke, it's such a gorgeous evening. Let's take a walk," Kendall said as she picked up a light sweater. "Sixty-five degrees in January. You can't beat this weather. It's perfect. I could live in Huntington Beach forever. We can walk down by the ocean and see the moon come out." They had purchased their first home five years earlier—a one-story stucco with three bedrooms, a big living room, and—most important—a fireplace. It was full of California charm. They both enjoyed the neighborhood and the carefree lifestyle.

"Great idea. I want to talk to you about something," Duke said as he grabbed a sweatshirt. There was a gentle breeze, and only a few other people were out strolling.

"Can you believe how wonderful it is to live here? To be able to walk on the beach in January? I love it," Kendall said, taking Duke's hand.

"Oh, I love it, too. This has been a wonderful place to live." Duke paused for a minute and then said, "Kendall, it's time for me to take a head job. I've been ready for several years, but I stayed here longer because I know you love your work so much. Would you be willing to move now?"

Kendall stopped and stood still, looking up at Duke. "I knew this day was going to come. I've been happy here, but I was afraid it couldn't last."

Duke hesitated a moment and then said, "Wyoming is the place—that is, if you agree."

"Did you make this decision without talking to me? Don't you think we should've discussed where we were going to go?"

"Honey, this is a good situation. A representative from the school came and talked to me at the stadium. I thought I was going to turn him down the same way I've turned down others over the years. But it's time. It's probably past time that I move on. I've stayed here because we both love California, and you were making such progress in your job. But if I don't go now, it's going to set back my career. Don't you think we're ready to make a move?"

Kendall knew that whatever she said would sound selfish. It really didn't matter that much where they went first. It was the beginning of the moving that she had dreaded. She agreed, though, that it was past time for Duke to take his turn and for her to sacrifice.

They walked along quietly for several minutes while Kendall tried to think of what to say and how to say it. She was heartsick but wanted to sound enthusiastic. Finally, she looked at Duke and smiled. "Well, where are my boots and my cowboy hat? If we're moving to Wyoming, I'll have to learn to ride horses."

"I'm so touched. There are so many people here," Kendall said as she walked around the room hugging everyone. The Blue Ribbon Club, the law firm hangout down the street with the wood paneling and horse paintings, had been rented for Kendall's farewell party. It was packed with lawyers, staff, and clients.

Rosa Rodriguez, a bouncy brunette with beautiful brown eyes, came up with tears running down her cheeks. "How can I get along without you? You've taught me so much. Now you're turning your clients over to me. I hope I can do half as well as you have done with all these women," she said as she threw her arms around Kendall.

"Oh, Rosa, you'll do great. You're ready. You've learned to speak up." Kendall laughed. "Here, I want you to meet one of my clients, Marianne Sanders. I am so proud of her. Her husband abused her for thirty years and she finally left him."

Kendall took the hand of a petite older woman standing nearby. "Marianne, I haven't seen you since I finished up your divorce. I hope you're doing well."

"Oh, I'm doing better than I've done in years. I feel like a butterfly that has come out of its chrysalis. You gave me the courage to leave my husband. Now I'm free because of you. Thank you, thank you. But I hate to see you go. Now, if I need one, I'll miss being able to drop in for one of your great pep talks," Marianne responded.

"I'll miss seeing you, too, more than you can imagine," Kendall said with tears in her eyes. "But I'm leaving you in good hands. This is Rosa Rodriguez. She will be taking over all my cases. If you ever need anything, call Rosa."

She left Rosa and Marianne visiting as she spotted a young colleague, Mark Peterson, who had recently joined the firm. "Mark, thank you for coming over to help me with the move. Couldn't handle some of those big things without your help."

"I'm the one who should be thanking you," Mark said. "That old desk you gave me is perfect for my barren apartment. And I enjoyed getting to know you better."

"Glad you can use it. It was the first thing Duke and I bought for our apartment. But we have a newer one now and didn't want to take the old one to Wyoming."

"Oh, I love it, and now I can brag that I have something that once belonged to the famous couple—Duke and Kendall Astin."

"I'm glad you like 'antiques.' But deciding what to take and what to get rid of for a move is a hassle. In fact, the whole moving thing is such a huge job. Of course, Duke took off immediately after he got the job and left me to do everything. You know—organize the house, put it on the market, sell it, and then hire a moving company. Have you heard that the three worst things in life are death, divorce, and moving? Thank goodness, I've not had to deal with the first two, but I'm now an expert on moving. I could write a book on the subject," Kendall said with a laugh. "But that's the last thing I want to write about."

"Let me come over and help you some more. Without Duke, you've had a lot on you," Mark offered.

"Thanks, but I'm finished now. Movers are coming tomorrow to start loading," Kendall said as she walked away to see some other friends. She was happy to have a chance to say good-bye to all these people who were such an important part of her life. It was bittersweet; she would miss them more than they would ever know.

At the end of the evening, Andrew Jamison stood up to give a toast. "Let's wish Kendall the very best and thank her for keeping us old guys in line all these years. Never one to be shy, she always told us what she thought. And she would never stop arguing until she convinced us that her way was the right way. But I must admit, she was usually correct. Here's to Kendall and Duke's future in Wyoming."

"Thank you, thank you to everyone," Kendall said, struggling to stay composed. "I've learned so much from all of you. I appreciate you being patient with me. I know sometimes I drove you crazy. But it's all been a joy to me. Now I want you to get your boots and cowboy hats and come on out to Wyoming. I promise we'll show you a good time!" Kendall forced a smile, knowing this was likely the last time she would see many of these people.

Chapter 10

1988–1992

Kendall sat by the window in the small commuter plane into Laramie. Two and a half months ago, she'd learned they were moving to Wyoming. Duke had left immediately to start recruiting players and hiring staff. The combination of selling the house and closing down her law practice had left her exhausted. If she were honest, she was also sad. But she was determined to put on the best face she could. She loved Duke, and she had to do this for him.

Looking out the window, she saw nothing but snow and barren land. Was this what they called the plains? Compared to flying into L.A. or Atlanta, it was shocking how small the city looked. In fact, she had heard that the whole state had fewer people than the city of Atlanta or even Fulton County where her family lived. At least the traffic would be light, and they wouldn't have to drive an hour to see any friends they might make.

This was the longest time Duke and Kendall had ever been separated. Even when he had been in training camp for pro football, they were still in the same town. She was looking forward to seeing him.

Entering the terminal, she had to laugh. No one could miss that tall, handsome man waving exuberantly to her—with a cowboy hat no less.

"Oh, baby, I'm so glad to see you! It's been way too long. I can't wait to show you around," Duke said as he threw his arms around Kendall and gave her a big kiss.

"I've really missed you, too. I'm sorry you had to miss all the fun of packing up the house and selling it," she said. "Great fun."

"But look what a fabulous job you did. It sold right off the bat. You had it looking so charming. It's that special touch you have. Now you get to fix up our new place. It'll be fun."

"Let me catch my breath first. I'm tired. You are so exuberant. I need to catch some of that energy from you."

"Come on, we'll go to dinner, and I'll tell you all about it. I want you to be happy here," Duke said as he led her toward baggage claim.

Country music played on a juke box in the Western-themed restaurant. As soon as they walked in the door, Duke waved over a man in jeans, cowboy boots, and hat. "Cody, I want you to meet my beautiful wife, Kendall. You're going to love her."

"I'm mighty pleased to meet you. Heard good things from Duke. You a lawyer?"

"Yes, I am. Glad to meet you, too," Kendall said as Duke waved someone else over. She could tell he was having fun and getting to know folks quickly the way he always did.

"Sit here, Kendall. Let's order something. The bison burgers and steak are both especially good here," Duke said as he pulled out a chair and helped her take off her coat.

"How about salmon? Could I get some fish?" Kendall asked.

Duke laughed. "Baby, this isn't the best place for fresh fish, but I'll ask."

"Okay, I love fish, but I'll find something else," Kendall said, thinking she was going to have to work hard to fit in here. "Tell me about your first impressions and what you've learned so far."

"The folks here have been great. I've enjoyed getting to know them. They really love football, too. They're dedicated. They have something I've never seen before. The towns are so spread out and the population is so small that they play eight-man football, sometimes even six-man. A coach told me he had to drive four hundred miles to play a league game. Can you imagine that?"

"No, I can't," Kendall said, trying to wedge a word in. Duke was talking so fast.

"They've had some good football players to come out of Wyoming, too. You remember Jerry Hill, who played on the Baltimore Colts Super Bowl Three and Five teams? He played at Wyoming. Lots of others from here, but they went out of state to play college ball—like Boyd Dowler for the Packers went to Colorado. We've got to keep them in state from now on. Lots of good coaches, too. I've met quite a few. They want me to speak at their convention next year in Casper. Told them I'd be honored."

Kendall had to smile as Duke rattled on. He was so excited about the state and already making plans for next year.

"The summers are warm, and the winter weather will take some getting used to, but I'm sure you can do it. I've already purchased some real winter clothing. You're going to love my Shearling sheepskin jacket. Folks say I look like the Marlboro man but with darker hair." Duke laughed.

"Well, I'm sure you look good in that jacket. Can't wait to see," Kendall said, smiling.

"We'll have to go shopping for you too," Duke said. "It gets cold and windy here. You'll need something heavier than your California jackets. You might need a whole new winter wardrobe. Maybe a fur-lined coat. And boots, of course. Long underwear if you're going to be doing something outside. With the wind, it'll seem colder than it actually is. But you're such a trooper, you'll adjust quickly. I'm sure of it. I think it'll be fun to live in a climate so different from what we've always known. It's nothing like Hawaii, California, or Atlanta."

"Gosh, you can say that again." Kendall felt that adjusting might be harder than Duke seemed to think. But if he could be happy, maybe she could, too. And a new winter wardrobe might be fun.

Picking up the menu, Kendall grinned at Duke. "This Georgia girl is excited to be in Wyoming with the Hawaiian Marlboro man. Who would've ever thunk it?"

Over the next four years, Duke had great success in Wyoming, going to three bowl games and winning two. Even though Kendall had a hard time figuring out what she was supposed to do, she did enjoy the people and the beautiful western land with its national parks. Her favorite spot in the state was Jackson Hole, where she and Duke learned to ski. The bowl game that fourth year was in mid-December, and Vickie and David came for Christmas. Kendall was more excited than she had been in a long time.

After a morning of skiing, Kendall and Vickie sat by the huge fireplace in the ski lodge. "I'm so happy you and David came. Isn't this a great place to spend the holidays? I love all the wooden beams and high ceilings in this lodge. Look at that huge Christmas tree. Isn't it magnificent? What a great place to relax! I don't know about you, but I'm exhausted." Kendall took off her ski jacket and propped her feet on an oversized leather ottoman.

"Me too. How do Duke and David keep going so long?" Vickie asked as she propped her feet next to Kendall's.

"Duke will ski all day. He loves it, and he's such a good athlete. He says all the surfing he did helps him. He says I'm too cautious. Of course, he's such a daredevil. He loves the black diamond runs and is always trying to get me on the moguls. No way. I'm not a good enough skier. I don't want to run into a tree and break something—or worse, kill myself." She laughed.

A waiter brought them both a hot buttered rum. "Now, let's sip these and relax. You must be careful with these rums. One will relax us quite enough. They're a tradition at this lodge in the winter. Delicious. Don't you think?"

"Yes, I'll say. Delicious but strong. We should be quite mellow soon." Vickie giggled and took another sip.

"I hope so. I feel happy today, and I'm glad we have an opportunity to be alone. You're my best friend, and we've always been able to talk about anything. To be honest, I've had a hard time in Wyoming. I haven't stayed busy enough. It's left a lot of time for me to think. You know I told Duke years ago that I didn't want children as long as he coached. I had hoped he would tire of coaching, but he hasn't, and now it's probably too late for us. I quit taking birth control pills a year ago and nothing has happened. It's hard to get pregnant in your forties. Sometimes it happens, but not often," Kendall said with tears in her eyes.

"Kendall, I know. We both delayed having children. I think it was the right decision for us," Vickie said. "But if you still want children, you can adopt or go to a fertility clinic. In vitro is becoming more and more popular and successful."

"I know. We're thinking about both options. But something always seems to get in the way. It hasn't been announced yet, but it will be soon. Duke wants to accept an offer from Kansas. We're going to be moving again. That is such an ordeal. We'll have to put any decision about children on the back burner again. I think it's so painful for us both that we just avoid talking about it." Kendall took Vickie's hand and squeezed it. "But I'm glad I have someone to talk to about it. I haven't uttered a word to another soul. Just talking to you makes me feel better. Maybe somehow, some way, this issue will work itself out," Kendall said. They both sat quietly for several minutes, mesmerized by the fire as it popped and sputtered in an orange glow.

Suddenly snapping out of it, Kendall said with a big smile, "That's enough about that. Let's enjoy this beautiful afternoon. I don't want anything to interfere with us having a joyous Christmas. Let's enjoy each moment because we never know what tomorrow will bring."

Chapter 11

1992–1996

Duke and Kendall settled themselves in Kansas, where Duke had even more success. During their four years in this new state, Kendall found volunteer work at battered women's shelters and taught occasionally. But she never worked to pass the bar because she knew they would not be there long.

Soon, head coaching offers were coming in from all over the country. By this time, Kendall had not completely given up on getting Duke to leave coaching, but she mentioned it less and less. He was addicted to the game and was happy. She didn't feel she could force him to quit, but she was not happy. She didn't like moving every few years and was beginning to wonder if it would ever end.

One evening after the season, they sat down after dinner to have one of their long conversations that had always meant so much to Kendall. "Duke, whatever happens now with all these offers coming in for you to coach, I want to be involved in the decision. The only thing I ask is that we quit moving. I would like to settle in one place. Preferably a warm place. My blood's too thin for ice and snow all winter. I think I would be so much happier. Don't you want that, too?"

"Yes, I do. And you should get back into the work you love. We've been moving around for my career. It's been a whirlwind, hasn't it?"

"Yes, a whirlwind is a good way to describe it. Wherever we go, you jump right in—as Grandpa would say, 'You're as happy as a pig in slop.' But it takes longer for me to find something to wallow in. It takes time for me to find where I belong and what I'm supposed to do. By the time I find it, we up and leave."

Duke laughed. "There you go again with your Southern expressions. But you're right. I can be happy about any place I can play ball.

But it's difficult for you. I appreciate what you've done for me. Now it's your turn. Let's figure out the next move together," Duke said as he put his arms around her and held her tight. "I want you to be happy, too."

Only a few days later, Duke came in from the stadium with news to share. "Kendall, please come sit on the sofa with me. We need to have a serious talk. I got a call today from a traditional powerhouse in the South—Mason Benton University in Benton, South Carolina."

"Oh, Duke, I've heard about the Benton Bears all my life. They had a great coach, Jack Barnes. Folks were always talking about him. It's great that they called you!"

"We'll see. They want me to interview. But I know you left the South when you came to UCLA. Would you be willing to go back?"

"Funny, I've been thinking lately about going back to that part of the country. I love the weather, the azaleas and dogwoods in the spring, and so many of the good people—friends and family," Kendall said. "Things have changed after all these years. And I've been away from my folks so long. I know they would be happy if we moved closer to them."

"We have to think carefully about it. To stay in one place, you have to keep winning, and there are so many great football programs in the South. Of course, I'll do everything in my power to win so we can settle down. There's something else we need to think about. Fans don't really know me there. I grew up in Hawaii half a world away. I don't imagine they've had any coaches that look like me. You know, with darker skin. There have been a few in the West and Midwest but not in the South. I don't know if they'll take to me," Duke said.

"I'm not worried about that. You're a very handsome man with dark skin from your Hawaiian heritage. I have no doubt the fans will love you; they always do. How can they resist that smile?" Kendall assured him. Then she couldn't help adding, "If you get fired, you can practice law with me."

"Kendall, you're my wife, and you love me, but I think it'll take a lot more than my smile to succeed. But if you agree, I'll go interview and we'll see what happens."

"If you interview, you'll get the job. And they'll be lucky to have you," Kendall said. She was correct. Duke flew down and interviewed. The university hired him to be their new head football coach and set the news conference for January 4, 1996.

This would be their last move; Kendall was certain of it. She was happy about relocating and glad they'd made the decision together. But she still felt anxious. Change made her nervous, and for some reason she was more agitated than usual. She just didn't know where all of this would lead. Had they made the right decision? She hoped and prayed that they had, but there was always the unknown.

PART 2

THE HIRE

Chapter 12

January 1996

Billy Bob Craven hadn't slept well. He was worried about the new football coach at the university. Who would it be? At about 6:00 A.M., he rolled over in the king-size bed to look at the picture of his wife Janice that he kept on the nightstand. Her beautiful face with curly brown hair and sweet smile was the first thing he saw in the morning and the last thing he saw every night. His heart ached for her. He missed her more than he ever let on to anyone. He kept thinking, why did she have to die so young?

He could hear her now: *Billy B., get yourself out of bed. Time's a wasting. Lots to do today.* She always had some project going on. She loved to entertain and put flowers everywhere. Whether it was having friends for dinner, doing a benefit for the Children's Hospital, or putting on a company barbeque, she loved them all.

This big old house with its white columns was magic to her. She called it her Tara. She would laugh and say she didn't know if she was more Scarlett or Melanie. Like Scarlett, she was strong, always said what she thought, and kept everything going. But she loved her man like Melanie loved Ashley. She would laugh and say, *But of course, Scarlett loved Ashley, too. Whether I'm Scarlett or Melanie, you are my Ashley.* It was silly, but she could make him laugh. At five foot six, with about thirty pounds of excess weight and balding, Billy Bob sure didn't look anything like Ashley Wilkes.

Janice could get him to do just about anything. He could see her now, coming through the bedroom door with the Santa costume from the Children's Hospital. *I volunteered you to play Santa for the children. Come on, Billy B., try these on.* As she buckled the belt around his waist, she patted his belly and said, *We might have to pad you a little bit, but not much. With your wonderful laugh, you're a perfect Santa. The kids will love you!* He couldn't believe that he'd made such a fool of himself. But he would do anything for her because she had loved him like no one else had ever loved him. Who would ever love him that way again? No one.

Now the house was quiet. The only sound was the low hum of the heat pump coming on to take off the chill in the air. There were no flowers, no laughter—only quiet.

When Janice couldn't get pregnant, she had begged him to go to the fertility clinic with her. *Please, Billy B. It won't be so bad.* But there was no way he'd do what you had to do to get your sperm in the cup. Lying there in the big bed without her, he thinks maybe he should have done it. There might be children now—pieces of her left in this world.

How could she get ovarian cancer in her early fifties? It wasn't fair. She'd been such a trooper through it all. *I will fight this, Billy B. With you by my side, we'll beat it together.* He went with her to every doctor in town. Determined to find a cure, he'd even taken her to MD Anderson in Texas and the Mayo Clinic in Minnesota, but nothing helped. They didn't beat it. It beat them.

At five foot three, Janice was naturally small, but she wasted away before his eyes. In the end, she only weighed about seventy pounds and looked pale and skeletal propped up against white pillows. That was one image he wished he could erase. With only days left, she had asked him to put the hospital bed in the sunroom where she could look at the garden and the fall trees. Sleeping on the sofa at her side, he listened to her struggling to breathe. He kept trying to get her to eat or drink. Nothing helped. About the only thing he could do for her was adjust her morphine drip. No longer able to talk, she would give him a weak smile.

One memory played over and over in his head. The late afternoon sunlight was coming through the window of the sunroom, and the trees outside were dropping their orange and yellow leaves. Inside, the air was still and smelled of sickness and death. He carefully took Janice's small, fragile body in his arms and held her like a baby. He felt tears running down his cheeks as he whispered, "My sweet wife, I will always, always love you." As he watched her take her last labored breath, he felt like his life was over, too. She was only fifty-four years old, but he still had years to live without her love.

At first, he was in shock; he couldn't believe she had died. Then he got angry. He hated all the platitudes people said to him: "So sorry for your loss," "She is out of her suffering," or "It was her time." His sister wanted him to go to the counselor at the Methodist church. He couldn't even leave his driveway without his busybody neighbor running over to insist that her psychiatrist could help him. But Billy Bob liked to be in control. No shrink was going to tell him what was wrong or make him any better. He was angry, and he planned to stay that way.

As long as he worked in the family construction business, he could stay busy and away from the house as much as possible. He told everybody what to do and they did it. He had power and was in control of everything around him. Somehow, that seemed to help a little.

But since his retirement, all he had in his life was the Athletic Department at Benton University. He had never played sports himself, but he and his fraternity buddies were loyal fans. As the business succeeded, he became a generous contributor to the program. After his company built the new stadium, he made sure he had a big skybox upstairs where he could invite his friends to watch the games. It was about the only thing that still meant something to him. In the past, folks at the university had listened to him and generally did what he told them to do. But things had changed. How could the new president not listen to him? He was selecting the coach with some damn committee of alumni and faculty. Billy Bob had lost control, and he didn't like it one bit.

Thinking he had lollygagged long enough, Billy Bob rolled out of bed, ambled to the bathroom to relieve himself, then got in the shower. As he toweled off, he thought about how he usually enjoyed hearing the scores and the small talk about sports on the early morning radio show. But his morning was different. Yesterday he'd had lunch with President Jansson at the university, stressing to him the importance of hiring Rocky Owens as the new football coach. Owens had been an assistant coach for the legendary Big Jack Barnes. Everyone loved Owens, who knew how things had always been done at the university. Even though Billy Bob had never played or coached himself, he was convinced the Benton Bears didn't need some hot-shot former quarterback nobody knew—some guy named Jonathan Wayne Astin. Dr. Jansson said the committee had narrowed it down to two candidates—Owens and Astin—but he wouldn't tell him which one they would choose, said he had to wait for the announcement the next morning. That was today. Billy Bob had been bothered by that but decided surely the new president had enough sense to do the right thing.

He was anxious when he turned on the radio. He had begun to lather his face with Barbasol shaving cream when he heard the announcer say, "Hello, all you football fans out there! We have a huge announcement for you." Billy Bob stood perfectly still and held his breath. Then the announcer said, "The new football coach is Jonathan Wayne Astin."

Billy Bob exploded. "No. No! That son-of-a-bitch president," he yelled as he threw the shaving cream can as hard as he could at the mirror on the back of the bathroom door. The glass instantly shattered all over the floor. He stood at the sink shaking, gripping the edge and mumbling to himself. "How could he? How could he? He's so stupid." He looked in the mirror at his red face, his drooping jowls half smeared with shaving cream. Quickly lifting the razor to shave, he immediately cut his jaw. "Damn it, damn it." He scowled. Now there was blood on his T-shirt and in the sink. He looked like a wild man, with deranged eyes and blood running down his face. He had completely lost it.

Calm down. He had to calm down and think. He put toilet paper on the nick and managed to finish shaving. Yes, breathe deep and think. "I'll get them sumbitches. They better watch out," he said. "By God, I know what I'm going to do." He walked over the glass in his slippers, making crackling sounds as he went. "Yeah, by God, I'll get them sumbitches," he said again as he grabbed the telephone and called his man Clyde Parsons at the warehouse.

"Hey, Clyde, I knew you'd be there early. Have you heard the news about our new coach?" Billy Bob asked.

"Boss, I just heard it on the radio. It's bullshit. Owens is our man. What can we do?"

"I'm furious. Those idiots at the university didn't do what I told 'em to do. I don't know what they're thinkin'. We got to get them sumbitches, scare 'em, and run 'em off. Most important, we got to do it as fast as we can. You got that? You know the program. You've done it for me before when I needed to harass someone. Make threats. You know I can't call. They all know my voice, but you can do it. Lay it on thick, ya hear me? Lay it on thick. We got to scare 'em. We got to run 'em both off—the coach and that damn president of the university, too. This is bullshit. I am fightin' mad." Billy Bob's heart was pounding, and he could barely catch his breath. "I'm gonna get the Reverend to make a call to the president as well. Yeah, we're gonna scare the hell out of 'em."

"Boss, don't you worry. I know the program, and I had already thought I should call. I'll tell 'em. Yes, this is bullshit," Clyde said. He hung up the phone, jacked up his pants, and started walking to the back of the warehouse where no one could hear him talk.

The air hung heavy and still; it was very warm for a January morning. Clyde felt the sweat beading on the back of his neck, and his white T-shirt stuck to his ample belly. He had already been in a foul mood before he heard the news. His wife Nora Jean was off tending to her sick mama and hadn't been at home to fix his usual breakfast—homemade biscuits, eggs, grits, red-eye gravy, and black coffee. A man couldn't survive on that pitiful cereal she expected him to eat when she was away.

The news had been on the radio and in the newspaper. He would call that sorry writer at the newspaper and give him a piece of his mind. He wouldn't provide his name; he never did. Never tell your name. That don't matter. Somebody's got to speak up. Making the calls made him feel important, too. He'd gotten in the habit of carrying a few numbers on the back of a card in his hip pocket—the sports department at the *Herald News* and the radio stations that had those call-in shows. He always dialed *67 because that blocked caller ID. Yeah, he was going to tell that young Stewart kid at the newspaper a thing or two.

"I want to speak to Jay Stewart," he muttered as a male voice answered the phone.

"Speaking. What can I do for you this morning?" a polite voice answered.

"You wrote that column about the new coach coming to the university, didn't you?" growled Clyde.

"I sure did," Stewart affirmed. "It's an exciting day around the state today, isn't it? Astin has a great reputation as a coach and as a person. We are lucky we got him."

"The hell we are! What you think you know? He don't deserve to be our coach. He don't belong. You hear me? He don't belong. He ain't one of us!" Clyde said excitedly.

"I'm sorry you feel that way. Who's calling, please?"

"You never mind what my name is. I just want you to tell that damn university president up there—what's his name? Tell him we don't like his choice of a coach. You tell him this too: if they stand up in front of the TV and say they picked Astin to be our coach, somebody just might blow that coach's head right off. You got that, boy? Blow his head right off! While they at it, they might get the president, too," Clyde shouted into the phone.

"Hold on, mister. Are you making a threat on somebody's life?" Stewart asked.

"You're damn right I am. We can't just sit by and let this happen. They say he ain't one, but he looks like a nigger to me. You hear me? We won't have it. Tell the president and tell the folks who read your paper. We won't have it!"

The phone went silent as Jay Stewart stood there, stunned. This was the worst call he had received in the six months he had been at the paper. He'd come down from the University of Virginia, excited to cover one of the legendary football programs in the country, but he wasn't prepared for some of the things he'd heard. But didn't the word "fan" come from "fanatic"? Some of these folks were certainly fanatics. Or maybe they were just plain crazy. All these thoughts flooded his head as he walked into his editor's office.

"Chief, I need help with this one. Another crazy call just came in. But this time I believe he made a death threat. In fact, I'm sure he did," Stewart said.

Editor Jeb Merton looked up from his desk, startled. "What did you say—a death threat? Who's it on?"

"He's targeting the new football coach and the president of the university, too."

"My God, the coach hasn't even lost a game yet. Can't the fool wait until then?" grumbled Merton.

"It would seem so. But he told me to tell them something about how, if they stand up at the news conference, somebody might 'blow their heads off.' What am I supposed to do?" Stewart asked.

"I'll handle it. Get President Jansson on the line immediately. That news conference is at 11:00 A.M. The man's probably just blowing off steam, but we need to let Jansson know what's happening. I hate this crap! It's a sorry way to start the new coach's life here with us," Merton said.

Chapter 13

This was a red-letter day for the young administration of the new university president, Axel Wilhelm Jansson. He had come south after serving as president of an Ivy League school in New England. He first arrived in the States as a high school exchange student from Sweden, but once he met his future wife, Glenda, he decided to stay. A Yale- and Stanford-educated man, he had always loved sports and had played soccer himself. He was excited about his first job at a major university with a top-notch athletic program. He knew what a good program could mean to an institution of higher learning, particularly if it was led correctly, with class. He was determined to have a clean program with none of the cheating that was such a problem in college athletics. That's why today was so special. Hiring Jonathan Wayne Astin was a real coup. A great coach with integrity, Astin even shared Jansson's love of history. They'd had a wonderful conversation over dinner when he came to interview. Astin's wife Kendall was an attorney, and he was looking forward to meeting her. He was thinking how he and his wife Glenda would be good friends with the Astins when the phone rang.

"Is this Dr. Jansson, president of the university?" the voice asked.

"Yes, it is. What can I do for you?" Dr. Jansson said.

"Just call me the Reverend. The Lord sent me a message last night. Appeared in a vision, clear as could be. I'm the mouthpiece of God. The Lord giveth and the Lord taketh away. He will strike down the heathen with his thunderbolt. The wrath of God will come as lightning from the sky and kill the pagan." The caller's voice had risen to a fever pitch.

"What are you talking about? Who is this?" Jansson asked.

"Never mind. Just call me the Reverend. The Lord was talkin' about the new coach. He is a heathen from a foreign land—the devil incarnate...." The caller rambled on, but Jansson hung up the phone.

He could still hear the voice raging. Religious extremists were all over the place. Had he just talked to one? The phone rang again. He hesitated but decided to answer it.

"Dr. Jansson, this is Jeb Merton, editor of the *Herald News*. We've talked several times at Rotary Club. I apologize for calling you at home, but I felt it was necessary. I wanted to catch you before you got going this morning. We've had a call to the office down here that you need to know about. Some man called—wouldn't give his name. It was a weird call. I hate to tell you this. I'm sure the man is some crackpot. But he says if the coach gets up at the news conference today...." Merton hesitated. "Ah, sir, he said somebody might—in his words—'blow his head off.'"

"What did you say?" Jansson asked in disbelief.

"Yes sir, he said, 'blow his head off.' But, Dr. Jansson, he said they might get you, too. I hate this, but I had to call you. This anonymous person is making a death threat on you and Coach Astin," Merton said apologetically.

"I'll get right on it. Thank you for calling." Jansson hung up and immediately picked up the phone again. "Get me Thornton Miles, and make it quick."

By 9:30 A.M., Dr. Jansson had campus security head Thornton Miles, local police chief Vernon Patterson, and about a dozen police officers gathered in his office. He was not in a good mood, and everyone could tell. "Listen to what I'm going to say, and listen well. I will say this one time and one time only," he began.

Dr. Jansson stood quietly for a few seconds and then spoke. "I have only been at this university for one year, but I know its history. I know that years ago when the university tried to integrate, the KKK was burning crosses on campus and demonstrators broke into violence. The National Guard was called in to keep the peace. I have heard that the president at that time—Dr. Simpson—called you all together and said that if another cross were burned on campus, there would be hell to pay. He might have been a former preacher, but he was hard-nosed. I know there was no more violence and no more crosses burned. We are at a similar crossroads today. We have some ignorant people threatening violence again. We have received two death threats on the life of our new coach. Some dumb folks don't approve of his dark skin or his origins or whatever the hell it is they don't like. There was even a threat thrown in against me. Now I want that news conference blanketed inside and out. I want two plain-clothed, armed guards on Astin and his wife at every minute today. The guards do not leave their sides. Is that understood? I want no incident whatsoever. History will not repeat itself at this university. One more thing: what I have told you is not to leave this room. I want this to be peaceful—no incidents. Understood?"

All the officers nodded and said, "Yes sir," as Jansson turned and left the room.

Chapter 14

Kendall would never forget the day the university flew them down for the press conference announcing Duke's hiring. They were picked up by a private plane—the first of many surprises that day. After they landed in Benton, a large black van with tinted windows pulled up right next to the plane.

When they stepped down out of the plane, they were greeted by a tall, slim, blond-haired man with a slight accent. "Welcome, welcome to our university. I'm Axel Jansson, university president. We're delighted you have decided to join us, Mrs. Astin...or shall I call you Kendall?" He reached out to shake Kendall's hand. "Duke speaks so fondly of you. I look forward to you meeting my wife, Glenda. I know you will hit it off, and she will be glad to help you in any way she can."

"Yes, call me Kendall. We're excited to be here, too. I look forward to meeting your wife. Thank you for coming out to meet us," Kendall answered.

"I wouldn't miss being here to pick you up and make you feel welcome. Everyone at the university is excited. Duke's reputation has preceded him. We feel so fortunate that you've decided to join us."

On the way to the university, Dr. Jansson shared information about the community, and Kendall immediately liked him. Everything happened so quickly that she hadn't had a chance to visit the campus, and Duke had only been there for his interview.

There were no leaves on the trees, but the campus was still beautiful with its stately neoclassical buildings. Dr. Jansson Axel pointed out various buildings—science, math, and of course history. He also showed them the president's home, which looked like Tara from *GONE WITH THE WIND*. Kendall thought there was no doubt this university was in the South.

Two other men rode with them in the van. They had been briefly introduced but never joined in the conversation. As they approached a large convention center, Kendall was wondering who the two men were and why they were there. They constantly peered out the windows as if they were looking for something.

When they entered the large conference room, there were cameras everywhere. She and Duke were led to the front of the room. She stood to one side and looked out at the throng of reporters. She could not believe how many people were there with pads and pens jotting down everything that was said. It reminded her of one of those news conferences you see on TV with the President of the United States.

Dr. Jansson gave a cordial welcoming speech and highlighted Duke's resume, talking about his years at UCLA and in the pros along with his coaching success. Kendall was particularly proud when he said, "But more important than his wins on the field is his reputation for integrity and the graduation rate of his players." She decided she was going to like this president, who had his priorities straight.

The room was hot with all the TV lights, and it was getting hotter by the minute. She had worn a pink wool jacket that she thought would be appropriate for a January day. But this day was proving much warmer than she expected, and she felt a little sick. Nonetheless, she kept smiling. Again, she noticed those two men who seemed to be glued to them as they monitored the room. Who were they?

The news conference was opened for questions. The room was full of mostly white men with only a few women. Kendall noticed there were very few black reporters. It was bright, very bright. It crossed her mind that Duke stood out in this sea of white, especially standing by the fair-skinned Dr. Jansson. Duke had a naturally dark complexion, but his many hours in the sun made him appear even darker. He looked rugged and handsome to her, but she wondered if everyone else saw him that way. After all, she had grown up in the South. This day and age, it shouldn't matter anyway. Besides, they all knew he was Hawaiian, and that was no issue. At least, that's how Kendall reassured herself.

Duke answered questions about what kind of offense he intended to run, how he planned to jump into recruiting, and his thoughts on hiring assistant coaches. There were a few unusual questions. One man asked, "Hey, coach, do you like barbequed ribs?" and everyone laughed. Another asked in a somewhat argumentative tone, "Astin, are you one of those 'academic coaches'?" It sounded like he thought that was a negative, like the coach shouldn't bother with the players' grades in class. The most troubling question was, "You're not from the South, so why do you think you were selected? You didn't play for Big Jack Barnes, nor were you one of his assistants." Kendall wanted to scream that a committee had selected Duke for his abilities. Why did it matter that he hadn't played for Big Jack? Thankfully, someone finally called an end to the questions. Then Dr. Jansson walked out with them as Duke kept shaking hands with everyone. The two mystery men stayed close to their sides.

Later, Kendall learned that the news conference had been carried live on all the network stations as well as CNN. But that wasn't her last shock of the day. She finally learned who the two men were and why they were there.

Chapter 15

Billy Bob Craven sat at his usual table at the country club. He met good friends from his university days, Tommy Lee Hampton and Roland Rigby, for lunch almost every day. It got him out of the house, gave him something to do. They liked to sit at the round table by the window. It had a nice view of the golf course, but more than that, they could have private conversations.

"I'll have a vodka and cranberry juice," he told the waiter. He always enjoyed a couple of drinks with lunch, but he needed them more than usual today. Meeting his friends here at the club was important to him. They liked to talk about politics and local gossip, but mostly they liked to keep tabs on the football program at the university.

"Hey, Tommy Lee, it's about time you got here. I'm already one drink ahead of you," he said to the man who sat down a few minutes later.

"You know I don't move as fast as I used to. But I'm not complaining. Boy, I'll have a vodka martini," he almost barked to the young black waiter. Tommy Lee was in decent shape for a man going on seventy. He'd been a legendary running back at the university, and he never quit moving. He still did a little running for exercise. His mind wasn't as healthy as his body; in fact, it never had been. But he'd been able to "stay on scholarship" his entire life. As a former Benton player, and later in the pros, he was used to someone taking care of him. In fact, through the years he had amassed quite a sizable fortune from endorsements, speaking engagements, and his inclusion on some land deals his friends sent his way. He had also become the one everyone looked to for the final word on decisions in the athletic department at the university. His okay was the stamp of approval.

"You okay, Billy Bob? You look frazzled today. What's that cut on your jaw?" Tommy Lee asked.

"Oh, it's nothing. Cut myself shaving this morning." Trying to change the subject, Billy Bob said, "You know, you ought to stop drinking those vodka martinis and switch to vodka and cranberry juice. Ole Doc Shorter told me cranberry juice is good for you. Of course, I don't think he knew I would be drinking a lot of vodka with it." Billy Bob laughed when Tommy Lee waved him off, just as the third member of their group walked up.

Roland Rigby was a tall, rugged-looking man with skin like leather from years in the sun. He had inherited money from his wealthy father, who had wisely invested large sums in Coca-Cola stock. Roland's inheritance had ensured that he would never have to work for a living. He'd gotten in some trouble as a kid—he had a mean streak, and his father had sent him off to military prep school before university. Roland had thrived there, and unlike other young men of his privileged class, he had volunteered for Vietnam. Craving the adventure, he went into special forces and became a ranger. He was quiet and never talked about his days in the military, but he had become something of a local war hero. He was prouder of those days in Nam than he was of anything else he'd ever done. With two failed marriages and a troubled teenage son, he hadn't been successful at much else. Now he loved to hunt and play golf. In fact, if he wasn't hunting, he was playing golf almost every day, like he'd done for years. His recreational activities became his life. As much as playing golf, he loved to bet on the games. If he couldn't bet at least twenty bucks a hole, he didn't care about playing golf. He loved to gamble on everything—college football, pro games, horse races. Going to Vegas with the guys or his son once every couple of months was a must. "Hello, you two. Let's get down to business. I got a golf game at 2:00."

Billy Bob immediately got serious. "I'm mad as hell today about that damn new football coach. They're having the news conference right now, introducing him to the world. I don't like him. He wasn't our choice. We wanted one of our own—Rocky Owens. Why did that new president have to go get some coach from halfway around the world? Is he an immigrant or something?"

"No, Billy Bob. He's part Hawaiian. You know that's a state now," Tommy Lee said with a laugh.

"Don't try to be funny. I know Hawaii is a state. But the guy is so dark—brown skinned. That's not good in this part of the world. Folks will wonder. You know what I mean," Billy Bob said seriously.

"But he was a super player out West and has a great coaching record," Tommy Lee said.

"I don't care about any of that. He didn't go to our university. Ole Big Jack must be rolling over in his grave. He would've wanted one of his boys that had played for him or coached with him. They would know how things are done around here. We'll never win with some 'academic' coach who's gonna insist on smart kids who do well in class. Hell, we just need to know they can play. We know how to get 'em in and keep 'em in school. It doesn't matter if they graduate. We just want young men who want to play ball. We won't be able to get all the great players the way we used to. You know what I mean?" Billy Bob nodded and winked.

"You talkin' about the time we gave that great running back a paper bag with $14,000.00 in it? I'll never forget that. Exciting. Those other teams wondered why he suddenly loved us so much," Tommy Lee said.

"Keep your voice down. You know we're not supposed to talk about that stuff. It's illegal as hell." Billy Bob looked around the room to see if anyone was listening. "But here's another thing, too. We give all the money every time they come asking. That gives us control of the program. We make the decisions, not some new president or a damn committee. That's what we're supposed to do. We just need to get rid of this guy as fast as we can, and that president, too. Now listen to me— what can we do to make life difficult for the new coach?"

"You know we can make it real unpleasant for him right from day one," Roland said calmly. "We can plain harass him. We got our guys in the media. Every time he loses a game—and he'll lose a few this year—they'll go after him. He doesn't have the usual talent on the team. We'll make sure the media folks make a lot of noise."

"That's easy," Billy Bob countered. "But what else? We can't wait for the season to begin; we got to start now. You know my company built the stadium. And when the school needed money for some faculty salaries, I gave them a half million a few years back. I'll let that president know I won't be real anxious to fork over the money the next time they come calling."

"Yeah, that's right. You've given an awful lot of money over the years—probably more than anybody," Tommy Lee said as he patted Billy Bob on the shoulder. "And since your company built the stadium, they ought to name it for you someday. But as for that coach now, you mentioned the media. We've got several around the state we can call and stir up some controversy. They've got connections with the police—a player gets a DUI or anything, and it's immediately out. They used to keep it quiet for us, but if we tell 'em to get it out, they will. That TV guy that's tied in with the national networks, we can call him and feed him rumors. He's good about saying, 'My sources tell me,' but he never verifies his source. He'll say anything to have a story and beat somebody else to the punch."

Billy Bob smiled. "Well, let's get going immediately. I want that coach to feel the heat from day one. Whatever it takes, we got to get rid of him as soon as possible. I don't like that foreign president either. He ain't from here; he's got a weird name. What is goin' on? All these foreigners invading. We don't want to lose control of the football program. It's always been ours—we paid for it. And you're right, they should name that stadium after me!"

Chapter 16

Elijah Ray Johnson was the leader of the Benton Bears. All the players respected him. He was quiet; he wasn't a talker like many of the guys who were always carrying on and horsing around having fun. Elijah just watched. Everyone looked up to him because he was such a great athlete, worked hard in the classroom, and put everyone else to shame on the practice field. But he never acted like a big shot or lorded it over any of the others. All the players wondered what the new coach was like, but they really wanted Elijah's opinion.

They were all waiting expectantly in the football meeting room, a large room with tiered theater seats that could hold over a hundred people. Today it was packed with players, staff, and trainers all waiting for the new coach to arrive. It was noisy, with questions flying around the room. Elijah sat on the front row being hammered by his teammates: "What have you heard about this new coach?" "Have you seen any of his NFL films?" "Man, was he fast!" "Did you see how he threw the ball?" "I wonder what it'll be like to play for him?" "I bet he can help us get into pro ball." When Coach Astin suddenly walked into the room, everyone fell silent.

He stood before them for a moment and looked around the room. He was a handsome, tall, muscular man who stood ramrod straight. He was in great physical shape and, in fact, looked like he could still be a quarterback in the NFL. His presence filled the room and demanded everyone's attention. He immediately took charge. There was tension in the air; everyone seemed uneasy. Then the coach smiled and the room lit up. "Men, I'm happy to be here as your new coach. I know you're wondering what it will be like to play for me. You don't know me, and I don't know you. But that won't take long to correct. I'll lay out what I expect of you, and I'll tell you what you can expect from me. It won't be complicated.

"Heads up, now; let's be serious while I give some basic information." Coach Astin looked out at the players, meeting their curious eyes. "First, you are student athletes, here to get an education while playing football. I expect you to go to all your classes and work to do the best you can. It's simple. Don't cut classes, and work to graduate with a degree from this university. If you don't go to class, you won't play football. Understood?" The players nodded their heads in agreement.

"Second, we'll have some simple rules that will be posted regularly pertaining to curfews and training schedules in the weight room. Of course, you will never be late for any meetings or for practice. If you're late, you won't play. Understood?" Again, the players nodded as the coach looked straight at them.

"Third, we will be honest. We won't break any NCAA rules. Don't take anything illegal from any booster. Understood?" He paused again, waiting for the group's agreement.

"Finally," he resumed, "and this is important. You are not here to play for me. You are here to play for each other. We will become a team together. If you learn to play for the team and not individual glory, you will succeed beyond your dreams. Work hard for each other, and we'll have great success. If you do what I ask you to do, we'll have fun, too." The coach smiled. "It's fun when you win. As I said earlier, it isn't complicated. I come from Hawaii, where there's a tradition of friendliness. We're an easygoing people. But don't be fooled; there's also the tradition of the fierce warrior. I apply that to the football field. I will be friendly and easygoing off the field, but once we step across the white line, everything changes. We become warriors, and we will win. Say, 'Warriors win.' Do you understand?" Coach Astin asked as the players mumbled back to him. "I can't hear you. Let me hear that loud and clear: 'Warriors win,'" he said as the team shouted, "Warriors win."

"That's better! Now that you know where I stand, I want to get to know all of you better. My assistant will be setting up individual meetings with each one of you. I want to know your academic standing, and I want to know what your dreams are. What do you want to do with your life?" the coach said. He wrapped up the meeting, explained that he was available for them but warned that he had some demands on him right away. Hiring a staff had to be a priority, and recruiting would require frequent travel. He reminded them that national signing day for new recruits was February 14, the second Wednesday of the month, so he had to get going. By the end of the meeting, they were shaking hands, high-fiving, and laughing. Duke was off to a good start doing what he loved, and the players sensed it. It was going to be hard work but fun, too. The players were jacked up as they yelled, "Warriors win."

Before he left the room, Coach Astin walked up to shake Elijah's hand. "I've heard wonderful things about you, Elijah. I know you're a great athlete and a leader of the team. I want to meet with you first. Please make an appointment with my assistant today. I want you to tell me about the team, and I want to know what your dreams are for your life. Would you do that for me?"

"Yes sir, I will," Elijah said, at a loss for words. Something's different about this coach, he thought. He knows my name and wants me to tell him my dreams. No coach has ever been interested in me for anything except football. I like this coach.

As he was leaving the meeting, all the players kept coming up to Elijah asking him what he thought. He was quiet for a few moments, and then all he said was, "I like him." The guys were pleased. If Elijah liked him, they did, too.

Chapter 17

Kendall saw very little of Duke after that first day. He was up at 5:00 A.M., off to the office or wherever the day took him, and he returned late at night exhausted. After all these years, she had gotten used to him leaving early in the morning and coming back late. As usual, Duke made a quick adjustment when they moved to a new place. He had an instant job, a purpose, and he hit the ground running. Of course, it wasn't as easy for Kendall. She had to figure out where they were going to live and what she was going to do.

Kendall had decided this move would be different. She had left their home in Kansas on the market with instructions for everything to be packed and shipped when the house sold. If necessary, their furniture would be put in storage until they found a place to live.

The university recommended an experienced real estate agent, Betty Friedman, who began showing Kendall every available house in town. The two spent so many hours together that Betty became her first friend.

It was a typical university town, with many of the houses around the university nearly a hundred years old. Some were two-story brick colonials, and others were Victorian with wraparound porches. Since these houses were within walking distance of campus, many faculty members and staff liked living there. The newer suburbs were farther away but didn't offer many choices.

At the end of a long morning of looking and finding nothing, Kendall said, "Betty, I'm beginning to get discouraged. I haven't seen anything that's right for us. I want a quiet place—a place to get away from the noise. We live in a fishbowl. Everyone wants to ask questions about football wherever we go. It's hard to have a private life."

"Wait a minute, what have I been thinking?" Betty said, turning out of the suburbs. "I assumed you wanted to be close to the university.

I know just the right spot for you, but you might have to build." She drove about ten miles out of town to Lake Bradford. It was a beautiful lake that was just beginning to be developed.

"Oh, Betty, I had no idea any place like this existed around here. It's wonderful!" Kendall exclaimed. The shoreline was covered with pines and hardwood trees and even a few weeping willows down by the water. The lake was huge, covering miles and miles of undeveloped property. The few lots that had already been cut were three to five acres with wonderful privacy. Kendall immediately loved the lake and soon found the perfect lot to build a house. It was on a little peninsula that jutted out into a wide expanse of the water. There was a one-hundred-eighty-degree view with a little cove on the left and a perfect spot for a boat dock.

By the time Kendall and Betty finished, it was getting late and the sun was beginning to go down. The afternoon sky was orange, with light sparkling off the water. The quiet was magical, only a few birds were chirping. They sat on an old log, had bottled waters, and soaked up the atmosphere. Suddenly Kendall spotted some loons in the water. "Betty, look out there. See the loons bobbing their heads in the water, just like in *On Golden Pond*? Duke and I can grow old like Katharine Hepburn and Henry Fonda: old grumps, loving each other and bickering all the time." Kendall laughed at the thought.

"I've always wanted to build a house," she said, "and this is the perfect spot." Kendall's mind started churning. Maybe, finally, they wouldn't have to move anymore. She was now in her late forties and might be too old to get pregnant. If she couldn't, maybe they could adopt a child or even two. She didn't need to ask Duke about this place; she knew he would love it, too. It would give them wonderful sunsets and quiet serenity. It was just what they needed to get away from the noise in the city and the stress of his job. This could be their forever home—one with children they had wanted their entire marriage.

Betty recommended that Kendall and Duke rent a condo nearby on the lake. "While you're building, keep your things in storage. The condo is furnished with a comfortable sofa and chairs and has window views of the lake. You can start enjoying the quiet and be near the building site. Nice fireplace, too." She also suggested a builder—G. B.

Carter —and said she would be happy to make an appointment for Kendall to meet him.

"The condo sounds great for us right now. And I'd love to meet the builder as soon as possible. I think our life in this new place is taking shape." For the first time in a long time, Kendall felt that she and Duke could be happy. She couldn't wait to tell him all about it. Surely nothing could happen to ruin their life here. They could live here for the rest of their days.

Chapter 18

Kendall had dressed carefully for her speaking engagement at the Rotary Club. It was the end of January, and she was still meeting people for the first time. As the coach's wife, she felt she needed to look professional but still be ladylike and feminine. She had grown up in the South and knew about the mystique of the Southern lady. She wore a navy blue suit with a light blue silk blouse. Her hair, which she now wore shoulder length, was fixed perfectly. She knew some people thought she was a radical feminist since she specialized in domestic law, but she would be herself and try to win them over. She was a little nervous, but she always was when she spoke to a large group. She figured that was fine because she had prepared well. She sat at the head table looking out at the audience of about three hundred.

Kendall could see the nervousness in their faces. They sat rigid in their chairs. They didn't know what she was going to say, and they didn't look too eager to hear it. The men outnumbered the women about ten to one. Women had been banned from such organizations for years, and even though they were now invited, their number was still small. At Rotary Club luncheons, women were still not sure all the men welcomed them. As Kendall looked out from the podium at this gathering of business and civic leaders, she took a deep breath. It was going to be difficult to win this group.

After the president of the club introduced her, she stood and took another deep breath. "I am delighted to be here. It gives me an opportunity to thank all the people who have welcomed us so warmly. I know you prefer that Duke be here today, but he's out recruiting, and you know how important that is." A few of the men smiled and nodded.

"I know some of you are nervous. I can see it in your faces. You're asking yourselves, is that woman a radical, feminist lawyer who's mad at the world?" She heard a few uneasy chuckles. "Well, you can relax. I like men. I love my husband—but I am an advocate for women. I am really concerned about what happens to them," she continued.

She decided to tell a funny story. "Did you hear what happened soon after our president Dr. Jansson and his wife Glenda arrived here? They were walking down the street, and a man who was covered with dirt popped his head out of a manhole. He immediately looked up and said 'Hello, Glenda, it is great to see you. You look great.' Glenda answered, 'Jimmy, thank you and so good to see you.' President Jansson could not help but be a little annoyed. As they walked away, he said, 'Who was that?' Glenda answered, 'That was Jimmy. We dated in high school, and he even asked me to marry him.' Dr. Jansson said, 'Well, aren't you glad you married me? I'm a university president, and look where he is.' Glenda looked up and smiled. 'If I had married him, he would be the university president.'" The audience burst into laughter. She could see them beginning to relax and respond to what she was saying.

"I would like to get serious for a moment. The women here will understand what I'm going to talk about, but it's harder for men sometimes. I want you men to think about your daughters and granddaughters. Think about what you want for them. I think it will help you understand."

She began what she called her fifteen-minute lecture on the legal history of women in America. Women had not been included in the Constitution, had almost no rights, and had to fight to have a voice. She briefly talked about the long struggle for the vote and how the truth was left out of history books. At the end, she said that in America's early history it was legal for men to beat their wives. Wife beating was permitted if husbands abided by the "rule of thumb," meaning the rod was no bigger than their thumbs. She continued up through the present time, saying that some men, unfortunately, still felt they had that right.

Kendall could see in their eyes that she had a good portion of the group listening to her. "The problem transcends all class lines and economic levels," she said. "More women die in America at the hands of their husbands or lovers than in automobile accidents, rapes, and muggings combined." She ended her remarks by talking about what could be done to raise awareness of the problem and, hopefully, make the lives of women better. She thanked everyone for giving her the opportunity to speak and sat down. To her amazement, she received a standing ovation. She was astounded. They had let go of their anxiety and listened. They got the message.

Afterwards, many attendees came up to speak to her. She had a brief conversation with an assistant district attorney, Byron Thomas. He said her suggestion to think about his daughter helped him understand. His daughter wanted to be a judge someday, and he knew it would be harder for her because she was female. Kendall assured him it was happening more and more and for him to continue to encourage her. The dean of the law school, Matt Brisbane, came over and said she should be in the classroom teaching and that they should talk later. A woman came up and asked if she would be interested in serving on the board of the new Spouse Abuse Center. Kendall responded that she would be delighted. She met so many interesting people—like-minded folks who shared her interests.

She left the luncheon feeling like she had found her place in the community. She and Duke could both be happy and make a contribution in the lives of the people. To be truthful, she floated out of that meeting. She was elated.

Chapter 19

February 1996

Kendall hardly saw Duke during recruiting in January and the first week of February. They were both so busy. Of course, she tried to help with recruiting, meeting the parents and hoping she could get an idea of who they were and what they wanted for their sons. But, by the time she and Duke got home, they were so exhausted that they fell into bed with only brief exchanges about anything else.

By mid-February, with recruiting wrapped up, they finally had a free night to enjoy. The condo at the lake had turned out to be just as comfortable and cozy as Betty had said it would be. They had a fire going in the fireplace and had eaten their dinner on TV trays. It was nice to be able to relax and just visit with each other.

"Recruiting went well, didn't it?" Kendall asked.

"Yes, I think so," Duke said, leaning forward in his chair. "We didn't get every player we wanted, but we got enough. Several of the guys are real blue chippers that might be able to help us next year. I think all the young men coming are good kids, even though some might have to be tutored to make up some deficiencies in their background. But they all really want to be here. The tradition of the program is very important. I can't wait to start working with them."

"I'm so glad," Kendall said. She began to report on what had happened with her. "I have visited with Dean Brisbane of the law school, and I will be teaching one course this fall—Women and the Law in America. It'll fit right in with my interests. And I've already told you about being on the board of the Spouse Abuse Center. Looks like we'll both be doing what we love to do."

Duke didn't smile; in fact, he showed no interest in what she'd just told him. Kendall was irritated. "Duke, you don't seem excited about this. Don't you understand that I have to find some meaningful things to do when we move into a new location? You just come right in and get busy with football. It's always football this and football that. If we aren't talking about something that has to do with football, you couldn't care less. I get so tired of it!"

"Kendall, I'm sorry. I can't help it sometimes. There's just always something going on, and my mind wanders. I do stay preoccupied about football. It's huge to everyone here. Can you forgive me and let me tell you a few things?" Duke asked.

"Okay, okay, let me hear the bad news. But please, try to show more interest in what I'm doing," Kendall pleaded.

"I will. I promise I'll try," Duke said, then hesitated before he began to speak. "Kendall, there are some things I need to tell you. I've been waiting until we had some time to sit down quietly. Do you remember those two men at the press conference the day we arrived? They stuck to our sides all day, and you wondered who they were. Well, they were armed guards in civilian dress. President Jansson ordered them never to leave our side that day. You saw all those police everywhere, too. There were death threats made on my life that morning. One was called to the newspaper, and one was called to the president's home."

Shocked and angry, Kendall struggled to find the right words. "I can't believe it. Why would there be death threats?"

"Various reasons, it seems. One was a crazy religious fanatic. They didn't pay much attention to him. Another came from some man who said I didn't belong here. I was an outsider. Even called me a nigger," he said sadly.

"What was he talking about? What does that mean, for heaven's sake? You have dark skin—part Hawaiian. And it shouldn't matter what color your skin is." She was getting madder by the minute.

"I knew you would get angry. Just remember, this is the Deep South," Duke said.

"Yes, I grew up in Atlanta. But a lot has changed since then. There were no blacks on our high school team, and now half the university team is black. I really can't believe this. I am furious." Her face felt hot.

"Calm down. We've got to talk about this rationally. There have been some other calls, too. Calls have come from big contributors who didn't like me being selected coach," Duke said. "These men think they should have more say about who the coach is. They don't think they were consulted. Actually, I think they believe they should control everything about the football program."

"Listen, Duke, you didn't have any control over how they selected you. In fact, this university went about it the way most universities do—with a committee made up of the president, alumni, faculty, and student representatives. You didn't make a single call asking for this job. They called you. They interviewed you. They selected you. You could have gone anywhere in the country. Now you have taken this job and you haven't done a thing wrong. This is absurd."

"I know, I know. You're right. But what do we do now? I want you to know everything that's going on. We must go into this with our eyes wide open," Duke said as he took Kendall's hand.

"What a way to start a job. I wonder if any other football coach has ever started a job with death threats and armed guards? It's unbelievable. How can you do your job effectively?"

"Well, so far we've been able to keep these death threats quiet. There have been questions from the media about why I got the job since I didn't play for the legendary Big Jack Barnes. Funny thing is he coached me in a college all-star game years ago and we got to be good friends. These folks don't know that, but I feel like he would approve if he were alive. He could shut them up quickly. Unfortunately, he isn't around to do that."

Duke sat quietly for a few moments before he said, "I really think if I do a good job and run a clean program, we'll be fine. Of course, I have to win enough games—you always have to win. But I believe we can, and we'll overcome the naysayers."

"Duke, I don't know. This is dangerous. Death threats. I'm worried. I'm really worried about your safety," Kendall said with tears in her eyes.

"I've met with Dr. Jansson and the authorities. The police and the FBI say that people who make these threats usually don't follow through. I tend to believe them. These folks aren't serious. They're just blowing off steam or something," Duke said to reassure her.

"But you don't know that. There are crazy people in this world. I think we have to take them very seriously," Kendall said.

"I'll be careful and do everything the authorities tell me to do. You don't take a job and walk away because of a few weird people. I choose to believe what the FBI says. The crazies probably won't do anything," Duke said calmly.

"Well, I guess we don't have any other choice. The administration is with you. Dr. Jansson is great. You do what you came here to do, and do it well. You show these people," Kendall said with conviction.

Duke had a smile on his face for the first time. "Kendall, I love your spirit. What would I do with an indecisive woman—or a woman who didn't have your courage? I feel the same way, but I wanted you to agree with me. I wanted you to know the truth. It isn't going to be easy, but if you're with me, we can do it." He laughed as he reached out to hug her.

"Of course I'm with you. I love you and I'll be right by your side. But I don't like it."

Duke put his arm around Kendall, and she leaned on his shoulder. They sat like that by the fire and talked long into the evening. They didn't know what they had gotten themselves into, but they didn't see that they had any other alternatives than to stick it out. They were too far into the project now. They would do the best they could, and surely things would work out in the end. That's what their rational minds told them, and that's what they said to each other. They were both disappointed with the turn of events. But truthfully, Kendall was more angry than anything, and she would stay that way to the bitter end.

Chapter 20

Toby Lane had been working construction since he finished high school. He liked being outside and getting to do something different every day. His father had been a carpenter and taught him well. He had become a darn good carpenter, and the pay was pretty good, too. If he couldn't be a pro football player like he had planned in high school, this was what he would do.

Toby was a big guy, about six-foot-three with muscular arms. Unfortunately, his stomach was too big now, and he couldn't get enough exercise. His wife Margie was a mighty good cook, too. You could say it really wasn't his fault that he was getting fat. Carpentry didn't provide much physical activity. And all the beer didn't help.

"Toby, pick up that trash by the door—those Vienna sausage cans, candy wrappers, and cigarette butts," said G. B. Carter, the general contractor. "I provide those big trash cans. When are you going to start using 'em, for God's sake?"

Toby got up from his lunch break and started picking up the garbage, but he didn't like it. He never liked anybody telling him what to do.

"Now don't look so irritated. That new coach's wife is coming to check out our work before she makes a decision on her builder. I don't want the job site to look a mess. You want to work on the coach's house, don't you?" Carter asked.

"Whatever you want, boss. It don't matter to me," Toby answered.

"But you love football. I always hear you talking about it in the fall. You played in high school. I thought you would be excited about this job."

"As long as they win, I'm happy. I like to bet on the games, too—you know, just a little, boss. If they win and I win, too, I'm happy," Toby said.

"Well, whatever. Let's at least make a good impression on this woman." He raised his voice a little and directed it to the others who were finishing their lunches. "Men, watch your language. No profanity, and no staring at the lady while she's on the site."

Toby was putting quarter round down in the great room as Mrs. Astin and Carter exchanged pleasantries. He could hear everything and was in a perfect spot to check her out. She looked pretty good for her age. She wasn't too old. But she seemed awful bossy to him. She asked so many questions and seemed to have a lot of ideas of her own. Toby hated women like her. They needed somebody to keep them in their place. He didn't put up with any of that talk from Margie. If she asked too many questions about his drinking with the guys or gave him instruction on how to do something, he let her have it. Yes sir, he let her have it. Toby decided right then and there that he did not like this Astin lady. If Carter did decide to build their house, Toby would have a hard time putting up with that woman. He didn't like her husband either. He was an outsider; he wasn't one of them. No matter if he was a good coach—he didn't belong. If truth were told, Toby resented the fact that Coach Astin had gotten to do all the things Toby had wanted to do. Life wasn't fair.

Chapter 21

Margie stood at the stove working on dinner and thinking about how she and Toby had met and decided to marry. They started dating in high school. Toby was a big, good-looking guy with sandy blond hair. Always the life of any party, he had loved to joke with his teammates and was always horsing around playing tricks on them. At the rec center dances after the football games, he would let loose and have a great time. For his size, he was an unusually good dancer. Sports—especially football—had given him confidence. They had also been an escape from his home life. Toby was the only son of an alcoholic father who had loved to whip Toby with a belt for the least reason when he was growing up. His mother was a demanding woman who was always after Toby, too. He thought his younger sisters got by easier while he was made to do the hard labor all the time. Toby had grown to hate his father and resent his mother. He couldn't wait to leave home and had been determined to be different when he grew up. His dream was to go to college and play football on a scholarship. The game was going to be his ticket for escape because his father had said he couldn't afford to send him. Margie had always wished that dream had worked out. If it had, she knew their life would be very different now.

Margie was a petite blonde, and her classmates had always told her she was one of the smartest girls in the class. She came from a poor farm family, with two older brothers who had taught her to take care of herself. She was quiet but had a feisty personality. She remembered how all the guys wanted to get her attention and win a date with her. But with his fun personality, good looks, and accomplishments on the football field, Toby had won the competition and became Margie's steady boyfriend.

Toby was sweet to her when they first started dating during their junior year of high school. The football team won the regional championship that year. He was a big offensive lineman, and when his senior year rolled around, he got a few articles written about him in the local newspaper. He even made second team on the all-state team. The two of them had fun going to the local hangouts and the movies. Toby drank some in high school. Everybody did, but he didn't seem to have a problem with it back then.

But then, his dream of playing football didn't work out the way he wanted. He got a feeler or two from a couple of small schools who said he didn't have quite enough size or speed. With the loss of a football scholarship came the loss of his dream of escape and a college degree. Toby was profoundly disappointed. In fact, that was around the end of his senior year of high school, when Toby started drinking more than he should.

But he had loved Margie and was so happy when they got married right out of high school. They wanted to have a big family and live on a farm in a house he would build for them. They immediately had their first baby girl, Lisbeth, twelve months later. After eighteen months, Jane Ann was born, and finally Carrie came along eighteen months after Jane Ann. They were all beautiful little blonde, blue-eyed girls. Toby and Margie both loved the girls, but they were a big responsibility. Toby spent long days on his construction job, and Margie filled every waking hour running after the three girls. After a few years, the strain began to show on the marriage. They both thought maybe they had rushed into too much too soon, but what could they do now?

Margie was tired and wanted to get the three girls in bed early just so she could have some time of her own. She also liked to get them in bed before Toby got home from work, especially if he'd been drinking. She served the girls chili, had a little for herself, and then got them all bathed and settled into bed.

Margie heard Toby drive up in his pickup truck as she was coming out of the girls' room. She had read them a bedtime story and they had all fallen asleep immediately. Maybe she and Toby could have a good evening tonight.

"Hey, how was your day?" she asked. She tried not to look too irritated despite the fact she could tell he'd been drinking.

"Not good. I had to work late. Carter was yelling at us all day. Do this, do that. Pushing us. He made me real mad," he grumbled.

"I guess he has to do that. I know y'all are running behind on that house you're building because of all the rain we've had," Margie replied.

"Are you taking his side? You think Carter is such a nice guy—try working for him every day," Toby snapped back.

"I'm not taking anybody's side. I'm just making a comment."

"That's not what it sounds like to me. I think you've got a crush on Carter. You're always talking about how nice he is. I guess you think he's cute, too," Toby said as his voice got louder.

"There you go again, Toby. I've only met the man a few times when I've come by the job site to bring your lunch to you. For heaven's sake, what's wrong with you tonight? Where's that fun-loving guy I married? We used to get along so well. I'm sick and tired of the way you act all the time now." Margie couldn't hold back her anger.

"Nothing's wrong with me except I'm tired. Have you got anything to eat around here? There's a basketball game I want to watch on ESPN. Bring me a couple beers." As usual, he didn't say please, just barked an order at her.

Margie put the beers in front of him along with a big bowl of chili. She didn't feel like arguing with him tonight. Let him drink, eat, watch TV, and fall asleep, she thought. That's a lot better than trying to talk to him. He'll just get mad, start an argument, and wake the girls.

She went into the bedroom and closed the door, thinking how much Toby had changed since they got married. Stay away from him, she thought, and maybe he won't hit you tonight.

Chapter 22

April 1996

Billy Bob was getting worried. Astin had a good recruiting class and went around to all the booster clubs in March, winning friends right and left. That damn guy was so smooth, telling funny stories and flattering the women, who all loved him. Billy Bob was trying to think of something when the phone rang. It was Officer Suttles, who'd promised to call him when anything happened with the football team. Billy Bob had given him a cash gift to help out with the little league team. He winked when he did, making it clear that the officer could keep it himself if he would help Billy Bob.

"Billy Bob, hope you're doing well today. I thought I would call you and let you know about an unfortunate thing that just happened. You know that Denny Durham? He's a damn good linebacker. I hate it for him, but he got a DUI last night late. I don't think anybody knows it yet. I know we kept it real quiet in the old days. What do you want me to do with it?" Suttles asked.

Billy Bob was gleeful. "Thank you for calling me. You did the right thing. This is bad for our football program. We can't have it. I'll take care of it. I know exactly what to do. You leave it to me. Thanks again."

After they hung up, Billy Bob called his friend Stubby Jones, who would know exactly how to stir up a controversy. "Hello, Stubby, my man. I've not talked to you in a while, but I'm calling you this morning with some breaking news that's not good for our football program. I think you might like to hear it." Billy Bob told Stubby all about Durham's DUI.

Stubby Jones had built quite a reputation as a sportswriter. It was his dream since high school. Of course, he'd have rather played sports than write about them, but he had no athletic ability. As a kid he was short, awkward, and rather uncoordinated. Kids made fun of him and called him Stubby, and the name stuck. In childhood games he was always picked last. In high school he never played a single organized sport. He tried out for football once, but he didn't make the team. He couldn't help but resent the football and baseball players who swaggered around school—big shots. But he found his way of getting into the mix. He was good with words and sort of liked to write, so he started writing for the high school newspaper. There was something macho about it, and he got to hang around the athletes. One job led to another in college, and here he was now, working for a big newspaper covering sports. He got noticed, he had some power, and he loved it.

In the beginning he had hustled, working hard to do something resembling research to run down interesting, noteworthy stories. That was the way it was done in the old days. Tell the readers something interesting—maybe uplifting—about the athletes, such as how they visited hospitals and gave presents to sick kids. But that was the old days. Now he just looked for the dirt. He didn't have to work at it; people fed it to him. He had people in high places who called him up to tell him controversial tidbits. Sometimes he couldn't believe how easy it was. The newspaper loved it, too. The more outrageous the story, the more newspapers they sold.

He'd even managed to get a call-in radio show of his own. Talk about easy money. You didn't have to do anything except open the phone lines, drop a few inflammatory remarks, make a few folks mad, and the calls started pouring in—the crazier the better.

Stubby had just walked into his office when Billy Bob called about Denny Durham. "No," he said, "I haven't heard about that. Star linebacker getting a DUI right before spring practice? That doesn't sound good. I already know about two players on campus who got caught with open beer cans. That's against campus rules. Sounds like the team has some drinking problems. I'll get right on it. We can make the afternoon edition with the DUI. Thanks, man. Let me know if you hear anything else." Stubby smiled, thinking how he could stir up a little controversy and make some trouble for that new coach. He was so thankful for friends like Billy Bob.

Chapter 23

After meeting with G. B. Carter and visiting the house he was finishing, Kendall decided she would hire him to build their new home. Carter was knowledgeable, easy to talk to, and just plain likable. Her uncles had been in the construction business, and she had heard a fair amount of construction talk all her life. Planning the build was a creative venture that gave her something to do while Duke was gone so much. The lot was cleared and leveled right away. Wanting to disturb the land as little as possible, she was on site that day to make sure they cleared only a minimum number of trees. Carter had a plan for a house built around a big lodge-like room that was just what Kendall wanted. They would only have to modify it a little to add porches facing the lake.

She couldn't wait to take Duke over to see the progress. It was the first full weekend he'd had off since their arrival. She was thinking about the house when Duke walked in on Friday afternoon. She could tell right away that something was on his mind.

"Hey, babe," he said as he gave her a hug. "Man, am I glad this week is over. It seems like there's a crisis a day."

"I don't want to hear it, but tell me anyway. What happened?" she asked.

"Sorry, I should be more positive. The kids are great and are working hard. I really like this team. I think we have good rapport. It's just these distractions the last couple of days. Denny Durham, our best linebacker, got a DUI. I have preached to these young men about the dangers of too much alcohol. I've told them if anything happens, they'll be all over the newspapers. But they don't listen," he said.

"It's too bad. But maybe they'll learn a lesson. Maybe this will get their attention before it's too late," she said, trying to encourage Duke.

"Get their attention, yes. But the sad thing for Denny is that I'll have to suspend him and keep him out of the spring game. He will hate that. No one loves to play more than Denny, and the spring game is a big event around the university. Thousands come to see it," Duke said.

"You had those two players with open beer cans on campus the other night, too," she reminded him.

"Yes, there's something funny about that. There must have been two hundred students at this big party on campus, and the cops walked through the entire group right up to the two players. It's like they were looking for the recognizable faces. The guys were in the wrong—true—but they felt like they were being targeted."

"You can't make excuses for them. It doesn't matter if everyone else was doing it."

"That's absolutely right. I told them that. But still, there's something strange going on. The newspaper had the story on Denny before I did. Somebody down at police headquarters called the paper before anybody let me know about it. Then the paper blew it up into a headline. Somebody is trying to make trouble for us, and they're succeeding. All I want to be thinking about is spring practice. It should be a fun time—and we have all of this to distract us. It's a damn shame." Duke was muttering as he laid his head back in the chair and fell asleep, exhausted.

Kendall figured she would have to wait to show him the progress on the house another day. Funny how often this seemed to happen—football stuff always taking over their life.

Chapter 24

May 1996

Despite the controversies with the suspension of their best linebacker and a couple of third string players, the spring game was a success. Immediately afterwards, Duke was anxious to get to know people better around the state and started making the banquet circuit. He won a lot of folks over with his charisma. Of course, Kendall knew the women would love him. With his charm and good looks, most women fell for him immediately. He was also making friends in the media. He was good at joking with them, telling funny little stories, and they could not help but laugh.

It was a beautiful, warm Saturday morning, and Duke and Kendall could have a rare day off.

"Duke, isn't this amazing? I love this time of year, with tender green leaves on the trees and flowers beginning to bloom. Let's sit outside and have our breakfast," Kendall said as she walked out on the deck with a tray of eggs, toast, and coffee.

"Great idea. It's so peaceful out here on the lake."

"Sit here at the table and tell me what's happening on the banquet tour. How about some good news for a change?"

"Okay, this is positive. I really like Jeb Phillips, who writes for *The Examiner*. He takes his job seriously and is careful to tell the truth. He's even written some historical novels. I think you would like him, too, if you could meet him."

"Oh, I'd love to meet him."

"He has started confiding in me. He pulled me aside at the press conference after the spring game. He wanted me to know about three wealthy, powerful men who are always stirring up trouble. They meet for lunch almost every day at the country club and plot ways to stay in control. They feel like the football program belongs to them and that they're the ones who should be running the show. They feel entitled to pick the coach and even the president of the university. They want to make life tough for me and run me off or get me fired. They have a group of sports writers that they call all the time. The three men are Billy Bob Craven, Tommy Lee Hampton, and Roland Rigby."

"Oh, like the Triumvirate in ancient Rome—you know, Julius Caesar, Crassus, and Pompey," she joked, pouring him another cup of coffee.

"Kendall, I doubt these guys know anything about Roman history, but they're very powerful, especially Craven, who has been one of the biggest contributors to the program. I've suspected there was something organized, and Jeb Phillips confirmed it. But he assured me that large numbers of the fans are coming around. I can see it at these booster club events. Of course, the students have been great from day one. Phillips says just stick to our program. He feels we'll win more games than folks expect, and things will start getting better." Duke sighed and took a sip of coffee.

"I really hope you're right. It just seems so crazy to me. You shouldn't have to give any energy to plots and conspiracies," Kendall said. She could see that Duke was feeling better, able to calm down and even be jovial about it all.

Kendall was feeling better now, too, and thought this was a good time to tell Duke what she was doing on the house. She got up and went inside to get some things to show him. "The house is going to be perfect," she said when she returned, spreading pictures on the table where they had been eating. "Look at these pictures I've collected from decorating magazines. I figure this is a good way to show the workmen what I want. Don't you agree?"

Duke glanced at them. "I'm sure that's a good idea, honey. How do the men feel about your being around so much?"

"I think most of them don't mind. I know Carter doesn't care. He knows I'm particular and want everything done correctly. I take coffee and donuts to the workmen sometimes. They seem to appreciate it. But there are a few that don't like me making suggestions."

"I know how some men are. They don't want to take advice or corrections from a woman," Duke said with a laugh. "You can be pretty bossy."

"Duke, how could you say that?" Kendall laughed too. "But I do want things done a certain way. I'm paying them, so I can hang around the job site if I want to. I know I have an obsessive/compulsive personality, but that isn't all bad. I'll make sure things are done just so. But you know I'm not bossy."

Duke could only smile. I'm glad you enjoy it. I'm gone so much. The new house keeps you busy and out of my hair."

"That's right. You worry about the Triumvirate and I'll worry about the house," Kendall said as she got up and began to clear the table.

They both laughed as Duke held the door for her to carry the tray of dishes inside. She then gathered her pictures and carefully arranged them in a folder. Finally, she walked over to Duke and put her arms around him.

"This is a good day. Let's just stand here and hold each other for a while." She knew they both felt it—the comfort, the easing of the stress.

"Yes, this is a good day. Let's savor it. Who knows what tomorrow will bring."

Chapter 25

Late one morning, Toby was working quietly in the back of the Astins' house. He had a bad headache. Thankfully, the weather wasn't too hot yet. He was wondering when the ninety-degree days would start when he heard Carter calling him. He slowly walked to the front of the house where Carter had some things spread out on the worktable.

"Look at these pictures of a fireplace opening I want you to build for Mrs. Astin," Carter said as he laid out images from a magazine. "She wants to put some blue and white tiles around the opening. After the masons finish the fire brick opening, I want you to build this frame like the one in the picture."

"Gosh, boss. I've never done anything like that. Copy a picture in a magazine? Why can't she just have a fireplace like other people?" Toby asked.

"Toby, she wants it this way. We're building her house and she's paying us. Now just build it and quit complaining. I swear, kid, you better stop your groaning and moaning all the time. You hear me? I'm losing my patience with you," Carter said as he looked Toby in the eyes.

"Okay, okay, boss. It's just that she's so particular. Always hanging around the job site telling us what to do. She gets on my nerves," Toby complained.

"I don't care how you feel. Just build what she wants."

"Yes sir," Toby said, but he didn't like it. Didn't that woman have something else to do, like cooking supper for that coach-husband of hers? Anything—just do anything, he thought, except come around here all the time telling me how to do my job. Damn uppity bitch acts so smart all the time.

He was just thinking somebody needed to put her in her place when his wife, Margie, and Mrs. Astin drove up to the job site at the same time.

Chapter 26

When Kendall pulled up at the job site, she saw a pretty young woman park behind her. With blonde hair and blue eyes, she was small and fragile looking but had a lovely smile. She had two little girls asleep in car seats in the back of an old Ford Explorer.

"Hello," Kendall said as the woman got out of the car. "Those are two precious little girls you have there. You must be a very busy mother."

"Oh, thank you. And I have another one that just started first grade. You're not kidding. They keep me busy. But I love 'em so much. You must be Mrs. Astin. My name's Margie Lane. My husband's working on your house. I'm so happy to meet you. We hope you and Mr. Astin are settling in. We're glad you're here. This home on the lake is going to be so nice. I love it."

Kendall was immediately drawn to this woman who looked almost like a teenager. How could she have three children at her age? "Well, when it's finished, I hope you'll come out here anytime and enjoy it. I love it, too. I wanted our home to be here because it's so quiet and peaceful."

"That's a nice offer, but I just come here to bring Toby his lunch. He's one of the carpenters on this job—the big guy over there. I get so busy in the morning I don't have time to fix his lunch and get all three of the girls up and Lisbeth off to school," Margie said as she leaned in to grab a bag from her car.

"You're sweet to bring lunch out to your husband. I'm sure he appreciates it, and he gets to see these little ones, which I'm sure he enjoys," Kendall said as she admired the two sleeping towheads and wondered why this Toby couldn't make his own lunch.

Margie looked as if she wanted to say something but decided against it. "Thank you, but I better run and give my husband his lunch.

He gets upset if I'm late with it," she said as she walked toward the construction area.

Kendall watched as Margie took the bag to the carpenter named Toby. He didn't look like he appreciated it at all and made no effort to come see his daughters. Kendall could tell that he didn't even say thank you. He just grabbed the bag and seemed to say something that was unkind. When Margie came back to her car, she was upset. She was fighting back tears and clearly embarrassed for anyone to see them. Kendall was concerned because she thought she saw a bruise around one of her eyes. From all her work with abused women, she knew what that could mean. Kendall would have to keep an eye on Margie. This young woman might need help.

Chapter 27

August 1996

As summer drew to a close, excitement mounted about the new football season. Kendall couldn't believe the hullabaloo being made over Duke and the team. Football was enormously important to these people.

With all his summer travels and now fall practice for the season, Kendall was seeing very little of her husband. On a hot Sunday afternoon in August, she decided to ride with Duke to a booster club meeting in the southern part of the state. She didn't always go with him but knew they needed some time together, even if most of it was spent in the car.

About a mile from their destination, she turned and asked Duke, "It's so hot—maybe one hundred but certainly in the nineties—and it's Sunday. Do you think people will come out today just to see a coach and his wife?"

"You haven't been to any of these with me. Just wait and see. The people will come," Duke assured her.

When they arrived at a huge warehouse-like building, the parking lot was full. Loud music played, and everyone wore school colors. The band was there as well as the cheerleaders. Fans started rushing over, pushing and shoving to get Duke's autograph. Kendall leaned over and said to Duke, "I see what you mean. You are quite the celebrity."

Soon fans started asking for her autograph as well. She wanted to say, "I'm just the wife," but fortunately she kept her mouth shut as she nervously scribbled her name. Then Duke leaned over and said, "I think you are a celebrity, too."

Kendall had another coach's wife tell her one time, "You know, we live in their reflected glory." At the time, Kendall hadn't known what that meant. She wanted to be a person in her own right and had always worked to establish a separate identity. But that Sunday afternoon, she realized the woman was right.

Charitable organizations had started asking her to serve on their boards. She was flattered when she was asked to serve on a hospital board, even though she knew they would have preferred Duke. He certainly didn't have time to go to board meetings. The United Way asked them both to do TV spots, and of course they did. Kendall was even asked to do a TV promo on her own for the Spouse Abuse Center. She was beginning to understand this celebrity by association, "reflected glory" stuff all too well.

When she was alone, some folks still didn't recognize her. But one day when she was at the grocery store, she handed her credit card to the cashier. "Oh, you're Mrs. Astin, our new coach's wife. Are we going to win this year?" the cashier asked.

Kendall was surprised by the question and said, "I hope so. They are sure working hard to make that happen." It was all very new to her, but she figured it was a part of the job. After that, she had to get used to not being anonymous in public anymore. She just had to remember to be polite and smile. As she greeted strangers, she couldn't help but wonder who was on their side and who was against them, working to get Duke fired. But from that day forward, she went to the drive thru at the bank and got cash to go to the grocery store, hoping it could help her avoid being questioned constantly. She guessed Duke was right: she was a celebrity now, too.

Chapter 28

Billy Bob drove up the long, curved driveway of the country club between giant magnolia trees. He was thinking it must be one hundred degrees today; it was blazing hot. Most folks around town took off for vacation at this time of year, heading to the mountains or the beach. He and Janice used to love to go to Ft. Lauderdale and take those nice cruises to the Caribbean. He hadn't done anything of that sort since Janice died. Usually, as fall approached, he looked forward to football. But this year was different.

When he pulled his Mercedes up to the club entrance, he tossed the keys to Benny, the young valet, who immediately started talking like he always did. "Hello, Mr. Craven. How're you today? I know you got football on your mind. I can't wait. Looks like the new coach is goin' to work out just fine. Lots of folks saying nice things about him now. They say you just got to get to know him."

Billy Bob grunted in response and thought there was no way he'd ever like the new coach. He strolled into the cool, air-conditioned lobby and headed toward the dining room. As usual, he was the first one to arrive. He quickly ordered a drink and was taking a sip when Roland walked up in a golf shirt.

"How in the world can you play golf in this heat?" Billy Bob asked.

"I started early this morning and just finished. Had to get a dry shirt on. My other one was soaked. But this heat isn't that bad. I can take it. You should have felt the heat in Nam," Roland responded boastfully.

"Well, I'm not superman like you are. This damn heat bothers me. Seems just about everything bothers me these days. I can't get my mind off that new coach."

"Cool it, Billy Bob, we'll think of something to get rid of him," Roland said as Tommy Lee walked up.

"Well, we three have got to get busy," Billy Bob said, taking a sip of his vodka and cranberry juice. "Usually, I can't wait for football. All those other sports like baseball, basketball, and such just fill in the time until football starts each fall."

"I know what you mean. It always makes me want to play again," Tommy Lee chimed in. "But these old legs can't do it anymore."

Roland waved the waiter over and ordered drinks for himself and Tommy Lee. "We may not be able to play," he said as the waiter left, "but we can enjoy it just the same. The betting somehow makes me feel like I'm participating—like I have skin in the game. The thrill is there all the time. And when you win big, there's nothing like it. It's a high. Well, I can remember one thing that was better, but that was gone for all three of us a long time ago." He winked and they all laughed.

Then Billy Bob turned serious. "Men, we have a real problem here. We want our team to do well, but we don't want this coach to succeed. How are we gonna get rid of him if he wins too many games?"

"Well, I just think some of that will work itself out. He's sure not going to win 'em all this year. He's got some weak spots," Roland offered. "I think he'll lose enough to keep the grumbling going."

"But that's not good enough," Tommy Lee insisted. "We've got to be sure he's not going to win too many games. I have an idea. What if we can get inside the team somehow? Some of the players aren't all that crazy about his discipline program. All his high and mighty integrity stuff gets old fast. I know Durham is mad as hell that he couldn't play in the spring game."

"You got a good idea there, Tommy Lee. I like that. Find a kid who owes us or an unhappy kid who feels like he's not being treated right. We can use him," Billy Bob said. He downed the rest of his drink in one gulp.

The waiter came back with the two drinks, nodding when Billy Bob asked for another. The three of them sat there for a minute thinking, and then Billy Bob spoke up again. "At one time or another, I've given jobs to parents of some of the players. That's still technically legal. The jobs are very important to those families. We can let the kid know that the job may not be secure if he doesn't cooperate with us. We get one of those players—a high-profile player—to slack off at crucial times. You know, give 90 percent instead of 100 percent. He might not catch every ball thrown his way or run as fast as he is able on his way to the end zone. That could throw a game or two. Know what I mean, guys?"

"Yeah, but I'm not sure it'll work," Tommy Lee warned. "These players are very devoted and want to win. It's built into them, especially the gifted ones. Besides, I don't see how we can get to them. It almost needs to be tried by someone their age who is close to the program. We sure can't call them in and offer money."

Roland took a sip of his drink and smiled. "I've got the perfect way to get inside the team. I don't know why it took so long for me to think of it. My son, J.J.—you know, from my second marriage—I'm old enough to be his grandfather. He's about the age of what a grandson should be since I had him so late in life. He had this harebrained idea of walking on the football team. He played quarterback at the private school, Heritage Academy. He did alright, but he's not the caliber of player that will make it at the university. He's a headstrong kid and won't listen to reason. I figured just let him go on and do it. I've never told him he couldn't do something. I figure he'll learn by trial and error. He's been practicing with the team. He's bragging about it to all his friends. I don't know how long the coach will let him hang around, but J.J. already knows the players well. Let me talk to him."

"What a break, Roland. Yes, talk to J.J. and see what you find out," Billy Bob said as the waiter came up with his second drink. The three men lifted their glasses to each other. Maybe they could figure this out after all.

Chapter 29

Elijah Ray Johnson had always been strong and could run fast. Running had always been fun and easy for him—the only thing fun and easy. The rest of life was hard. Elijah was the oldest of six children. He loved and admired his mother, Maybelle, who was tough as nails. She had always worked two jobs just to put food on the table. They'd lived in the public housing projects. He'd never known his father, who left when he was a baby. That wasn't unusual. In fact, Elijah didn't know anybody in the projects who knew his father. In his own household, there were at least three different fathers who bailed.

They lived in the projects with their grandmother, who took care of the kids while their mother worked. Maybelle had always cleaned houses for white women during the day and cleaned office buildings at night. As Elijah got older, he began to think about how he could help his mother. By his senior year in high school, he was already six-foot-two, weighed 215 pounds, and was a star running back. College recruiters began attending his games as early as his junior year. They went to all his football games, and when basketball season started, they were at all those games, too. Elijah was happy doing what he loved to do—running, jumping, moving. These things were his gift, and performing was thrilling for him. It would be wonderful if he could get paid for his ability.

Elijah had always been quiet. He could move like a gazelle, but he didn't say a word. Talking made him nervous. He just watched and listened. When recruiters started talking about money, cars, and so-called jobs that boosters provided where you didn't have to work hard, he said nothing. But he knew his mother wouldn't do anything dishonest, and neither could he. His mama had always taken him and his siblings to church and preached to them to do their schoolwork, make something of themselves, be honest, and stay out of trouble. Her words always rang in his ears.

Finally, one recruiter mentioned something about helping his mama get a better job that paid good money if he'd agree to play for them. That didn't sound dishonest to him. Mason Benton here in town was where he wanted to go anyway. It was close enough for his mama and brothers and sisters to come to his games. In fact, when he was a kid, he had sold Cokes at the games just to get in the stadium. Now he would get to play there. It was a dream come true.

February of his senior year, he signed a grant-in-aid letter of intent, which provided books and tuition. Since his family was so poor, he also would qualify for a Pell grant that paid $2,300.00 a year. An alumnus had arranged for his mother to work at Craven Construction. She was so happy, and that made Elijah happy. Things were beginning to look up for his family.

As soon as Elijah started at the university, he became a star. He worked hard in the classroom and did okay in academics. He contributed on the football field as a freshman, but by sophomore year he played a lot. Now as he was entering his junior year, folks were talking about him being a number one draft choice for the NFL.

When Coach Astin came to town, Elijah was apprehensive at first. But that didn't last long. When this coach talked, you could tell he really had the players' best interests in mind. He asked about their families and their academics. Almost immediately, Coach Astin became the father figure Elijah needed. He was a role model, and Elijah wanted to be like him. He liked the discipline system and training program.

Astin had arranged private meetings with each player to get to know them. When it was Elijah's turn, the coach had asked him what his dream was for his life. Elijah somehow felt comfortable with this new coach and felt he could be honest. He didn't think he had ever said it out loud to anyone, but he decided he would tell this man. "Coach, I just want to do what you did. I want to play in the NFL a few years, buy my mama a house, and then coach other young players to be good men."

Coach Astin smiled, patted Elijah on the shoulder, and said, "Elijah, I believe your dream will come true, and I will help you to make sure it does." From that minute, Elijah decided he would do everything he could to make sure Coach Astin succeeded at the university.

Chapter 30

The week before the season started, Kendall went to the first meeting of the board of the Spouse Abuse Center. She liked the men and women who attended and listened eagerly as they talked about the new building they had purchased. They also discussed the campaign they were getting ready to launch with the local newspaper, *The Herald News*, running a series of front-page articles on the problem of spouse abuse. The local TV station was on board, too, and had asked if Kendall would make the service announcement. After the meeting, she and the director, Mary Denton, headed to the station to make the promo, which would run for the next six months.

When they arrived, a young man named Burt met them and took them back to the studio. "Mrs. Astin," he said, "I'm happy to meet you and welcome you to our community. I can't wait for the football season. It is mighty important around here. But you've probably figured that out by now."

"Oh, yes, I know football is important," Kendall assured him. "Everywhere I go, folks remind me."

"You're important, too. That's why we wanted you to do the spot today," Burt said as he attached a microphone to the lapel of her jacket and the transmitter box to the waistband of her skirt. He then pointed to a teleprompter. "Read this message and we'll do a few takes."

"This is my first solo TV spot. I've done some with Duke, but he usually does most of the talking. I'll do the best I can," Kendall said. She read over her remarks a couple times and then nodded at Burt. "Okay, let's do it."

Kendall read the message with feeling, highlighted the seriousness of abuse, and explained how the community had purchased a building to house the women and children. She asked for contributions to help pay off the building's mortgage and to provide funds for daily operation expenses. In bold numbers at the bottom of the screen was a telephone number a woman could call if she needed help. Kendall only had to do a couple of takes before she got the quality they wanted.

"Mrs. Astin, you did very well. You sound like a pro," Burt said. "I sure didn't know abuse was such a problem. Folks will learn a lot, especially coming from you."

"Thank you for your kind words. I'm glad it went okay. TV is new territory for me. I hope it will help."

"Well, if the practice of law doesn't work out for you, you can go into TV. You are a natural," Burt said as he led Kendall and Mary back to the entrance of the building.

Kendall thanked Burt as they walked out. She was anxious to make a request of Mary. Once he shut the door behind them, she said, "We've been talking about the Spouse Abuse Center, but I've never seen it. Would it be possible for me to visit? I don't even know where it is."

"That is by design," Mary said. "We don't want anyone to know where it is. You understand, I'm sure. We have to make it a safe place for the women. Their abusers shouldn't be able to find it. But since you are now on the board and have made this promo for us, I trust you to keep our secret."

"Of course, I won't tell anyone. I understand completely the danger of it getting out," Kendall said as she got in the passenger seat of Mary's car. Mary drove through the commercial part of town to an area of doctors' and dentists' offices. A large, two-story office building had signs advertising medical services and listing the names for each office. Mary pulled around back and they got out of the car. Before they went into the building, Mary pointed out a long, four-car garage where cars could be locked in and hidden. She explained that an abuser, looking for his wife, will ride all over town searching for her car, so the center had to be sure they were hidden.

As they entered the building, Mary explained, "A lot of people think we have a residential house. This business location is easier to disguise, so to speak, if people think there are only offices here. There is no outside entrance. You have to go through one of the offices to get upstairs."

"Well, you could have certainly fooled me. I would never think the center was here," Kendall said.

There was a receptionist sitting at a desk. Mary introduced her. "Kendall, I want you to meet Gloria Potts. She looks like a nurse or simply a receptionist, but actually she is trained as an armed guard. She doesn't let anybody in if they aren't cleared."

Gloria immediately stood up. "Mrs. Astin, I'm so glad to meet you. I'm Elijah Ray Johnson's aunt. His mother, Maybelle, is my older sister. We are so proud that you and your husband are at Benton. Elijah has already told us how much he likes his new coach."

"It's nice to meet you, too. Duke thinks Elijah is a great young man with a wonderful future in the NFL. I know your family is proud of him," Kendall said.

"Oh, they are," Mary said with a laugh. "We hear about Elijah and his accomplishments on the football field all the time. But what I want you to know is that the women in the family are talented, too. Maybelle and Gloria are both tough women. You don't want to cross them. Gloria's husband is a police officer, and she is trained to use weapons and protect this building. If she has a problem with an abuser trying to force his way in, she has a buzzer that alerts someone upstairs to call the police. There are two other guards, and the three of them have rotating shifts so that we have protection 24/7. We can sleep at night knowing they are here to protect our women."

"Mary, you know I love working here and protecting these women. Their crazy husbands better not try to get in here. If they do, I'll stop 'em," Gloria said, smiling.

"Gloria, I believe you will," Kendall said. "And I'll be sure to tell Duke I met Elijah's aunt."

When they went upstairs, Mary said, "You must remember that these women usually come here with the clothes on their backs and that's all. They don't have time to pack belongings when they're fleeing an abuser. They're running for their lives. Providing clothes for them is another one of our expenses. We take donations of clothing that is appropriate for job interviews. Of course, we also need to provide children's clothing."

They finished their tour by looking at the bedrooms for the individual mothers. There were cribs and single beds in the same room with a larger bed for the mother. The rooms were very clean and painted in happy colors of yellow, light blue, and green.

"I must say I'm impressed," Kendall said. "I've been sympathetic about this issue for years, but seeing this place is really moving. I can't imagine what a woman must feel when she comes here. It makes me even happier about what I'm doing to help you. I hope it will be meaningful."

"Oh, it will be. Running this message during football season in this town with the coach's wife making the pitch, folks will listen," Mary said with a smile on her face.

Here they go again with that celebrity stuff, Kendall thought. In this instance, though, maybe it'll mean something and make a difference.

Chapter 31

Jason James Rigby, always called J.J., was the only son of Roland Rigby and his second wife Jesse, who was twenty-five years younger than Roland. His mother and father divorced when J.J. was still in middle school. Roland and Jesse got joint custody, but J.J. liked to stay with his father. His mother had moved to Nashville, thinking she would be the next Dolly Parton. She even got breast enlargement surgery to enhance her resemblance to Dolly. And since she'd gotten a new, younger boyfriend, J.J. didn't see her very often. That was fine with him. His father let him do just about anything he wanted to do—stay out late, drink beer, take one of his expensive guns and go hunting with his friends. Yes, J.J. couldn't complain. He even had a cool Ford Mustang to drive. Good-looking, with dark hair and brown eyes, he did pretty well with the girls, too. He weighed about 180 pounds and was five-foot-eleven but wished he were a little taller. That would make him a better football prospect. He had done well in high school and felt he was good enough to play college football. He planned to show those college coaches they had made a mistake by not signing him on a scholarship. Even though his father didn't agree with him, J.J. was sure he was good enough for the team and had walked on at the university to play for the new coach, Duke Astin. J.J. didn't expect his father to support him in this effort. His father never seemed to think J.J. could do anything.

Truth be told, Roland was in his seventies with a young son he wasn't sure how to parent. They didn't communicate well. At least he had decided to let J.J. have free reign. He didn't expect much, but he was glad his son wanted to live with him and not his mother. Roland loved J.J. but obviously had no idea how to show him.

J.J. came home to see his father, who had called earlier in the day and said he had something to tell him. J.J. was staying in the dorm during football pre-season and working out with the team. He had fallen asleep on the sofa waiting for his father.

"J.J., wake up. I want to talk to you," Roland said as he came in the room.

"Oh, Dad, give me a minute. I've been working hard. They're running my butt off at football practice," J.J. said as he sat up and rubbed his eyes.

"How long are they going to let you hang around over there? You don't have a chance in hell to make the team. You're just trying to impress the girls," Roland said, laughing.

J.J. didn't appreciate the way his father was talking to him. The man never believed in him. Never encouraged him. The only time they seemed to get along and not bicker was on the golf course or on hunting trips. Those two activities were all Roland cared about. J.J. had figured out a long time ago that maybe if he could get good at those things, his dad would be impressed. He'd become a good shot with a rifle, and he wasn't a bad golfer either. But his father didn't seem to notice these achievements. He paid little attention to anything J.J. did.

"Yes, I do have a chance. I know they have three All-American quarterbacks. They're all taller and stronger than me now, but I'm catching 'em. If one of 'em gets hurt, I'll move up. You just wait and see," J.J. said defensively.

"You think you're gonna suddenly grow a few inches and get stronger overnight? You've finished growing, and you should've been working out with weights for a year to get stronger, but you haven't. You're crazy to be doing this. Wasting your time when you could be working on your golf game," Roland said as he sat down.

Dad is just his old self today, criticizing me as usual, J.J. thought as his father rambled on.

"Listen, I want to talk to you about something important. I just had lunch with Tommy Lee and Billy Bob, and we don't like the new football coach. There's a lot of grumbling going on. Lots of folks think he wasn't the right choice for this big job. We wanted Rocky Owens, who coached with Big Jack, to be the coach. The new president made Billy Bob think he was going to name Rocky, and then he up and double-crossed him. Things have always been done a certain way around here. You have to bend the rules a little to succeed. We're afraid Astin is going to ruin our football program. We want to get rid of him and do it quickly. He can't win too many games this year. If he does, it'll be harder for us to boot him. We've been creating controversy when we can, but that's not good enough. This may sound a little far out, but we want to get inside the team and see if one of the players will help us. Now, you can't say a word about this. This is confidential, but we need your help." Roland looked squarely at J.J.

His father had never asked him for help on anything—especially something his powerful friends wanted him to do. J.J. sat up straight. "Yeah, sure. I'll help if I can. What do you want me to do?"

"I know I've been critical of you trying to make the team, but maybe it'll be worth it after all. You know Billy Bob has given jobs at Craven Construction to some of the players' parents. Good jobs, too, that pay decent money. It's legal, and the parents really appreciate it. But they're beholden to him. We want a prominent athlete to let up in a game just a little. Not too much to be noticeable but enough to throw the game. Maybe he misses a crucial pass and doesn't give 100 percent all the time. You get what I mean. We want to let him know that his mama's or daddy's job might be in jeopardy if he doesn't go along with us," Roland said.

J.J. didn't know what to say. He knew how hard the guys worked, but he also knew he'd do what his dad wanted. "That sounds devious to me. A little scary but exciting. I'm not crazy about Astin either. Do you know which player?"

"Yes, there are several, but the most prominent is Elijah Ray Johnson. His mama has a job and is doing well at Craven. She has six kids, I understand, and that job must be important to her family. Do you know Elijah?" Roland asked.

"Oh, yeah, everybody knows Elijah. He's a great player and a leader, too. He works real hard all the time. But he's quiet, never says much. I don't know what he thinks about the coach."

"Well, I imagine none of the players like all his new rules. The players were upset when those guys were kept out of the spring game, weren't they? I'm sure a lot of 'em think Astin shouldn't be the coach," Roland said.

J.J. couldn't help feeling pleased that his father was asking him to do something this important. Maybe his dad was changing the way he felt about J.J. This would be a chance for him to show his father he could do something that mattered. "Yes sir, I'll get right on it and talk to Elijah. I'll be very careful and not let this get out. Thanks for including me," J.J. said as he got up off the sofa. He waved good-bye and walked out the door to go back to the dorm. He felt excited and wicked, and he liked it.

Chapter 32

After her visit to the Spouse Abuse Center, Kendall drove over to check on the construction. The house was all framed now, and she could walk around in the rooms. They were just the right size—not too big, not too small. And the views of the lake were spectacular. She could see it from the great room, from the kitchen, and from the master bedroom—just as she had planned. She was so excited and couldn't wait to show her parents and brother when they came to the game next week. She planned to bring them out and give them a tour. She was proud and knew they would love the place.

She was visiting with Carter, the contractor, when Margie drove up. Margie and Kendall had gotten to know each other better during the summer months. When Margie brought her three girls to the job site, they'd go down to the lake together and sit on a blanket talking while they watched the kids play. These were wonderful times. Kendall had gotten to know the girls' names—Lisbeth, Jane Ann, and Carrie. They played so well together, inventing games and finding treasures. They picked little bouquets of twigs, dandelions, clover, and an occasional wildflower. They were adorable, and she was developing such affection for them. Kendall noticed that the oldest, Lisbeth, was particularly attentive to her mother, occasionally asking Margie if she was okay. Sometimes it seemed like Margie was trying to time her visits just to see Kendall. Margie was still a little shy. Kendall sensed that she wanted to talk to her about something but was afraid.

Today Margie left the girls in the car and seemed nervous. She looked very tired and thinner than the last time Kendall had seen her. There were bruises on her arms.

"Hello, Margie," Kendall said, trying to put some cheer into her voice. "It's so good to see you. How are you?"

Carter had just headed off toward a corner of the house, and Margie quickly said, "Not well at all. Mrs. Astin, I am not doing well." Suddenly, Toby walked up and pulled her away.

Kendall was alarmed. Toby was never gentle with his wife. He never looked at her fondly like a young father should look at the mother of his children. She had always sensed that something was wrong, and now she was sure of it. She walked back to her car and acted as if she were arranging some things in the front seat. She wanted to catch Margie when she left. Soon Margie walked back to her car, fighting back tears yet again. Kendall quickly went over and handed her a card.

"Margie, I know we can't talk now. But this is my home phone number. I want you to call me any time, day or night, if you ever need help. Remember, any time. I am here to help you." She smiled broadly, in case Toby was watching, and touched Margie's shoulder. Then she got in her car and waved as if nothing was wrong.

Chapter 33

Rocky Owens had been an assistant coach with Big Jack. He had been young when he started coaching, and Big Jack had mentored him. As the former assistant to the beloved old coach, some folks thought he might be the new head coach instead of Duke Astin. But Rocky knew better. He had never been a head coach and never wanted to be. He had loved being a line coach, horsing around with the players. He was always trying to hush the folks who came up to him saying he should be the head coach. One thing he knew was what was going on in the athletic dorm. He had always been in charge of the dorm for Big Jack, and he still walked in sometimes to say hello to the guys and just hang out. He had a couple of things he wanted to talk to Coach Astin about and made an appointment after practice.

"Team is lookin' mighty good out there today, Coach. I appreciate you letting me come to practice," Rocky said, shaking hands with Duke. "I know you've been closing practice to reporters and visitors as we approach the opener."

"Rocky, you're welcome any time you want to come to practice. You can give me some pointers, I'm sure," Duke said with a chuckle.

"No, Coach, I would never do that. You know a lot more about quarterbacks and all that stuff than I do. But there are a couple of things I want to say to you. There are some fans around here that keep saying I should have been selected head coach because I coached for Big Jack. I try to tamp that talk down. I'm not as qualified as you are, and quite frankly I'm enjoying retirement. I want you to know I'm on your side and don't participate in any of that bullshit."

Duke nodded. "I've heard some of that talk and a lot of other talk, too. But I don't pay any attention to it. I have too much work to do to listen to gossip. But I appreciate you coming by to say that to me."

"But Coach, there's something else. I know something that I need to tell you about. I used to be the dorm monitor for Big Jack, and I still go over to the football dorm and hang out some. I enjoy saying hello to the guys. I always liked that job, and it feels good to be back over there. I hope you don't mind," Rocky said.

"Of course not. I'm sure the guys love to see you. You're one of the legends around here."

"I don't know about the legend bit, but I do know problems when I see 'em. I don't know if you realize how many of the players have guns in their rooms. A good number of the guys like to hunt—you know, deer, turkey, whatever is in season. They want their rifles for weekends and off days to go hunting. Then there are some young men who grew up in real rough sections of town, and they believe they must have a gun to protect their families. Some of them come from cities with gangs and such. It all boils down to a lot of guns, and they think they must have them in their rooms for safekeeping. Now, there was a scuffle the other night. Some players got in a fight. I don't know what it was about, but someone threatened to get out his gun. I managed to calm them down. But I believe you should get those guns out of their rooms."

"Damn, I didn't know about the guns. That's dangerous. Something could easily blow up with that many guns around. I've never had that problem anywhere else. Or I didn't know about it if I did. Thank you for telling me, Rocky. We'll get them out," Duke said.

"I'll tell you what you have to do. There are more now, but we had a few in my day. You have to get some kind of legal form giving you permission to search their rooms. You find the guns and put them in your office in one of those big closets. You tag 'em, and they check 'em out if they want to go hunting. If they're going home, they can take 'em out. You know what I'm saying, Coach?"

"Sure, I do. That makes sense to me. The players are probably not going to like it, but I'll get on it right away. Thank you so much, Rocky. I really appreciate your help with this," Duke said as they walked out of the office together, continuing their conversation.

Chapter 34

Duke entered the team meeting the next day in a serious mood. "I have an important matter to discuss with you today," he said as assistants began handing a sheet of paper to each player. "I'm asking you to sign these forms that give the assistant coaches permission to search your rooms while we're having our team meeting this morning."

The players looked around worriedly, wondering what was going on. This form was an invasion of privacy.

"Men, I've been told that a number of you have guns in your rooms. I know a lot of you guys like to go hunting, and some of you think you must have guns with you when you go home. But dorm rooms are no place to keep guns. I know a few of you got in a scuffle the other night, and someone threatened to get out a gun. Someone could have gotten hurt. Worse than that, someone might be killed. I want no guns in any room. If the assistants find guns in your room, they will take them to my office. They will be labeled, and when you go hunting or go home, you can come get them. There will be no discussion of this decision. Guns will be removed from all rooms. Now let's think about the opener this week," Duke said as he continued with the meeting.

J.J. looked around the room and could tell a lot of the guys were pissed. Guns were important to these guys. The nerve of this coach taking their guns away from them. J.J. even had one of his father's rifles in his dorm room. He was sure a good number of the guys had guns. He even believed Elijah might have one. He came from a rough neighborhood where he might need a pistol in case someone tried to break in or something. But even though J.J. didn't like it, this decision by the coach played right into his plans. Elijah would probably be just as pissed as everyone else.

Chapter 35

Duke and Kendall arrived back at the condo at the same time, late in the afternoon. "Well, this is a nice serendipity," Kendall said. "Both of us home at the same time. Just like any normal couple home from a day at the office. Let's sit out on the deck and enjoy the view. It's warm, but there's a slight breeze. I'll get us something cold to drink." When Duke didn't answer, Kendall could see that something was bothering him. "I can tell you're tired. So am I. And I've got something troubling to talk to you about, too. But I'm so happy to be home and to see my handsome husband." She gave him a quick hug and a kiss.

"Thanks, that'll be nice. I am tired. The heat was really bad today, and it drains everyone—players and coaches. Everyone is working so hard," Duke said as he sat on the chaise lounge.

Kendall went inside for a few minutes and returned with a cold beer. "Now, just relax. It's the reason for being out on the lake. Isn't it nice? Okay, I can tell from the look on your face that something else has happened. What is the crisis today?"

Duke tried to laugh, but it was halfhearted. "Yes, the daily crisis. This one was a surprise. Just when things have been going so well on the field, I found out a lot of our guys have guns in their rooms. I had the assistant coaches search their rooms, and we took the guns out. Of course, now a lot of the players are mad. Not good timing—right here before the first game."

"My God, guns. You know how worried I get about the proliferation of guns in our country. Why people think they have to have so many guns is beyond me. I can't believe it. How did you find out about this?"

"Rocky Owens, who used to coach for Big Jack, came by practice yesterday. He said he had something he wanted to talk to me about. He was Big Jack's dorm monitor, and he still goes by to see the players in the dorms sometimes. Thank goodness he did, because there was a fight and a player threatened to get out his gun. Rocky was able to break it up, and we avoided a disaster," Duke said as he wiped his brow. "We collected thirty-two guns. Can you believe it? And some of the players are very upset with me for doing it."

"Duke, you had to. If they get upset, that's too bad. They'll get over it. I know it's just before the first game of the season, but maybe that's good. They're going to have the opener on their minds," she responded.

"I hope so. But I was surprised. Even Elijah had a gun. I pulled him aside today to ask him about it. He said going into his neighborhood was dangerous and he had to protect his family. There are gangs in the projects where they live. I told him I was sorry, but I had to get the guns out of the dorms. He seems to understand, but I don't know. He's so quiet. It's hard to know what he's thinking." Duke sighed and looked at Kendall. "Okay, that's my crisis. What's yours?"

"Well, you know that young woman named Margie I've been telling you about? The one who comes to see her husband, that carpenter Toby who works on the job site? She always looks fearful, and he snaps at her all the time. I can tell he doesn't like me, and he doesn't like me talking to her either. When I saw her today, I asked her how she was doing. Before her husband walked up, she said she wasn't doing well. He quickly pulled her away. I think he's abusing her. She usually has a bruise somewhere on her body. I gave her a card when I was leaving. I told her to call me if she needed me, that she should call any time, day or night. I'm so worried about her."

"Kendall, I know you really feel for this young woman. You're doing a noble thing with the Spouse Abuse Center, but this could be trouble. Toby sounds like a dangerous man. Should you get so personally involved?" Duke asked with a worried look.

"I'll be careful. I know how to handle men like Toby. But I worry about you. You have all these threats against your life, and you just shrug them off. You never take anything seriously. Now you want me to be careful. I can never get you to be cautious. It really bothers me."

"I know, I know," Duke said. "I know I tell you that these people who make threats are just blowing off steam. They won't do anything. But Toby sounds too close to home."

"You're one to talk. Your players all have guns, and they're mad as hornets at you. Sounds like we're both in a little trouble." She lay down on the chaise and snuggled up in Duke's arms, wanting to be close to him.

"Oh, Kendall, you've always been so good for me. Helping me not to obsess. Sometimes the pressure gets to me, but I can never let it show. You're the only person I can be honest with. I'm so grateful. Couldn't do this job without you by my side," Duke said as he held her close.

"Let's just bury our heads in the sand tonight and not think about the folks with guns who don't like us one bit," she said, laughing nervously. "Don't think about the players, the first game, or what folks are saying. Just look at that beautiful sunset across the water, listen to the crickets beginning to chirp, and think of how lucky we are to have each other."

"Baby, I know how fortunate I am. I don't tell you often enough how much I love you. I'm always worrying about football. It'll all work out just fine. I need to come home early more nights and sit out here on the deck with you. Pretend we don't have a care in the world," Duke said.

"That sounds like a wonderful idea. Why do I feel I can't believe you?" Kendall smiled up at him, but she was serious. "A new crisis will always pop up. What will it be tomorrow? But we won't worry about what will happen tomorrow. We have this beautiful evening together. Nothing could be better." She stretched up and kissed him. "Yes, no worries about tomorrow."

Chapter 36

Elijah was exhausted and thankful that he had time to stretch out on his bed and rest. It was ninety degrees during practice today, and the humidity was higher than usual. Before he drifted off, he wanted to check something in his playbook. He was just getting it off his desk when he heard someone tapping quietly on his dorm room door. Surely it wasn't a teammate wanting to talk; they were all too tired.

"Yes," Elijah said, puzzled when he opened the door and saw J.J. This dude never had anything to do with the black players.

"I'm J.J. Rigby."

"I know," Elijah said.

"Yeah, well, I know you don't know me very well. You may know my dad—Roland Rigby—he's a big donor to the football program. He thinks you're a great player. And I do, too. Man, I hope you get drafted number one in the NFL. I'm sure you will. Where do you want to play—which city? New York, Green Bay, Chicago?" J.J. asked nervously, as if he were intimidated.

"I don't think about it. Just think about us now," Elijah said with no expression.

"Yes, that's right. I'm a walk-on quarterback. I hope I make the team. I think I have a pretty good chance. What do you think?"

Elijah just stood there looking at J.J. He didn't ask him to sit down.

"Man, I know you were as mad as all the guys about Coach taking our guns," J.J. persisted. "I was pissed. He got one of my father's expensive rifles. I know he took a handgun from you. It's not right, making us sign those forms, going in our rooms and taking our guns." He paused as if waiting for Elijah to agree.

Elijah thought it was too bad about J.J.'s daddy's expensive gun, but he didn't say anything. He figured Coach Astin had to do what he did. It was dangerous for the guys to have guns in the dorms. Elijah had seen plenty of fights break out in the projects when guns were fired, and people got killed. Of course, he knew this kid had never seen anything like it growing up in his big mansion.

Elijah sensed that J.J. was having a hard time figuring out what he wanted to say. After a few moments of hesitation, J.J. cleared his throat. "Ah, you know, man, it could make some players not give their all in the game. You know, not catch a pass or run as hard as they could. Don't you think?" Again, he looked at Elijah expectantly.

Elijah was thinking this guy was crazy. None of the players would sacrifice the game that way.

"Hey, doesn't your mother work at Craven Construction? Does she like her job?" J.J. asked.

Elijah frowned and finally said, "Yes."

"Well, it has been nice talking to you," J.J. said quickly. "Just think about your mother and her job." He turned and rushed out of the room.

Elijah didn't know what the hell J.J. was talking about. Why had he come at all? What a strange conversation. What did Coach taking up guns have to do with his mother's job? As Elijah opened his playbook, he tried to clear his mind. He had more important things to think about than worrying over that kid. And no, J.J. didn't have a good chance to make the team, not with the excellent quarterbacks they already had.

Chapter 37

J.J. went by his house late that afternoon after practice. He was waiting for his dad when he came in from his golf game.

"Came by to talk to you, Dad. I got some news for you," J.J. said as he greeted his father.

"Okay, shoot, kid. I need to shower before dinner. It was mighty hot out there today on the golf course. I had a great day—took several hundred off Tommy Lee. It was fun," Roland said.

"Well, Dad, I had a good day, too. But first, I got to tell you something that you're not going to like. Coach Astin took all our guns away yesterday. We had to sign some form giving permission to allow coaches to search our rooms. The assistant coaches did it while we were in the meeting. None of us had a chance to get them out and put them in our cars. I hate to tell you this, but you know that rifle you got when you went hunting in Wyoming last year? You said you paid a lot for it. I know you love that gun, but I took it to the dorm to show it to some guys," J.J. said, watching his father nervously.

"You took that gun to the dorm? Damn it, J.J., that's one of my favorites. And now you're telling me the coach has it? I don't believe this. Sometimes you're so stupid. Can't you do anything right?" Roland's face was turning red.

"I'm sorry. It's in the coach's office, and I can get it back if I promise to bring it home. No problem. I'll do that right away. But I have something good to tell you, too. Please relax and listen." J.J. wished he didn't sound so much like he was begging.

"Okay, okay. What do you want to tell me? It better be good."

"I went to see Elijah today. I figured he had a gun, too and would be pissed like all the guys are. I went to his dorm room so we could have privacy like you told me to do. We made some small talk—you know, about going into the NFL. I told him about you being a big donor and a fan of his. He seemed to appreciate that. Yeah, he was happy to hear you liked him. Then I asked him if he was upset about Coach taking his gun and he was. Now, Elijah is quiet and doesn't say much, but I could tell how upset he was. He was grumbling and mumbling about it. He's pissed. I also asked him about his mama working at Craven Construction and whether she likes it there." His words were tumbling out.

"Slow down, son. He said his mama appreciated her job. Correct?" Roland asked.

"Oh, he said 'yes' loud and clear to that," J.J. affirmed. "And I said he shouldn't give 100 percent on every play, like he should miss a pass sometime because he's so mad at the coach."

"Son, it sounds like you did what we asked you to do. Do you think he got the message?" Roland asked.

"Yes, yes sir, he got the message. He even nodded to me when I said I thought I had a good chance of being backup quarterback. Yes, it went perfectly." J.J. smiled at his dad.

"Good job, J.J.," Roland said as he gave his son a pat on the back. "But you better get that gun back or there will be hell to pay."

PART 3

THE SEASON

September 1996

Chapter 38

It was a hot Labor Day weekend and finally time for the first game of the season. The city was jammed with excited fans making their way to the stadium. Kendall's parents, William and Martha Ann; her brother, Randy, and his wife, Sue; and her and Duke's best friends, David and Vickie Flynn, had survived the traffic and—thankfully—had arrived safely.

Getting off the elevator and walking into Kendall's box, David wiped sweat off his brow.

"Am I glad to get into this air conditioning! It' blazing out there. How are those folks in the stands going to make it today?"

"Some of them won't," Kendall assured him. "I'm sure some will faint and be carried out of the stands. They wouldn't sit out in this heat for anything other than football. Maybe at the beach in a wet bathing suit with a beer in hand." She laughed. "But football is mighty important to these folks."

"I'll say. But I worry about the kids who have to play in this damn heat," David added. "At least they've been practicing in it, which gives them some advantage over the poor suckers in the stands who've been living in air conditioning—something I am elated over at the moment. Man, does this cool air feel good."

"Well, welcome to my little box. It's not huge like the one President Jansson and his wife have. Of course, they'll be entertaining about a hundred people in their box. Most of them will be talking, hardly paying attention to the game. I can't watch the game in one of those crowded boxes. I only want family and close friends here with me. I know you'll hang on every play and never make a negative comment. At least you'd better not." She shook her finger at him.

"We know better than that. We don't want to get that bad look from you or, heaven forbid, hear your angry words," David said.

"You're absolutely correct. If you don't behave, I'll put you back out in the heat."

"No. I'll behave, I promise."

"Seriously, I'm glad you all can be here today for our first game. You're my family, and it's so nice to have you. There's plenty of food, so please enjoy yourselves. Isn't this wonderful? The bathroom's in the back. You can sit in the padded, tiered seats out front or on this comfy sofa back here in the middle, where you have a coffee table and TV screen. You know me. If things get too tense, I'll be moving to the sofa to watch the game. Nobody can see me back here, bent over in a fetal position. It's a hideout. Somehow that puts distance between me and the game. Does that sound weird?"

"Whatever works for you," Randy said. "I remember all the stories you've told us through the years about what people said to you in the stands. They didn't know what trouble they were getting into. Tell us what that guy said at an NFL game in L.A. when he had all the players' wives sitting in front of him. But more important, tell us what you said to him."

"Randy, I can't repeat what that guy was saying. He was foul-mouthed. I think he had started drinking way before the game and was feeling his oats. He was yelling at the defensive back, whose wife was sitting right there. Fans never think that players' family members sit in the stands, too. Well, I couldn't stand it, so I turned around and very politely said, 'Excuse me, that player's wife, Angela, is sitting right here in front of you. Would you like to meet her?' He suddenly looked embarrassed and shut his mouth, thankfully."

"Good you said something. Maybe the guy learned a lesson that day."

"I don't know, but there were a lot of experiences like that. One time a guy started criticizing Duke before the game even started. I tapped him on the shoulder and said, 'Let me introduce myself; I'm Duke's wife. Let's not have that today, if you don't mind.' He looked shocked and stopped. But it doesn't always work like that. A friend of mine whose husband is a coach said she did that one time and the guy got worse."

Everyone laughed. Randy chimed in, "I guess it just goes with the job."

"Now you sound like Duke," Kendall said. "He told me one time that the fans buy the tickets, and they have the right to yell whatever they want to yell. But I told him I had some rights, too. I shouldn't have to listen to them. When I see injustice, I have to make it right. It's the lawyer in me. At any rate, the result was I got Duke to work it out in his contract that I always sit upstairs. I think he did that out of fear of what I might say to a fan yelling obscenities."

"That was probably a good idea," David said. "It would be a bad headline in the newspaper: 'Coach's wife in shouting match with irate fan.' We all know you've never been shy about saying what you think. You said you were speaking to the fans 'politely.' I'm not sure that's true. But for whatever reason, we're glad to be here with you."

Kendall was glad they were with her, too. She was a bundle of nerves, but this chatter helped get her mind off the game. As usual, she didn't want to eat anything. She'd had some toast that morning, but her anxious stomach had taken her appetite. She understood when Duke told her some players would throw up before games. She identified with them. Needless to say, on this first day at this new school where Duke had gotten death threats, she was close to being physically ill.

But they won the game, and everything went beautifully. They were expected to win, but they won big. Their quarterback played a great game and Elijah scored three touchdowns. The kicking game was good, the defense outstanding. It couldn't have gone better.

"Well, what fun! I think I'll have a hamburger and some French fries. That is, if you folks have left any," Kendall teased.

"Watch out, Kendall. If Duke has a good season, you're going to gain a lot of weight," David quipped.

"I'll take a few pounds for a game like this every week," Kendall said as she took a bite. "This is the best hamburger I've ever had." She wiped ketchup off her mouth. "Now, maybe the naysayers will realize how lucky they are to have Duke as their head coach."

After the game, she and Duke ended the day by taking the gang out to see the new house. "I can't believe how beautiful this spot is, right on the lake. I can see why you've been raving about it," Kendall's mother said. "I love all the trees, and the view is spectacular."

It made Kendall happy to see how everyone admired the setting and the house. The back patio was pretty much finished. She had left food and drinks in coolers. The sun was beginning to set over the lake and turned the sky a gorgeous orange. "Listen to the night creatures—crickets and tree frogs. I love it when they begin to make their night sounds," Kendall said. "The glorious sunsets are what immediately sold me on this place. I want all of you to come often and enjoy this wonderful place with us whenever you can." They sat watching the sunset, eating, sipping wine, and laughing late into the evening. It was a lovely day, and for a change, they were all happy and relaxed. No thoughts of death threats.

Chapter 39

The Triumvirate met for lunch on Monday after the first game. Of course, Saturday's game was the main topic of conversation.

"I just can't help but be happy today," Tommy Lee admitted. "I love it when the team wins and when they cover. I know we don't like this coach, but didn't you enjoy the game?"

"Hell, no, I told you we had to get rid of the guy, and winning like he did Saturday is going to make it harder," Billy Bob said. "I thought Elijah was going to let up some. Then he went and scored three touchdowns. Roland, are you sure your son talked to him?"

"Oh, yes, and Elijah was mad about the coach taking their guns and putting them in his office. He told J.J. he was pissed. They had a friendly conversation, even though Elijah doesn't talk much. J.J. was sure he got the message," Roland said.

"Heck, Elijah is a great player," Tommy Lee noted. "He probably couldn't help himself. Once he gets on the field and the adrenaline starts flowing, a player like that can't hold back. I told you I thought it would be hard to do what you want to do. Don't you all think that kid sort of reminds you of me in the day? I kept thinking about me in the Cotton Bowl when I made that eighty-yard run. The way I cut back off that sideline. I looked like I'd been shot out of a cannon. Y'all remember, don't you?" Tommy Lee was getting excited. But Roland and Billy Bob were not smiling.

"What's wrong with you, Tommy Lee? You've got your head in the clouds. You're just an old man wishing he could still play ball. Stop it, you dumbass. I don't care if this coach wins six National Championships. He'll never be our coach. He doesn't belong. He isn't one of us. Don't forget what I'm saying, Tommy Lee. If he stays, we'll lose control of the program. Get that smile off your face. And Elijah better watch it, or his mama's job might suddenly disappear." Billy Bob had a determined look on his face. "Roland, talk to your son again."

"Okay, I'll talk to J.J. again," Roland said quickly.

"One more thing. I know they're trying to keep this business about guns out of the newspapers. That's what we used to do, keep things quiet. But no more. I'll get in touch with that sportswriter—the one named Stubby with the call-in show—and that guy linked to the national networks. We got to start talking about the problem with guns, and that incident in the dorm can be made to sound a lot worse than it was. We got to keep something stirred up all the time. Have you two got it?" Billy Bob said with authority as the other two nodded their heads. "Scare 'em, keep the heat on 'em. Maybe somebody should go after the coach with one of them guns."

Chapter 40

Fifty young men had walked on and tried to earn a place on the football roster. Duke always loved walk-on players and usually kept one or two on the team. They hadn't been given scholarships, but they wanted to play so much that they were willing to play on the scout team and participate in all the practices just to get noticed. Almost half of them dropped out immediately once workouts started. Another twenty went slowly, one by one, as they realized the talent and work involved. By the time of the first game, only five were left. Duke decided to let them at least dress out for the first game. After all, they had gone through all the drills, and it would be a reward for them to put on the uniform, run out on the field, and sit on the bench. Duke had decided to keep two of them for the season—an undersized wide receiver with great hands and an offensive lineman who was a good long snapper, too. He'd have to tell the other three they hadn't made the team. Duke had asked his administrative assistant to make an appointment with each of them.

The first two had already come in for their appointments. They thanked Duke for the opportunity and said it had been a thrill to dress for the opener. One big lineman put his arms around Duke and said he would never forget it. It would be something he could tell his grandkids about someday. As he was walking out of the office, he told Duke to let him know if he needed any extra players for scout teams in spring practice. Duke was wishing the guy was just a little bit stronger; he would like to have that kid on his team. Then J.J. Rigby walked in.

"J.J., how are you today? I hope you're having a good day," Duke said as he shook J.J.'s hand.

J.J. was nervous. "Fine, Coach," was all he could say.

"Listen, I know you want to make this team. I appreciate that you came out and did all the drills with us. You've worked hard. But you know we have three All-American quarterbacks, plus a couple other guys, all with good arms who are strong and agile. They have every-thing a quarterback needs to succeed. You're not quite tall enough, and your arm needs to be stronger. I'm sorry we can't keep you on the roster. Now, I can call some of my coaching friends and see if they need a quarterback. Maybe a smaller school would be a better fit for you," Duke said warmly.

After pausing a few seconds, J.J. said, "When I got to dress for the first game, I thought that meant I'd made the team. I've already told some folks that I'm on the roster. This isn't fair. What do I tell them now?"

"I'm sorry you feel that way. I never told you that you would be on the team. The other walk-on players that I have seen today didn't get that message. They knew it was a gesture on my part. I wanted to re-ward you for your work in pre-season practice," Duke explained.

J.J. couldn't hold back his anger. "Who do you think you are? You come in and tell me I'm not good enough for your team. Do you know who my father is? He's given a lot of money to this program. I'll tell him what you've done to me, and he'll tell his friends." J.J. was getting louder and louder. "You know, there are a lot of folks around here who don't think you should be coach. My father has connections. There are some things going on to get rid of you, and I hope they work," J.J. said as he stormed out of Duke's office.

Duke sat there silent for a few minutes. He knew this kind of young man. He had run into a few at Punahou and UCLA. J.J. came from a privileged family and had always gotten everything he ever wanted. Now Duke wasn't letting him have something. But the kid didn't deserve to be on the team. It wouldn't be fair to the other players. Plus, he didn't want a kid with that attitude among his players. He was a troubled kid, and Duke could see it. If this decision caused trouble, so be it. It was the right thing to do. He assumed J.J. didn't want him to call any of his friends at other schools. That was fine with Duke because he couldn't honestly recommend him to any of them, especially after that conversation. It was too bad. Now he had to get back to work and get ready for the next game. What was a little more trouble? He had a crisis a day—maybe this was the one for today.

As J.J. was leaving Coach Astin's office, he remembered that he wanted to pick up his daddy's gun. He showed his identification, and then Astin's assistant went to get the gun from a big locked closet down the hall. Walking to his car, J.J. decided he wanted to shoot that beautiful expensive gun before he gave it back to his father. They had a farm about ten miles out of town where the targets stayed up all the time. He, his daddy, and his friends could go out there for target practice anytime. It was fun to shoot guns and work on his aim with the targets. There was something macho about knowing how to use a gun well. J.J. had been allowed to do it for years, and he'd become an excellent marksman. It would help him blow off steam, too.

J.J. had ammo for the gun in the trunk of his car. When he got to the farm, he grabbed it, loaded the gun, and began firing. What a fine weapon. It was so smooth and easy to use. Man, he loved this gun. He had been firing for about thirty minutes and hitting the target beautifully when he heard a dog yapping over to the side of the field. It was annoying, and the dog just kept barking as he came toward J.J. and the target range. Whose dog was that? There were no houses close by. It must be a stray, J.J. thought. When it came into view, J.J. saw that it had a straggly coat and was thin as a rail. Yes, that was a stray for sure. But the dog wouldn't stop yapping. Annoyed, J.J. suddenly took aim and shot the dog in the head. Bang. The dog went down and wiggled around for a second or two in agony. J.J. smiled. Somehow, killing that damn dog made him feel better. He could go home now.

Chapter 41

The next two games were big wins, too—one at home and one away. Duke had explained to Kendall that they were smaller schools, Western Kentucky and Virginia Commonwealth, that were scheduled early in the season. The Bears were expected to get wins against them. He said the next game would be tough against a big rival. Kendall promised herself she wouldn't worry about that game yet.

She was having a good day. Her law class had gone well that morning. She couldn't help but laugh about one of the female students, Jennifer Alston, who was from a small town in the state and had a strong Southern accent. Every time Kendall asked a question, Jennifer's hand shot up. "Mrs. Astin, let me tell ya'll what I believe…," she would begin and then go into a long explanation. Jennifer annoyed some of the other students, especially the men, but she was usually correct. Kendall thought how much Jennifer reminded her of herself in the early days of law school. But she'd never heard a Southern accent like Jennifer's. She didn't think hers had ever been so strong, or at least she hoped not.

Kendall was excited about this class of twenty-five, with nineteen women and six men. The women gave the men high marks for being strong enough to take the class and debate with them. So far, the class had a good feel to it. It would be interesting to see how the rest of the semester went. Kendall was thinking about her class as she pulled up to the new house.

A lot of final decisions were being made. She had come to discuss the fireplace opening in the office/library. The border that Toby had built didn't look correct to her. They would know for sure when they tried to place the tiles she had saved to put in last. As she and Carter tried to see how they would fit, they both realized the border was too small. Now Kendall wished she'd said something earlier, but it couldn't be helped.

"I hate to say it," she said to Carter as Toby walked up, "but this whole thing is going to have to be rebuilt. I measured it carefully and explained what I wanted, but there must have been some mistake."

"Hear that, Toby? You're gonna have to rebuild this opening for Mrs. Astin," Carter said.

"What d'ya mean? I did exactly what she wanted me to do. There ain't nothing wrong with that opening," Toby said defiantly.

"That's enough. You will rebuild the fireplace," Carter said quickly.

"No sir, ain't nothing wrong with that fireplace. It looks fine to me. I'm only going to build it once!" Toby said angrily.

"All right then, you go on outside and wait for me. We're gonna have a talk before you leave. I'll be talking with Mrs. Astin a few minutes first," Carter said as Toby stomped out of the house.

"Mrs. Astin, I agree with you that the fireplace opening needs to be redone. I apologize for that young man. He's a good carpenter, but I've given him too much slack. I'm going to have to fire him today."

"I know he doesn't like me. He doesn't want me to make any suggestions or correct anything he does. But I hate to get him fired. He has a wife and three children," Kendall said.

"Oh, I'll pay him for a couple weeks until he can get on with someone else. We don't have that many expert carpenters around town. I'll let someone else deal with him. I've lost all patience with him."

As Carter and Kendall finished their conversation, they heard Toby revving up his truck and peeling rubber down the blacktop. "Well, maybe I won't have to fire him. I think he just quit," Carter said. "Unfortunately, the kid brought it on himself."

Kendall suddenly felt a sense of dread for Margie, thinking this might set Toby off and he would take it out on her.

Chapter 42

Toby stopped by the liquor store on the way home to make sure he had a good supply for the weekend. At least he wouldn't have to deal with "that bitch" anymore. He would work for someone else—anybody that didn't have women standing around tellin' him what to do. He didn't like the way Margie was always talking to that woman either. She would come home saying, "Mrs. Astin is so nice. She's really smart. Did you know she's a lawyer? Isn't she pretty?" He was sick of that talk. There was something about that Astin woman that made him think of his mother and how she was always after him to do this and do that. He would make sure Margie forgot about her. He never wanted to hear her mentioned again. He was sick of that damn coach husband of hers, too.

As Toby drove his pickup truck off the asphalt onto the dirt road that led to their farmhouse, he began thinking back to when he and Margie first married. He'd been so proud that he could build a house for her with his own hands. Margie had been pleased, too. Remembering the first time he brought her out to see it, he got tears in his eyes. He had picked her up and twirled her round and round as they giggled like two kids. They'd been happy back in those first years. He had finally gotten away from his abusive, alcoholic father and his demanding mother. Now, he wondered what had happened. He knew Margie wasn't happy anymore either. She always said it was his drinking, but he didn't agree. It was his work. Sure, he was a good carpenter, but that wasn't what he wanted to do. His dream had been to go to college, play football, and then move into pro ball. Maybe coach after that. He knew he'd have been better at all of it than that new coach Margie talked about all the time. God, he had done exactly what Toby had always wanted to do. That Astin guy got all the breaks, with big money and an easy life. Now Toby had to hear about him and his damn wife day and night. He was sick of it.

Toby got the good feeling he always got when he entered the house. It wasn't big, but it had a certain charm about it. He knew the craftmanship was good. He had built the small frame house on a piece of land on his daddy's farm. It had two bedrooms, a kitchen, and a good-sized living area that had enough space for the kitchen table and chairs. The most outstanding feature in the big room was the gun rack he'd made of antlers and hooves from a big buck he'd shot. Two rifles were prominently displayed. There was a big brown Lazy Boy chair in the middle of the room in front of the TV, along with a little table where he set his drinks and a drawer where he kept his Glock. He had to have guns to protect his family from intruders. Everybody needed guns for protection. This house was all they needed, and Toby liked it just fine.

When he started looking around, he didn't see Margie and the girls. He found a note that she had gone to see her mama and daddy on their farm nearby. She had left fried chicken, corn on the cob, beans, and fresh biscuits for his dinner. He thought to himself that was good. He wanted to be left alone tonight. He would find some game on TV— Friday night was high school games. He would drink a few beers first, chased with some shots of Jack Daniels. Then he would have dinner alone. He deserved to relax. The university had a big game tomorrow, and he could watch the pro games on Sunday. He had big bets on all of 'em. He was going to make a lot of money this weekend. That would make him feel a lot better. Yep, he was sure he was going to win big.

Chapter 43

Duke knew this fourth game of the season against a tough North Carolina team would be their biggest challenge yet. The team seemed overconfident, and he was doing everything he could to keep them grounded. The distractions weren't helping—all that stuff about him taking up the guns was blown way out of proportion. Every week now he had to do a call-in coach's radio show; he dreaded it and thought it was a waste of time. But he had to do it. Half the folks called in saying dumb stuff about football or the gun issue, and the other half tried to say nice things to counter the first group. There were writers like that Stubby what's-his-name, who had nothing good to say about the football program. But thank heaven for Jeb Phillips, who had a big audience and was the rational balance. Why couldn't Duke just think about the football game and not be bothered about all this other stuff?

The game with North Carolina went about the way Duke was afraid it would go. It was a defensive battle, and both teams had a hard time scoring. At halftime the score was tied at 7-7. He and the staff made some adjustments and hoped it would be enough. The second half was better but not spectacular. With just a few minutes left in the game, the Bears were seven points ahead. They were driving down the field, running Elijah over and over. The offensive line struggled to block North Carolina's huge defensive line, but Elijah kept managing to get a few yards each carry. With just a few seconds left in the game, the team was on the ten-yard line. Duke thought about giving it to the big guy one more time. But everyone was so tired, and he couldn't risk a fumble where the other team could take it the length of the field. They were seven points ahead, so he told the quarterback to take a knee and run out the clock. The game was finally over, and they had won. It wasn't pretty, but a win was a win.

Duke expected to hear the crowd cheer, but he heard something else. It was a mixture of cheers along with boos. What was going on? They had won the game. What was wrong with these fans? Duke turned to his offensive line coach, Mac Andrews, as they walked off the field. "What's going on? Are those boos I hear?" he asked.

"Yeah, Coach, we didn't beat the spread. We were thirteen-point favorites today. You know—the gamblers aren't happy," Mac said.

"What do you mean, man? I never pay any attention to the gamblers. That stuff is illegal anyway. Isn't it?" Duke answered in disgust.

"Yes, it's illegal in South Carolina, but they do it anyway. In fact, I have a buddy in the FBI, and he says the money bet in this state is huge." Mac shook his head.

"You don't mean it! Well, I'll be damned," Duke said. "Now I understand the boos. But that's just tough. We got a win today, and it wasn't easy. I'm happy for the team. You have to win the games when you don't play well to have a good season. That's exactly what our team did today. The fans should know that—a win is a win! They'll just have to get over whatever money they lost. What can they do about it, anyway?"

Chapter 44

Toby threw one of the kitchen chairs across the room. He couldn't believe it. Why hadn't that damn coach run the ball in the end zone? He didn't cover the spread. Toby had just lost $500.00, and it was that coach's fault. God, he could kill that guy! Doesn't he know the spread? he thought. If he doesn't, he should. Anybody with any sense knows the spread.

Margie ran in from the bedroom. "My goodness, Toby, what's wrong?"

"The damn coach told his quarterback to take a knee and the game was over. He didn't beat the spread. I just lost a lot a money," Toby yelled.

"The team won. How can you lose money if you bet on them?" Margie said.

"You don't understand the spread. How can you be so stupid? I've explained it to you a hundred times. They don't just have to win; they have to win by the right number—the spread." Toby was growing even more frustrated.

"I know, I know. I just don't understand gambling, and I don't understand why you do it. You get so upset when you lose. Why can't you just stop betting on the games?"

"There you go again, telling me what you want me to do. I guess next you'll tell me to stop drinking. I will drink and gamble if I want to, woman. It's none of your damn business," Toby growled.

"Yes, it is my business. You're losing money we need for groceries and the girls. When you get paid, you go straight to the liquor store before you come home. Yes, your gambling is my business." Margie was crying now, struggling to get her words out.

"I take care of you and the girls. Look at this house I built for you. Now all you do is bitch and moan. I'm sick of it." Toby wondered what she'd say if he told her he'd quit working for Carter and wasn't building the house for her precious Mrs. Astin. She might really be mad. But he'd just lost money, so he figured he'd save that news for another day.

"If you don't like it here with us, why don't you leave and do your drinking somewhere else," Margie yelled as the girls came running into the room, their faces full of fear. With that, Toby exploded and hit Margie across the face. She grabbed the girls and hurried into the bedroom, locking the door behind her. Toby got another drink, sat down, and checked to see which game was on TV now. He figured she would cry a while and get over it. She always did. He knew how to keep Margie in her place.

Chapter 45

The next morning, Margie tiptoed into the kitchen to fix breakfast for the girls. Toby was still passed out in his chair, with empty beer cans and a shot glass on the small table. Margie was afraid, but Toby usually woke up in a better mood. Sometimes he would apologize and say he wouldn't do it again. But once he started drinking, things would change. Sure enough, that's what happened as he began to come out of it.

"Margie, I'm sorry I got tough with you last night. I hate for the girls to be upset. But I wasn't myself. I haven't told you something that I need to tell you. You know that Mrs. Astin that you love so much, that bitch, as I call her. She came over to the jobsite Friday afternoon all worked up about the fireplace opening I built. She said it wasn't right, the proportions were wrong. There ain't a thing wrong with that fancy fireplace opening. She had the nerve to say I didn't do it right. What does she know? But that damn Carter agreed with her. I've had it with that woman. I told her and Carter point blank that I wasn't going to rebuild it. I shocked 'em both. You should have seen the look on their faces. Carter told me to go outside, and he'd talk to me later. He stood there being so apologetic to her. It was sickening. I knew he was going to fire me, so I got in my truck and hightailed it out of there before he had a chance to do it." Toby couldn't keep the pride out of his voice.

"You mean you were fired. You don't have a job. What are we gonna do?" Margie asked.

"You don't worry, little lady. First of all, I can get on with another company. There are some other companies always lookin' for a good carpenter. And anyway, I'm gonna make a lot of money today. I've got big bets on several pro games. Honey, I'll make several weeks' wages this afternoon. You just wait and see," Toby said as the three girls walked into the room.

"Daddy's sorry, girls. I had a bad day at work Friday, and then the football game didn't go the way I wanted it to go yesterday. But today is a new day, and Daddy's fine," Toby said as he reached out to them. But they ran to their mother and put their arms around her legs. They knew their daddy couldn't be trusted and could change quickly.

True to form, Toby started drinking as soon as the pre-game talk shows came on. He settled into his Lazy Boy as if nothing had happened. Margie was sick and tired of his apologies and attempts to be nice. He didn't mean any of it. But what could she do? Today, she would just try to stay out of his way. She had to think and think fast. She didn't want to get hurt, but more than that, she didn't want the girls to see Toby hit her again.

Chapter 46

By late afternoon, Toby had already lost money on the first pro game. He didn't get overly upset, saying he didn't have much bet on that game. Margie was relieved, but she couldn't relax. She was more afraid than she had ever been. Toby was getting worse all the time. His outbursts were more ferocious and his blows more frequent. What had happened to the fun-loving man she had married? She and Toby used to laugh and have good times together. He wasn't the same person now. It was awful for the girls to see him raging and then hitting her. She couldn't allow it to continue. Her daughters would be scarred by the abuse just like their mother. She was especially worried about Lisbeth, who was old enough to know what was happening. Margie had to protect her girls, but how?

She took the three of them into their bedroom and tried to distract them. She got out the Old Maid cards and lay on the bed with the girls, turning the volume up on the little TV in their room. She was lost in thought when the ad came on with Mrs. Astin talking about the Spouse Abuse Center. Suddenly, Margie thought maybe she could talk to Mrs. Astin. She was so nice. Margie had always been embarrassed to tell anyone that Toby hit her, but she felt like Mrs. Astin would understand. Margie still had the card in her wallet with Mrs. Astin's phone number, and she had told Margie to call her anytime day or night. Yes, when Toby went job hunting the next day, that's what she would do. Having some kind of plan made her feel a little better. She would remain calm, fix dinner, and try to get a decent night of sleep.

Once the girls were playing happily, Margie went into the kitchen to fry some hamburgers and warm up a can of baked beans. When she took Toby's dinner over to him, he didn't look happy. She was uneasy as she asked, "Is your team winning?"

"Hell, no. What is wrong with these 49ers today? They were supposed to win. Damn it," he said as he downed another shot of Jack Daniels.

Please, let him get some wins today, Margie prayed. She didn't care as much about the money as she did his tirades. He had been drinking all day. She decided to feed the girls, give them their baths, and get them ready for bed. She would stay in the bedroom with them, try to keep them busy with a bedtime story, and stay away from Toby.

Periodically, she could hear him cussing. She wanted to ask him to stop because of the girls, but she didn't dare. She didn't want to set him off. It was getting late in the evening. She didn't even know who was playing or how much he had bet. She just wanted the games to be over. Finally, the girls were getting sleepy, so she put them to bed. She thought maybe she would go to bed, too.

Things were going fine until about 11:00 PM, when the Sunday night game went into overtime. Toby was glued to the TV. Margie couldn't sleep. She tiptoed to the kitchen to get some water and see what was going on. The Packers kicked a field goal to win the game, and Toby exploded.

"God dammit, the Bucs lost, too. This has been the worst day." Toby was furious. Margie was trying to think what to do and where to go when he looked up and saw her. "Well, I guess you're happy. All but one of my teams lost today. I lost a bundle," Toby hollered.

Margie didn't know what to do or say. She froze. She wanted to get to the girls' bedroom, but he was blocking her.

"Aren't you happy I lost? I know you are. You bitch. You're bad luck for me," Toby yelled.

"I didn't have anything to do with it. You're drunk. Just let me go to bed," Margie pleaded.

But Toby wouldn't let her pass. "No, you don't approve of anything I do. Always complaining about this or that. I've had it with you, woman," Toby yelled as he hit Margie.

"No, please, leave me alone. I just want to go to bed," she said as she backed up against the wall. She kept trying to get past him, but he had her pinned.

"No, woman. Say it. You don't approve of me. Always telling me what to do. I hate women who do that—just like that Astin bitch." Toby pulled back his fist to hit her again, but he lost his balance as he lunged at her. Margie ducked, and his fist went through the drywall behind her, making a gaping hole. While he was pulling out his arm, Margie wiggled past him and ran for the girls' bedroom. She slammed the door and locked it quickly. She was terrified.

The girls were awake now, crying, and they ran into her arms. She held them tightly and prayed over and over that Toby would calm down. Please, God, make him pass out—anything to get him to stop his raging. All of a sudden, she heard the drawer of his table opening. He fired the Glock twice. Oh, God, what is he doing? She was frozen with terror. Toby kept stumbling around, cursing and yelling. Margie wondered if he would shoot them and himself. Maybe he would just shoot himself. God, please, let us get through this night alive.

Chapter 47

Margie lay awake all night. Thankfully, she was finally able to get the girls to go back to sleep. She kept humming and whispering that everything would be okay. She just prayed that she was right. Toby kept stumbling around. She heard him crushing beer cans and spewing obscenities at Carter, Coach Astin, Mrs. Astin, and herself. She just kept hoping he would pass out. At about 3:00 AM she heard him picking up the phone to call someone. How was he even able to dial a phone? She couldn't hear everything he said, but she could make out some of it. He was saying he was going "to shoot you both." Who was he calling in the middle of the night? He was slurring his words. Anybody who heard the message would know he was drunk. Please, God, just let him pass out. That was all Margie wanted. She now knew what she was going to do.

Sometime after 4:00 AM, all was quiet, and Margie knew Toby was out cold. She waited, and around 5:30 she picked up the phone in the bedroom. She quickly dialed the number and got a sleepy answer on the other end. She whispered, "Mrs. Astin, this is Margie. You told me to call at any time, day or night. I'm afraid Toby might try to shoot me and the girls. Maybe himself. What do I do?"

Suddenly awake, Kendall tried to get her thoughts straight and make sure she said the right thing. "Margie, stay calm. Let me think. I know you and the girls need to get away from there. Can you get out of the house? Where are the girls? Where is Toby?" Kendall asked.

"I think he's passed out in front of the TV. He was up all night. I haven't heard him for over an hour. I have the girls in the bedroom with me," Margie whispered.

"Can you get past him with the girls?" Kendall asked.

"I can try. I have seen him pass out like this before, and he's usually out cold for a while."

"Margie, listen carefully. Get the keys to your car. Don't try to pack anything. Come in whatever you have on. You must get out quickly and quietly. Tell the girls not to make a sound. Put them in the car and come meet me. You know where that McDonald's is on Sycamore? I'll get dressed and be there when you arrive, okay?"

"Yes, I'll do it. See you soon." Margie hung up and began to wake the girls.

"Girls, I want you to get your slippers and robes. Be as quiet as you can. Don't make a sound," Margie said as she put on her bathrobe. "We're going somewhere safe. Follow me."

When she opened the bedroom door, she saw Toby sprawled in his Lazy Boy in a deep sleep. The room was full of beer cans and trash. She noted the gaping hole in the drywall and two bullet holes high above it on the wall. The gun was still on the table by Toby.

The girls were quiet as mice. Margie was hardly breathing as she turned the doorknob on the front door, and it opened without a sound. They tiptoed out the door and ran for the Explorer. She buckled the girls in and prayed Toby wouldn't wake up. She slipped into the car, turned the key in the ignition, and slowly drove away. They had made it out of that house, and she would never go back.

Chapter 48

Kendall was sitting in her car at the front of the McDonald's parking lot when Margie drove up. She rolled down the window to speak to Margie. "Thank God, you made it. Now follow me. I'm taking you to a safe place."

They drove a few blocks to the nondescript doctor's building. Kendall led Margie back to the secure four-car garage and motioned for her to pull into one of the spaces. A woman waited for them. Kendall helped get the little girls out of the car. After locking Margie's car in the garage, the woman smiled and led them into one of the offices. They went past a woman sitting at a desk and up some back stairs, which took them into a beautiful, sunny room that smelled of fresh-brewed coffee. Several women about Margie's age were sitting at a table on one side of the room. The woman led her to a spacious bedroom with three single beds and a crib, along with a private bathroom back in the corner. The walls featured colorful pictures of children playing. Blinds covered the two windows. The woman told Margie that this would be her bedroom. It looked so peaceful; she loved it immediately. They were invited to come to the kitchen area, where the girls were given cereal and a muffin with juice. Margie stood stunned. People were being nice to her and waiting on her and the kids. It felt so good. She sat down with a cup of coffee and breathed a sigh of relief as tears welled in her eyes.

"Margie, this is Sara White," Kendall said, gesturing at the woman who had shown them around. "I wanted to get you safely inside before I introduced you. Sara is one of the women who are always here to help you and the others. This is the Spouse Abuse Center you might have seen me talking about on TV. I'm so glad I came here to visit a few weeks ago and knew where to bring you. I called Sara as soon as you called me this morning. Sara told me to bring you and the girls and that she would get your room ready. You can stay here as long as you need to stay. You will be fed and clothed. There are some classes for both you and the girls. Lisbeth won't get behind in school. You can take some courses, too. There are classes for job preparation and such. We'll talk about those later. There are TVs and movies, games for the girls to play, a toy box for the little ones. We hope you'll find everything you need."

"Oh, I'm so grateful. I don't know what to say except thank you," Margie whispered.

"There's no need to say anything. I know you and the girls are exhausted. Let's get you all fed, and then let's put the little ones back to bed. I imagine you've been up all night," Kendall said.

After the girls finished their breakfasts and Margie had nibbled a muffin, Kendall walked back to her bedroom with her. Together, they tucked the girls in, and then Margie quietly told Kendall everything that had happened the night before. She was talking fast, but Kendall got the story in spurts. She realized that Margie needed sleep, too. She put her arm around her shoulder and pulled the fragile woman to her. "Margie, I'm going to help you get through this nightmare. Please go to sleep and know you are safe. I'll be in touch shortly. God bless you, Margie. You are a brave woman," Kendall said. Margie got in her own bed and was falling asleep as Kendall slipped out of the room.

Chapter 49

On Monday Duke got up at 5:00 AM and went to the office as usual. The staff had spent Sunday afternoon grading the film of Saturday's game and were looking at what needed to be changed for the next game. They had started the game plan on Sunday night and would get back to it this morning. Despite the close game, there was a jovial mood in the room.

"Saturday, I sure got an education about gambling in this state," Duke said with a laugh. "I've never paid much attention to point spread and stuff like that. Never been interested. I have enough to think about in the game without having to remember that stuff. I'm not about to change. Let's get busy and see if we can win another game."

At that moment, his assistant Donna tapped on the door. "Coach, I know you don't want to be interrupted when you and your coaches are meeting, but this is an emergency," she said.

"What is it this time? I can't believe all the distractions. Men, I'll try to handle this while you continue with the game plan," Duke said.

"Coach, this is terrible. You're not going to like it," Donna said as they headed into her office. "I got here at about 7:30 and started listening to the answering machine messages that came in over the weekend. One came in at 2:48 AM this morning that is very troubling. I don't know what to do, but I knew you had to hear it."

"Okay, go ahead and play it," Duke said, dreading what he was going to hear.

When the message started, Duke immediately knew the caller was drunk. He was railing about the game and the fact Duke had not covered the spread. "You son of a bitch, you cost me big bucks this weekend. You idiot, don't you know the spread? It's all your fault I lost so much. I'd like to get my hands on you and wring your neck or worse. You know what I mean." The caller laughed. "Also, you know that wife of yours, that bitch has been all over the TV making those announcements. Well, she better watch it, too," he said, slurring his words. "Yeah, she's a bossy bitch. Telling people what to do all the time. I hate women like her. I'd like to shoot you both. Now that's a good idea, just shoot you both." The caller's voice began to fade away as if he'd dropped the phone.

Duke pounded his fist on the desk as the message clicked off. He couldn't believe it. Of all the things that could happen, he never dreamed that someone would threaten Kendall. He had already received death threats and been assured that nothing would come of them. But this was over the top. Furious, he looked at Donna. "Get Police Chief Patterson over here right away, and Ben Lawson, the FBI man who lives in town. I want them to hear this message in person, and I want to talk to them immediately. They keep saying these messages don't mean anything. Well, damn it, now someone's threatening my wife. This has to stop. Those cowards making threats. I'd like to see them in person. Teach them a lesson."

Unable to calm down, Duke sat in his office trying to figure out what to do. Should he call Kendall and upset her? It was the middle of the season; they couldn't just pick up and leave town. Was the caller serious? He sounded like he meant what he was saying. He was raging. Duke must have sat there longer than he realized because before he knew it, the chief of police, Vernon Patterson, was knocking on his door. Duke briefly greeted him and played the message.

"Coach, I'm so sorry this has happened," Chief Patterson said. "Some jerk made a big bet on the game and lost. He probably bet again on the pro games Sunday and lost. He was drunk as a skunk and picked up the phone to blame you for his own stupidity. Damn shame. And I hate that he's naming your wife. Now, most of the time these fools don't do anything. They usually don't follow through on their threats. But in this case, I think we have to take him seriously. There's something about this message; he seems to know your wife or her whereabouts. I want you to call her right now and have her come straight to this office. I don't want her alone at your home. Then I want her to disappear for about a week. She shouldn't go see relatives or anywhere else someone might expect her to go. While she's gone, of course, we'll try to find out who this is. Now, Coach, he threatened you. Are you familiar with guns at all?"

"Hell, no," Duke answered angrily. "I've never been interested in guns, never hunted, was never in ROTC. I know nothing about guns. I'm not comfortable with them. But if you put one in my hands right now, I might try to shoot somebody. I have never been so angry in my life. This is God awful."

"Well, Coach, I was going to give you a gun, but you might shoot somebody or yourself. So I think I'll hold off on that." Patterson smiled, trying to bring some levity into the situation, but Duke didn't return it. "I'll put an armed guard on you 24/7. He will be plain-clothed, and no one will notice. But I want to be cautious. There are crazy people out there."

"You can say that again. I've lost track of how many death threats I've gotten since I came here. You guys keep telling me to ignore them. But damn it, having one on my wife is a different matter. I feel so sick about this. It's crazy to think that what I do for a living has put my wife in danger."

As Duke picked up the phone to call Kendall, he was still mumbling, "That son of a bitch. I'd like to get my hands on him. Also, wonder how that chickenshit would do in an Oklahoma drill. He's a damn coward."

Chapter 50

When Kendall walked back in the condo, the phone was ringing. Her cell phone had been off since last night. She checked the caller ID and was surprised to see Duke's name.

"Hey, babe," she said. "I thought you were in meetings this time of day on Mondays."

"You're not going to believe what I have to tell you. I'm so sorry." Duke paused. He was gripping the phone tight enough to break it. "Some sorry son of a bitch left a message on the answering machine at the office. We think he called during the night after the pro football games went off the air yesterday. He was probably a gambler who lost big money on our game and the pro games on Sunday. For some reason, he started ranting about you and your public service announcement. The caller made a death threat against you. The chief of police wants you to get out of the condo right now and come down here. Pack a few things quickly and get down here. He wants you to vanish for about a week," Duke said, rushing through the words.

"What are you talking about? I can't leave town. I have to teach today. I was about to get dressed for class. This is crazy. You always say they don't follow through on these things. No, I can't leave town," Kendall said emphatically.

"I know you're a brave soul. But I heard the message. The guy sounds dangerous. Please, just pack a few things and come down here as soon as you can," Duke said.

Kendall was sure it was a hoax, just some guy sounding off. But she agreed to do what Duke asked. He sounded really upset. She put some clothes and cosmetics in her small carry-on bag and got in the car. She arrived at the office about forty-five minutes after their conversation. When she walked in, Duke introduced her to the chief of police Vernon Patterson and an FBI agent named Ben Lawson.

"Kendall, we've all listened to the message and agree that you should leave town for a week while they investigate. Maybe the guy will cool off," Duke said with concern written all over his face.

"But don't you think this is just another hoax?" Kendall insisted, looking at the three men in turn. "We've been told that nobody follows through. Duke has gotten so many of these threats, and nothing has ever happened. Besides, I'm teaching a course in the law school. I can't just not show up." She was holding her ground.

Duke immediately spoke up. "This is different. This threat is on you, baby, and I insist. We all insist. You can get someone to take your classes while you're gone. It'll only be a week. Please, I'll feel so much better if you're somewhere safe. This guy sounded serious."

"Let me hear the message," she said.

"No, you don't need to hear a drunken fool saying horrible things about you. I don't want you to hear it," Duke said with conviction.

Patterson couldn't help admiring this beautiful woman who was so brave. He had seen her at Rotary and been impressed. Here she was, dressed in her "lawyer suit," looking determined and self-confident. In fact, he admired both Mrs. Astin and the coach. They were devoted to one another. Patterson hated that they had to go through this crap.

"So it's three to one," Kendall finally said. "I guess I'm outnumbered."

Patterson and Lawson breathed a sigh of relief and then said they would be back in touch. After they left, Kendall sat down to talk to Duke about what they should do.

"I hate that what I do for a living has put you in danger. I hate it," Duke said.

"Duke, don't worry. You've told me he was drunk. Whoever he is, he probably doesn't even remember that he made a threat. But if it makes you feel better, I'll go away somewhere. But you said I couldn't go to family, so that cuts out Atlanta. I really don't want to go anywhere, but I could hide out somewhere. Maybe I could go to the beach or something."

"Are you crazy, Kendall? You could be followed, and you wouldn't be safe in some hotel room."

Suddenly, Kendall knew exactly what she would do. She would go to the Spouse Abuse Center. She would hide in that safe place and help the women. She would get to know Margie and the girls better. Yes, she liked that idea. At least she would be doing something useful. She told Duke and he agreed. It was a perfect place for her to vanish. Nothing bad could possibly happen there.

Chapter 51

Toby finally began to come out of his drunken coma at about 9:00 AM. He had a terrible headache and needed some water. As he stood in the kitchen, he began to look around. The house was awfully quiet.

"Margie, where are you? I'm sorry about last night. I know I got a little upset," he said. Then he saw the hole in the drywall and the two bullet holes. Where did they come from? Could he have done that? He noticed his fist, all cut up with scratches. Gosh, Margie will be really mad. Guess I'll have to apologize.

He went in the two bedrooms. No one was in either one of them. The beds weren't made. That wasn't like Margie. She always made the beds. Where could she be? He opened the door and looked outside and saw that her car was gone. Maybe she went to her mama's and daddy's the way she had Friday night. But there was no note. He walked over to the phone to call Margie's mama.

"Hey, Mama, how you this morning? I was wondering if Margie and the girls are over there. They aren't here this morning. If she isn't there, would you check and see if they're with one of her brothers?" He could have done this himself, but those guys were tough, and they didn't like Toby one bit. Toby was still looking around, as if his family would simply appear, when Margie's mother called back saying the boys hadn't seen them.

"Is everything okay, Toby? Margie wouldn't leave without letting you know where she was going. I'm concerned. Please have her call me when she comes back," she said.

Toby was getting put out with Margie. How could she leave and not tell him anything? Since her car was gone, he decided to get in the truck and try to find her. He didn't know where to look. She didn't socialize with her old friends much anymore. He started driving, sure he would see her car somewhere. Maybe she had taken the girls to that

McDonald's on Sycamore. No, she wasn't there. He kept driving, looking everywhere in town, but he couldn't find her. What was going on? He was just plain mad at that woman now. Finally, he decided to go back home. Maybe she was there by now. But she wasn't. Damn that woman. This wasn't good. He'd have to teach her a lesson. This wouldn't do. Since he didn't have to go to work today, he decided to have a beer.

Then Toby had an inspiration. I might take me a vacation. No work today, so I'll go to Grandpa's old cabin in North Carolina. I love that place. The woods are so dense and full of game. I can get lost there for days, or even weeks, and not see anybody. I won't tell a soul. I'll go by the liquor store and get me a good supply of booze. Then I'll put my rifles in the truck, pick up some food, and head out. I'll show that woman. When she comes home, I'll be gone. That will stress her out. Let her worry about where I am. Give her some of her own medicine. I need to be alone in the woods, shoot some game, drink liquor, and relax. Nobody to tell me what to do. It'll be just what I need for a while. But I'll be back. Yes, I'll be back. I have some scores to settle.

Chapter 52

Margie was surprised when she saw Kendall walk back into the Spouse Abuse Center with a carry-on bag late that morning.

"Well, I'm back, ladies. You won't believe what's happened. I guess you can say I've been abused, too, but not by my spouse. It's some unknown man out there," Kendall said as she entered the room. "Please carry on with what you were doing. I'll join you."

Margie was sitting at the dining table, talking with three other women as Sara led the discussion. But they all wanted to hear what had happened to Kendall. Margie took the bag from her and put it aside as they all leaned in to listen.

"A death threat was made during the night against me and my husband. Some drunk man called and left a message on the answering machine at the football office. They think it was a gambler who'd lost a lot of money over the weekend and was blaming Duke and me. It sounds crazy, doesn't it? I think it's just a hoax. No big deal, but the police chief thought I should leave town. Isn't that ridiculous! I had to call the law school and get someone to teach my class for a week. They told me to vanish. Wanted me to go out of town, but I said no way. I was irritated. Then I had the idea to come here. Called the director and cleared it with her. I insisted that I pay for staying here, but she won't hear of it. I'll make her take something. So, ladies, I'm here to stay for a week." Kendall slapped her hand on the table with a smile on her face.

"I plan to help out," she added. "Sara, let me know what I can do. Help with meals, take care of the children, or clean up. I want to get to know all of you better. Please call me Kendall and not Mrs. Astin. I'm one of you."

Margie sat there frozen. Of course she was glad to see Kendall, who had been so good to her. But she immediately started thinking about Toby. Was he the caller who made the threat against Coach and

Mrs. Astin? She remembered Toby saying, "shoot you both." Could he have meant the Astins? She was afraid it could be him. Should she say something now or think about it for a while? She decided to think about it. If it was Toby, she would feel terrible. Could she have made Toby so mad that he did something this horrible? She couldn't think straight yet. Yes, she told herself, think before you say anything.

The women, who all knew too well what it felt like to be threatened, began trying to console Kendall. But Kendall assured them she was fine. She was certain that whoever it was wouldn't follow through on the threat. They never do, she said. Margie wasn't so sure.

As they left the table, Kendall put her arm around Margie and said, "I really want to get to know you better. I want you to tell me what your dreams are for yourself and the girls. I feel like you're smart, and I already know how brave you are. Feel free to tell me anything. You can trust me. I want to help you and the girls."

Margie responded with tears in her eyes, "You are so sweet and kind to me. I'm going to have to get used to people being nice to me. I haven't seen much of that for a long time. I'm so grateful. I can't tell you how happy I am to be in a safe place. I'm relieved for the girls. I've been worried sick about what they've seen and heard in our home. I would love to get to know you better, too."

Margie was sincere about everything she said to Kendall. But could she tell her what she feared? Could she tell her that she was afraid Toby was the man on the phone?

Chapter 53

Knowing Kendall was safe was a comfort to Duke, and he was able to throw himself back into his work. The team was responding well and working through all the distractions. He was proud of this bunch of young men and had great affection for them. He was concerned, though, about the small injuries some of the guys were dealing with. He was especially worried about Elijah's slight groin pull. But Elijah had the heart of a warrior and wouldn't let up. There were a few problems on the offensive line, too. The roster was thin. They hadn't had time to build depth at each position. That would take several years. But these young men were fighters.

Duke was sitting at his desk one afternoon mulling over these problems when his assistant Donna knocked on his door. "Coach, you have a very special guest. He didn't have an appointment, but I knew you would want to see him. Have you heard of Tommy Lee Hampton?"

A member of the Triumvirate had come to see him. What could he want?

Duke stood and warmly greeted Tommy Lee. "Yes, I've heard of you, Tommy Lee. You were an outstanding player here. I'm glad you came by to visit. What can I do for you?" he asked.

"Coach, I'll not take much of your time. I'm not asking you to do anything you're not doing already. I know you don't have all the talent you'd like to have, but somehow you're getting those boys to play over their heads as a team. I really appreciate that. Now, some of my friends are going to be mad as hell that I came by to say that, but I don't care," Tommy Lee said with conviction.

"Well, I can't tell you how much I appreciate that, especially coming from you," Duke said as he patted Tommy Lee on the back.

"Yeah, I thought I should come by and let you know. I'm sure you've heard that some folks don't approve of you and have been working to make things hard for you," Tommy Lee said.

"Yes, I've heard, but I try not to pay any attention to them."

"You're right not to pay any attention. You see, they aren't real football people. I played and they didn't. Do you remember when our team went to the Cotton Bowl back in my playing days? You might remember I had a great eighty-yard run in that game. Folks around here still talk about it all the time. Legendary. So I understand what it takes to play football well, and they don't. I wanted you to know I'm on your side now," Tommy Lee said. "I can't help but compare Elijah to me when I played. Very similar."

"Thank you so much, Tommy Lee. Coming from you, that really means a lot," Duke said.

As he was standing up to leave, Tommy Lee added, "My only regret is that I'm too old to play for you. I still miss playing. I had more fun being on a team than I've ever had in my life. I mean that sincerely." As tears began to form in his eyes, he added, "Yes sir, my football days were the best days of my life."

Tommy Lee lingered a few more minutes but soon told Duke he had to get going. He knew Duke had a lot of work to do getting ready for the next game. When he left, Duke was moved that he'd wanted to come by and say what he had. It seemed to be a real breakthrough. He also had to laugh at the old-timer bragging about himself, but he still appreciated his support. And Tommy Lee was one of the big three, the Triumvirate. Billy Bob Craven had not come around and probably never would. Of course, Roland Rigby's son J.J. would make sure his father was against the team, too. But winning over one of the three was a good sign. Yes, things were looking up.

Chapter 54

October 1996

Billy Bob was worried. The team didn't look great in the fifth and sixth games of the year, but they won both of them. The damn coach was winning too many games. At least Elijah seemed to be trying to let up a little. Billy Bob didn't think he was playing as great as he had at the beginning of the year, but he was still looking pretty good. The seventh game was coming up, and he would see how Elijah looked in this game.

Billy Bob had invited some friends down from Chicago. They were a powerful group of businessmen who were always fun to have at the game. Craven Construction had built warehouses for them for years and were now building a casino in North Carolina. They loved the Chicago Bears, so it was only natural that when Billy Bob started asking them to come sit in his box for the Benton games, they jumped at the chance. They'd been coming to one game each year now for fifteen years. Billy Bob never asked them anything about their business, but he knew they were very successful and made tons of money. They all favored black suits, white shirts, and pearl cuff links. Billy Bob was sure that whatever they did wasn't completely legal. He knew better than to cross them or ask too many questions. He might be guilty by association, but the less he knew the better. He could always plead ignorance.

Everyone was shaking hands and greeting each other after a year's separation. The food and libations were going fast. He would have to make sure they were replenished soon. This was going to be a fun day. The guys loved Tommy Lee and his stories about the old days and Big Jack. But Tommy Lee was getting on Billy Bob's nerves these days. The old jock had gone over completely to the other side—he now loved the new coach and this team. If he said one more time that Elijah reminded him of the way he used to play, Billy Bob would throw up.

Suddenly, he could hear Tommy Lee getting wound up on the other side of the box. "You guys are going to have a ball today. It's so much fun to watch this team play. They may not always be the best team, but they find a way to win. They're fighters. You're going to love to watch this great back, Elijah Ray Johnson. He reminds me of the way I used to play. Do you remember the Cotton Bowl back in the day when I made the eighty-yard run?" Tommy Lee was into it again, and Billy Bob was about to throw something when he had a thought.

He sidled over to Antonio and spoke quietly, trying to make it sound like he was joking at first. "Tommy Lee is driving me crazy talking about what a great player he used to be. Don't you know how to get rid of people that irritate you? What would you do if you needed to get rid of someone?"

Antonio looked startled. "Tommy Lee is a good guy. I like him. You aren't serious, are you?"

Billy Bob gave a nervous laugh and said, "Of course not. Tommy Lee irritates me, but he's a friend. I would never really want to harm him." He lowered his voice and leaned closer. "However, I would like to get rid of that coach out there. I hate the guy. Everybody knows it. I don't try to hide it. He might be winning now, but he's bad for the team in the long run. Me and my friends, who give big bucks to the program and have always been in charge, are losing that power because of him. Got to get rid of him." Billy Bob looked at Antonio seriously.

"Keep your voice down. Don't talk to me about things like that out in public. Never. Do you understand?" Antonio said sternly with a scowl on his face.

"Sorry, sorry, I just meant maybe Coach could have an accident," he whispered. But he'd suddenly started sweating and knew he'd overstepped.

Antonio was quiet for several minutes and then leaned over and whispered, "You are a friend. You've been good to us all these years. We owe you, man. Sitting up here in this fine box. I'll help my friend. You understand? Give me a few days and call me late next week. I'll have a plan, but we'll have to talk in person—not on the phone. Never in public around other people. In private. Do you understand?"

Billy Bob knew he'd made a mistake and was nervous. But still, he couldn't believe how easy it was for Antonio to get the idea of what he wanted. Billy Bob nodded in agreement, saying apologetically, "Yes, I understand, sorry. I'll call you late next week. Thank you, my friend."

Chapter 55

Kendall enjoyed her week in the Spouse Abuse Center, even though she hated to miss her classes in the law school and her time with Duke in the evenings. But she had learned so much. It was impossible to know what these women experienced unless you heard them say it.

In a discussion one afternoon, Carol, who came from a prominent family, said, "My husband had been what we call a social drinker at first, but his drinking got heavier and heavier. He couldn't handle it. Then, when he lost a ton of money on the stock exchange, he blamed me. How he came up with that idea I'll never know. I had only asked him a few questions. But he started hitting me. He was a big, strong man. I couldn't fight back. When we went to parties with friends, I had to wear a lot of makeup to cover the bruises. Then, when he lost his position at the real estate firm where he worked, he went crazy. I thought he was going to kill me. One day when he was drunk, I pretended to go in the kitchen to fix dinner. I managed to run out the back door of my house, jump in the car, and drive here. If I hadn't, I honestly don't know if I would be alive today."

At that point, a young woman named Mindy, who looked no more than twenty, told her story. "My husband sure didn't have enough money to put any in the stock market. We were just plain poor. If we were lucky enough for him to have a job, we lived paycheck to paycheck. We had one baby, our precious little Jamie. But my husband got involved in meth. Then he got violent. It was horrible. I knew if I didn't get away from him, Jamie and I both might die." Tears streamed down her face.

"You two are perfect examples," Sara said gently, handing Mindy a box of tissues. "It doesn't matter if you have money or not. Very often, the same things happen. A violent man who can't control his addiction takes it out on his partner who can't defend herself. You're lucky you got away. I can tell you stories about those who didn't get away and who were killed, and then their spouses committed suicide."

Kendall sat and listened to these women in amazement. She was impressed to see how they were working to get their lives back together with the help of the workers in the center. She felt privileged to sit and listen quietly as they talked about what they hoped to do in the future.

The most meaningful relationship for Kendall was the one she formed with Margie and the girls. They had been smothered in the house with Toby, but now they were coming alive. The three little girls were learning to play and have fun like children their age should.

One afternoon, Margie began to open up to Kendall. "You'll probably be surprised to know that I was a good student in high school. I would've liked to have gone to college—Toby and I both wanted to go, but our folks were too poor to send us. So we decided to get married right out of high school and started having babies. And you know the rest of our sad story."

"I'm not surprised you were a good student. I can tell you're intelligent. What were your favorite subjects? Did you ever think about what you might like to study?" Kendall asked.

"Oh, I loved math. I did fine in English and history, but I wasn't that creative. But numbers fascinated me. You can solve puzzles. You learn how to use them, and they don't let you down. Yes, I love working with numbers. What can I do with numbers?" Margie laughed.

"A lot of things! I don't think I've ever told you that my father taught accounting his entire career at Georgia State University in Atlanta. He was probably disappointed that I didn't go into his field, but I wanted to go to law school. I'm sure he'd be happy to talk to you. You might be able to go to college yet."

"You're so sweet to think that, but I don't have any money, and I've got three daughters to raise. Here I am hiding from my husband, who obviously has an addiction to alcohol. I'll have so much to overcome that college is probably out of reach for me," Margie said, wringing her hands.

"No, never say never. You could divorce Toby if you don't love him anymore. If you still love Toby, maybe he can go to a recovery program. That will be your decision. Just don't give up. I'm sure my father could help you get a scholarship to GSU in Atlanta. I don't know, but I always believe there's a way. You'll want the girls to go to college, too. I can tell they're smart like you, especially Lisbeth," Kendall said as her mind began to churn. Whatever happened, she knew she wanted to help this young woman and her three girls.

The week at the center flew by. As much as Kendall enjoyed it, she was glad to get back into the world again. But she wasn't prepared for the onslaught from the media. The newspaper had published an article about her being threatened and having to go away for a week. She hated that it made the news, but everything about her and Duke made the news. When she came home, reporters from all over the country called to interview her. She refused them all. She didn't want the drunken caller to get any more publicity. She just wanted it all to die down and go away. There was still a guard at their condo 24/7, and the police had a female plain-clothed officer come and sit in the back of her law class. Kendall couldn't believe the fuss the police were still making. She knew there was an ongoing investigation of the threat, but nothing had come of it as far as she knew.

She had missed one home game and didn't go to the away game, but she was back for game seven against an Alabama powerhouse. Her family came from Atlanta, as did David and Vickie. Everybody had been so worried about her, and there were relieved hugs all round. They kept asking where she had been, but she refused to say. David was making jokes the way he always did. "Kendall, I hear you've been on vacation. Come on now, tell us the secret place you went—the beach at Monte Carlo, maybe?" He laughed.

"You'll never know," she said, joining in the laughter. "All I'm saying is that it wasn't luxurious, but it was rewarding!" Now she hoped the game would be as rewarding and they could all leave happy today.

She was nervous as she always was at games—sick stomach and all. It was another one of those nail-biters that were so close. The team seemed tight. The quarterback couldn't complete a single pass in the first half. If he did throw a decent pass, the receiver dropped it. Thank goodness, Elijah was running well—not great, but gaining just enough yards to make first downs. Of course, Kendall knew about his injury and hoped he could keep playing. But early in the third quarter, the worst happened—Elijah went down. She always hated for players to get hurt, especially a player like Elijah. He was so conscientious and gave it his all every play. He was supposed to be a number one draft choice. She felt awful for Elijah and knew Duke would be upset, too. They just had to make it through this game with a win, no matter the score. Since their bad experience earlier in the season, she couldn't help looking at point spreads. Even if Duke didn't pay attention now, she did. If they managed to pull out a win, she didn't think they would cover the point spread. Finally, the game was over, and they had won by three but, as she feared, hadn't covered the six-point spread. There were some boos like she expected, but not as many. She had learned to say what Duke said—a win is a win. She was happy but knew some of the fans wouldn't be.

Chapter 56

Billy Bob said goodbye to all his guests from Chicago, who were half looped but content after the game. Billy Bob pulled Roland aside and asked him to stay and have a word. Roland didn't usually sit with Billy Bob at the games since he had his own skybox, but Billy Bob had asked him to sit with him today to entertain the Chicago guests. Roland gave his own box to his son J.J. so he could entertain some of his friends. The kid had been having a hard time lately. Maybe being upstairs impressing some of his friends would make him happy.

"Roland, it was a mighty close game today," Billy Bob said. "I heard some boos after the game. I don't think they completed a pass in the whole first half. The team didn't cover. Lots of folks will be upset by that."

"They almost got beat, but they didn't. They're still undefeated. Sure, the game wasn't pretty. Yes, folks will be upset that they didn't score enough points. But, like I've heard that coach say—a win is a win." Roland moved closer to Billy Bob so they wouldn't be overheard.

"But Elijah went down," Billy Bob said. "That was a good thing. I wonder if he's faking an injury to hurt the team. He seems like he's been letting up in the last few games."

"We'll never know. But you shouldn't do anything to the kid's mama," Roland said. "He did what you wanted him to do. Even if he couldn't bring himself to let the team down and actually has a real injury, it's all the same to us."

"Okay, okay. I won't fire the kid's mama. But we gotta think of something. Stir up some more stuff to show the folks aren't happy with the coach. I've had an idea. Lean in. I don't want anybody to hear this. I was thinking that you could get your son J.J. to do something else for us. He did a good job talking to Elijah. I want him to go over to the coach's office late tonight and throw a big rock through the window.

The office will be easy to find. It's the end one with the big windows. Then we'll get our people down at the newspaper and the talk show guys to start talking about how the fans don't like the coach and are throwing rocks through his office window." Billy Bob had a gleam in his eyes. "What do you think about that, Roland?"

"It might work. I know that ever since that coach told J.J. he wasn't good enough to be on his football team, J.J. has been mad as hell. Nothing seems to make him happy. It's all he can think about all the time. He isn't doing well in school. Of course, he's never done too well, but this is worse. Half the time he doesn't go to class. The kid doesn't seem right in the head sometimes. This might be the very thing he needs," Roland said with a smile. "I think he would love to throw a rock through the coach's window."

Chapter 57

J.J. had always loved going to the football games at the stadium. It was great living in a university town, having a father who was a big booster with a skybox. Ever since he was a little kid, he'd spent time in that box. When his parents were still married, they never missed a game. And when he was as young as four or five, his mother would fill a bag with matchbox cars and his little toy soldiers, and he would play on the floor during the game. His parents would sit with their friends in the leather chairs, watching the game while he entertained himself. Of course, there was food everywhere—hamburgers and hot dogs on the countertops and popcorn, cookies, and fudge on the coffee table. He could even get drinks out of the refrigerator that was under the counter. Nobody paid any attention to him during the games, but that was fine with him. He ate and drank anything he wanted. He loved lying on the floor playing. He'd even found a secret hiding place under the back counter where the food was displayed. One day he discovered a loose baseboard under that counter. He would drive his cars in the imaginary tunnel. Sometimes his soldiers would hide from the enemy there. He might even stash a cookie or two in case they ran out.

As J.J. got older, he watched the game with his parents and their friends. Those were fun days, when he was the only child present and all the women told him how cute he was. It was also the time in his life when he decided he wanted to be a football player, too. Look at all the attention they got, and people cheered for them when they did things well. His father and mother never paid much attention to him, so he figured football might be a way for them to notice him more. His father was such a tough guy, and you had to be tough to play football. But it really didn't work. His parents began to fight all the time and ended up getting a divorce when he was in eighth grade. His mother took off to be a country and western singer, and his father started going to Las

Vegas all the time. J.J. was left on his own with sitters who didn't pay him much attention either.

But the skybox never lost its appeal. He loved it when his father went out of town and told him he could invite his friends up for the games. It was a big deal to many of them, who had never sat upstairs. J.J. could tell they were impressed. Naturally, he was happy today when his father said he was going to sit in Billy Bob's skybox with their friends from Chicago. J.J. wanted to invite some of his old teammates from high school who were now at Benton, along with some new friends. But he especially wanted to invite Marilyn Pope, his ex-girl-friend, to sit in the box. She had been a cheerleader when he played football at the academy. They had gone out together, and J.J. still liked her. She was beautiful, with long brown hair and a great figure. She was smart, made excellent grades, and didn't party much. Their rela-tionship tanked when she said she'd grown tired of some of his moods and told him they couldn't date any more. J.J. was crushed, but now he would try to get her back. He knew that would make him feel better. She had accepted his invitation to come today, but only if J.J. agreed it wasn't a date. She would be part of a group of friends only. That was fine with J.J. It was a start.

J.J. was glad to see Juanita, who had been serving the box since he was a kid. He told her his friends would be hungry and she would need to keep the refreshments coming. She laughed and told him that's what she expected. Everything went well, and the group was finishing up the food after the game when Roland came to the door of the box and mo-tioned for J.J. to step outside. "Son, could you come here a minute. I need to talk to you for a second," he said as he waved to the other young folks.

"Sure, Dad, we've had a great time. We ate and drank a lot of stuff. I had to get Juanita to replenish everything. I knew you wouldn't mind," J.J. said as he stepped out the door.

"That's fine, son. Glad y'all had a good time. I need to talk to you where no one can hear. This is important. I just had a talk with Billy Bob. You know we're worried about the coach winning so much. We've got to do something else to distract attention from the wins and show that lots of folks still don't like him. Billy Bob and I hate the guy and are doing everything we can think of to get rid of him. Billy Bob had this idea and he wanted me to ask you to carry it out." Roland spoke in a low voice and kept looking around to make sure no one could hear.

"Sure, you know I hate that coach. Most of these guys in here today were happy—especially my old girlfriend, Marilyn Pope. Do you remember her, Dad?" J.J. asked.

"Never mind your ex-girlfriend. Listen up. This is important. Concentrate. You've been acting a little strange lately. Can you concentrate on what I'm about to say?" Roland asked, annoyed.

"Sure, Dad. Nothing is wrong with me. I can do whatever you ask," J.J. answered casually.

"Okay, okay, here's the plan. Billy Bob wants you to go over to the coach's office building late tonight and throw a big rock through one of Astin's windows. They're big windows, and they shouldn't be hard to find."

The idea thrilled J.J. "Sure, I know where it is. I was just in his office. Remember when he told me I wasn't good enough to be on his team? That jerk. Every day I think how he shouldn't be the coach. I would love to throw a big rock through his window. Too bad he won't be in the office so it could hit him, too." J.J. smiled. He was really going to enjoy this. Everybody would be talking about it and wondering who did it. It was a great idea, and he was glad his father and Billy Bob had asked him to do the deed.

Chapter 58

Every Sunday morning Duke went to his office to record his television show discussing Saturday's game. He didn't mind it as much as the call-in show he had to do later in the week. When he walked in the door, preoccupied about what he was going to say, he heard a commotion. What was happening? Then he saw several assistants moving furniture and sweeping up shards of glass.

"What in the hell happened in here?" Duke immediately blurted.

"Coach, your guess is as good as mine," a cameraman said as he held up a big rock. "We came in early to set up equipment for the show the way we always do, and glass was everywhere. Someone threw this at your window."

"What next? I've got to tell you, I haven't thought of this. We've had death threats—so many I can't count them—and now we have a rock through the window. I can't believe it," Duke said as he rubbed his head.

"What are we going to do, Coach?" the cameraman asked.

"What we always do. Clean up the glass and go on about our business. Let's try to keep it quiet. We don't need this to get out," Duke said.

"Too late. The phone was ringing when we came in the door, and we answered it, thinking it might be you. But it was a newspaper man wanting a quote. How could they know about this so quickly?"

"Damn it. From the time I started this job, the newspapers have always known everything before I do. They called some renegade officer in the police department. Heck, they might pay him, who knows," Duke said. "What this tells me is that it was planned and done deliberately to cause trouble. But guess what? We're just going to move on as if nothing happened. I'll make a joke about it. Some folks think I'm stupid and don't know anything about gambling. I'm going to say, 'If our quarterback had thrown the ball as well on Saturday as someone threw this rock, maybe we would have won Saturday by a better score and beat the spread.'" He couldn't help but laugh. Yep, he thought to himself, make a joke about it. Irritate the dumbass who's responsible.

Chapter 59

Toby had always enjoyed going to his grandfather's old cabin. It was quite a drive to Andrews, North Carolina, but it was worth it. The cabin was in the Nantahala National Forest surrounded by miles of dense woods with giant trees and beautiful creeks. As a kid, he had gone camping, hiking, and whitewater rafting on the river. But when he got older, he mainly just went hunting. Now it was the isolation he enjoyed; there was nobody to bother him. He could get lost. There wasn't anything to do really. He could listen to an old radio, but the reception was bad. He couldn't get his football games and place his bets. For a week, he sat and drank liquor all day while he cussed Margie, Coach Astin, Mrs. Astin, and Carter. But after a week, he was ready to go home.

As Toby neared his farmhouse, he couldn't help smiling. Margie thought she could irritate him by disappearing with the girls. He had given her some of her own medicine by just up and leaving himself. He was sure she was out of her mind with worry about where he was. But when he drove up, her car wasn't there. Well, damn, he thought. I wanted to walk in and startle her. Now I'll just have to go in and wait for her to come back.

But when he walked in the door, he realized the house was just the way he had left it a week ago, with crushed beer cans and trash everywhere. There was the big hole in the drywall, and the bullet holes. If he'd done that, he did feel bad about it. He honestly didn't remember, and that was sort of scary. He had the fleeting thought that maybe his father had once done something similar, but he put it out of his mind. He would have to apologize to Margie. Yes, tell her he was sorry, and she would forgive him like she always had.

Toby sat and thought for a long time. Finally, he got up and started cleaning the place since Margie wasn't there to do it for him.

He figured he would have to find something to eat. Tomorrow he would get another job, probably with Ambrose Construction. They had tried to hire him once before. But first, he was going to look for Margie and the girls. She couldn't get away with this. He wouldn't stand for it. He was mad now, and after he apologized he'd have to teach her a lesson. Where could she be?

He was trying to figure where else to look for Margie as he sat down in front of the TV with canned chili and a beer. He flipped through the channels, searching for a game to watch, and came across the public service announcement Mrs. Astin had made for that Spouse Abuse Center. All of a sudden, he knew the Astin woman had something to do with Margie disappearing. Why hadn't he thought of her before? She was always talking to Margie when she came out to the construction site, and Margie thought she was great. She and her coach husband lived out at the lake in that condo. Toby would have to go out there tomorrow. Yes, somehow that bitch and her sorry ass husband were helping Margie. He would make 'em pay.

Chapter 60

On Thursday, Billy Bob called Antonio. He was thankful he had this "special friend" in Chicago who knew how to get things done without anybody knowing how it happened. It was exciting—like James Bond or something. Billy Bob did exactly what he had been told to do. Antonio had instructed him to meet him the next day. Billy Bob was to fly his plane to Charlotte, North Carolina. He was to land on the tarmac where small private jets landed and go straight to Antonio's airplane, which would be sitting there waiting for him. The meeting would be completely private. No one would know about it.

Billy Bob had followed his instructions and was walking onto Antonio's plane. "Good to see you, my man. Hope you're doing well today," Billy Bob said as he hugged Antonio.

"I'm doing okay. I know I got tough with you when you started talking about getting rid of someone at the game. Never ever talk like that in public. Do you understand?" Antonio said immediately.

"Oh, I know. I'm sorry. I wasn't thinking. Never ever in public. So sorry," Billy Bob said nervously.

"Okay, take it easy. Now we can talk. You know I told you I owe you. You've been good to us all these years. You had my family down to all those games through the years. And you did a good job building those warehouses and now a casino for us, and you never say nothin' about 'em to nobody. We got a big operation goin' in your state," Antonio said as he smiled. "Yeah, you don't ask questions. I like that. You've been our friend and done good by us. Now, I'm not gonna ask you any questions either. You understand?"

All Billy Bob could do was nod. He was anxious and wasn't sure how this would go.

"Now, Billy Bob, I'm going to a send one of my men down there. He'll watch that coach every day for a few weeks. My man won't be noticed. He's good at that. He'll figure out the coach's schedule and settle on the best time and place. You'll never meet him. You'll know nothin' about it. Do you understand what I'm saying?" Antonio asked.

Again, Billy Bob nodded and said, "Yes, but your man should know the coach has one or two armed guards at all times."

"That won't bother this man at all. He's an expert at what he does," Antonio said with confidence. "The coach might have an accident or something. You know what I mean. He might run his car into a tree."

"That's good."

"Now, Billy Bob, as I've been saying, you're my friend, and I'll do this for you. But I'm gonna ask you one time. Are you sure you want to do this, 'cause there ain't no going back afterwards?" Antonio asked with complete seriousness.

Billy Bob swallowed and took a deep breath. "Yes," he said, "this is what I want to do. It's for the best. This coach must go."

Chapter 61

J.J. threw the big rock just the way they'd asked him to. It wasn't easy. The first couple of rocks were too heavy, and he couldn't get them high enough. But when he finally succeeded, the sound and sight of the shattering glass was so exciting. It was like a perfect high spiral soaring through the air to a great receiver, who then took the ball to the end zone. The sudden pop of the glass caught the streetlights just right and sent glittering sparkles into the air. He wanted to scream but only jumped up and down. He was smart enough not to rouse any of the security folks who stayed on the other side of the building. But what a thrill it was, and it made him feel important. Yes, he had really done something no one else could do. Now his father would be proud of him.

He loved hearing people talk about the broken window on the radio, and there was even an article in the paper. He was dying to tell somebody he had done it, but his father said not to do anything so stupid. Then the coach started joking about it on his TV show. He said if he had quarterbacks who could throw that well, they could score more points. Ha ha ha. Everybody laughed.

J.J. screamed at the TV. "You had somebody on your team that threw that big rock. You told him he wasn't good enough. You sorry SOB. I hate you!" He was home alone, but he didn't care if someone heard him. How could the coach dismiss him from the team the way he had? He would never get over it. That coach had ruined his life. J.J. had to think of something else to do to him. Astin was just laughing, and Marilyn thought he was so handsome. J.J. would think of something else to make him pay.

Chapter 62

Over the years, Kendall had learned that if she stayed busy, it helped get her mind off the stress of the games. That way, she didn't have time to think and worry so much. It was strange about the stress—it never went away. If the team was weak and didn't win, there was stress. But if the team was good, there was also stress. The more the team won, the more nerve-wracking it became. Everybody wanted them to win all the games. Then there were the death threats, and she worried what would happen next. It was really making her crazy.

One night when Duke walked into the condo, Kendall couldn't help it. She had to vent. "I'm so tired of being nervous all the time. The stress is eating me up. The only things that seem to help is getting busy teaching or working at the house. Thank goodness, I have those things. I am human. But I'm not as strong as you think I am, or at least my show of strength sometimes fails. I sure don't have you around to help me."

"I'm really sorry you feel that way," Duke said earnestly. "There's so much going on. I know I work all the time. But things have gotten better. Can't you enjoy any of it?"

"No, I'm sick of it all. I remember when I loved the games in college and in the pros. But it's different now. I always seem to have a knot in my stomach. I try to encourage you and be optimistic, but I have to be honest. Sometimes I wish you were doing something else. I sure as heck wish you were more interested in what I'm doing," Kendall blurted out.

"I'm interested in what you're doing. I'm proud of you, Kendall," Duke said. "You know I love you."

"Yes, I know you love me, but you're never here for me. Even when you come home, I can tell you're still thinking about football. And what about the house? When have you been over there? Are you interested at all in the construction? Do you have any opinions about anything to do with the house? Do you even know how to get to the lot?" Kendall asked.

"Of course, I'm interested. But I know you'll take care of it. You don't need me to make decisions. That's one of the good things about our relationship. You are self-sufficient, and I appreciate it." Duke looked at her with sincerity and concern.

"But you can just let things roll off your back. You laugh things off. It's that easygoing Hawaiian nature you have. I don't have it. I'm a worrier, and sometimes I think we need to worry. Who has armed guards everywhere they go? I'm tired of living like this. Sometimes I just want to run away."

"Babe, I'm sorry I haven't been more attentive. I don't pay enough attention. I said I would do better, and then I seem to forget. Please tell me when you need help or if I need to do something. I don't want you to be unhappy. I know this isn't the life you wanted. It's the life I wanted. Football is too important to me. I guess I'm addicted or something, I don't know," Duke said.

"Some nights I lay awake and can't sleep. A lot of the time, I can't eat because my nerves are so bad. Why do you think I wanted to build a house way out on the lake? Because it was far away and peaceful. And we've never had children. Sometimes I think about the beautiful children we could have had," Kendall said as she started to cry.

"Kendall, Kendall, I am so sorry," Duke said, putting his arms around her. "I know I'm obsessive when it comes to football. I'm sure it drives you crazy, and I'm disappointed about not having children, too. I tell you what, let's keep talking about this. Maybe at the end of the season we can reassess my use of time and make some adjustments. I promise I'll be more attentive to you. What do you say to that?"

"That would be good. Yes, let's keep talking. I feel like I have to get it out or it's going to eat me alive. You know I love you, but we must keep talking," Kendall whispered through her tears.

"Tomorrow's Thursday, and I'll leave practice in time to go over to the house. I want to see what's happening. Of course, I'm happy about the house. I'm proud of all you do—your teaching, work with abused women, and building houses. I couldn't do this without you," Duke said.

"Yes, let's go over to the house tomorrow. I would love to show you what's happening. We could take something to eat, sit, and watch the sunset, and anticipate what it'll be like to live there after the season," Kendall said as she wiped tears off her face. "I feel better now, but we have to keep being honest with each other. I can't keep it bottled up anymore—I might explode. Like you said, let's just get through these last few games of the season and see what happens."

"How did I get to be such a lucky man? I have a wife who's a brilliant lawyer, teaches in the law school, builds a house, gets death threats, and tells me not to worry about anything. And she is also beautiful," Duke said.

"Wait a minute. There you go with that charm of yours. You're not going to get off the hook so easily, telling me all those things. I'm going to hold you to your promise. I will be watching!" Kendall said with a smile.

At least they had always been able to talk things out—that was their saving grace. She just wished Duke would be more concerned about some of the things that worried her. Oh, well, he couldn't change in one conversation, but he was trying. Maybe things would get better.

Chapter 63

Around 5:00 Thursday afternoon, Kendall got home, kicked off her shoes, and was looking forward to showing Duke the progress they had made on the house. She was thinking about what she could pack for a picnic. Suddenly the phone rang, and it was Duke.

"Kendall, how about you come pick me up and we'll go to this little French restaurant in an old house on Mercer Avenue. They'll put us in a private room in the back where no one can bother us. We'll go by the new house later for a visit by flashlight. You'll have to bring me into the office tomorrow, but it isn't an early day. I'll just leave my car here. What do you say—how about a real date tonight?" Duke laughed. "I've even insisted to my guard that we don't need a chaperone."

"Oh, Duke, I'd love that. I'll be there in thirty minutes. I can't wait," Kendall said as she started putting her shoes back on.

She jumped in her BMW and drove as quickly as she could to the football offices to pick up Duke. They needed this. It had been so long since they were able to have a real date night, and she knew it would do them good.

"I love this charming restaurant," Kendall exclaimed later as they sat together drinking wine. "Why haven't we been here before? And the salmon was delicious. Fresh flowers on the table. All the things I love. It reminds me of that French restaurant where we had our graduation dinner. Do you remember?"

"Sorry, I don't remember that restaurant. I'm just glad you like this one. I want to see that happy smile on your face. Have a little more wine. I enjoy hearing you laugh," Duke said as he poured her another glass of chardonnay. They sat and laughed about the good times they'd enjoyed, until finally they realized it was getting late.

As they were leaving, Duke insisted on driving. "This is our date night, and I'm taking you out like I did in the old days. Plus, I think you've had a little too much wine," he joked.

"Well, some handsome guy kept refilling my glass!" Kendall teased back. "I am happy tonight, Duke. What a charming place. I really enjoyed it. Why don't we do this more often? I think we can manage this maybe once a week. What do you think?"

"I don't see why not. Maybe I'm getting things in perspective a little better," Duke said. He began telling her about how he was going to start leaving things at the office. They were soon lost in conversation and didn't notice the black sedan following them.

Suddenly, Duke looked in the rearview mirror and realized the car was right on their tail. "What the heck. That car is right on us. People who drive like that really annoy me. I'm going to speed up and get him off our rear." But when he sped up, the car sped up as well. It even seemed like the driver was trying to hit the back of their car. Duke sped up again, and so did the other driver.

"Kendall, he's trying to run us off the road. Every time I speed up and try to get some space between us, he speeds up and closes it. I'm going to try to speed up one more time. Hold on," Duke said as he went even faster.

"My God, Duke, how fast are you going, sixty or seventy on this single-lane road?" Kendall hollered. "This is dangerous. It's so dark. There are no streetlights along this stretch. We could have an accident!"

"I think that's the idea. But I'm betting I know this road better than he does. I drive this road every morning and night. There's a very sharp curve coming up. I'm going to wait until the last second to turn. Hold on." Duke pressed the gas and gripped the wheel.

Terrified, Kendall closed her eyes and prayed. Duke suddenly made a sharp turn to the right, and their car felt like it went up on two wheels. But he was able to straighten up and speed on down the road. Unfortunately for the other car, it plunged into a deep ditch.

"Oh my God!" Kendall exclaimed, shaking all over. "I was terrified. I don't even want to think about what could have happened."

"We could have been hurt bad or worse, that's what happened. Sorry son-of-a-bitch. We'll skip going to the new house tonight. I'm calling Chief Patterson immediately."

As soon as he walked in the condo, Duke had Patterson on the line. "What the hell is going on, Chief? You guys keep telling us they don't act on these threats, but tonight some coward followed through. Tried to run us off the road. Somebody tried to kill my wife tonight. He drove into the ditch, and I'm going back up there right now to beat his brains out. You'd better get somebody out here to watch Kendall." Duke was raging now, out of control.

"Hold on, hold on. Where was this?" Patterson asked.

"On that single-lane county road right before you get to the lake. That stretch with no streetlights. Damn fool was right on our bumper. I kept speeding up, then he sped up. We were going seventy, eighty before it was over. I made a quick turn; he went in a ditch. I'm going up there now. No one is going after my wife." Duke felt hot, the anger boiling inside him.

"Two men are on their way now. Duke, hold your horses. Don't leave Kendall. If you go by yourself, you're playing into their hands. That's the dumbest thing you could do. Stay where you are, and let us take care of it. Come to my office first thing in the morning, and I'll tell you what we find tonight," Patterson insisted.

Duke stood there shaking for several seconds, trying to get control of his anger. "Okay, okay, but it's only because I can't leave Kendall. I'll stay here. But you better get that sorry son of a bitch, or I'll find a way to get him. I promise. I'm sick and tired of this crap. No more Mr. Nice Guy here. I've had it," Duke said. He slammed down the phone and mumbled, "That sorry ass coward trying to run us off the road. This crap about 'they don't act on these threats' is over. What's their next trick?"

Chapter 64

After a sleepless night, Kendall and Duke got up early and drove to Chief Patterson's office. They were in a state of shock. Duke was calmer but still mad as hell. Patterson was already there waiting on them.

"I understand you two had some excitement last night," Patterson said as he tried to shake Duke's hand. But Duke was not in an affable mood.

"I wouldn't call it excitement. I would call it terror," Kendall said as she sat in one of the two chairs in front of the chief's desk. Duke was too restless to sit and started pacing instead. "If it hadn't been for Duke's knowledge of the road and the fact that he drove like a bat out of hell, we could both be dead."

Before he spoke, Duke stood there and stared at Patterson. "Things have changed big time," he finally said. "You've been saying these folks usually don't act on their threats. But now they have. What are you going to do about it?"

"I agree that things have changed," Patterson said. "We've got to be more diligent. But let's take it one step at a time. Let me report on what we did last night. After your call, two of my men went straight out there. They had to get a tow truck to get the car out of a ravine. There was no one in the car and no sign of injury. Whoever it was must have been able to leave on foot. We're checking for anybody who shows up in the area looking suspicious. We tried to get prints and looked for bloodstains. We're still looking at the car for evidence of who was driving. But we did find out it was a rental car—black Ford sedan rented under a fake ID. For one thing, we know this was well thought out and planned. Might say professional. We're dealing with a smart cookie here. But know that we're working hard on this and all the threats."

"We're really upset this morning. But we do appreciate what you're doing. Please understand our anger," Kendall said as Duke stood there, biting his tongue before he said too much.

"But I want to know why your guard wasn't with you. What happened?" Patterson asked.

"That was my fault," Duke admitted. "I was taking Kendall out for a date—a real date night—and I didn't want a guard tagging along. I told him we didn't need a chaperone. That's on me, not him. I take responsibility. We won't do it again, I promise you. You know, as soon as things seem to get better, something like this happens. If last night taught me anything, it's that we can't get complacent. This danger is real. We have to be on guard all the time for what might happen next. I've been too easygoing all along. Kendall has been right. I should've taken this more seriously all along. We have to wonder every day what will happen tomorrow."

"It's good you get the message," Patterson said as he reassured them. "Your guards will be with you twenty-four hours every day. But don't take any more chances. Especially at night. I think it's more likely they'll try something at night rather than during the day. But be cautious all the time. And no more late date nights alone. Sorry, but those are real tempting to someone out there."

Chapter 65

Since Toby got such a great inspiration about Mrs. Astin helping Margie, he decided to delay applying for a new job. That could wait. He would ride out to the Astins' condo on the lake. It wasn't far from the site of the new house. Even though he didn't know for sure which one they were renting, he knew Mrs. Astin's car, and that would tell him which condo to watch. He found her car easily. He didn't know what kind of car Coach Astin drove, but he figured he'd already left anyway. Then he noticed a second car parked out front with someone inside. Who could that be? Toby would sit there all day if necessary. Maybe he would see something, or maybe Mrs. Astin would get in her car, and he could follow her.

Just then, someone got out of the other car in front of the condo. It was a big guy, and he reached back into the car and got a pair of binoculars. He lifted them up and pointed them toward Toby. He thought he better get out of there before the man had a chance to come over where he was. He started the truck and sped away. He'd have to park further down the road the next time he came. But he was surer than ever that the bitch Mrs. Astin was helping Margie, and he would follow her another day. He would come at different times, being careful that no one saw him.

Since the man with the binoculars had interrupted his search, Toby decided he would go on over to Ambrose Construction and get a job. As he drove into their parking lot, he saw Mr. Ambrose coming out of the office.

He parked quickly and hurried over, sticking out his hand. "Mr. Ambrose, I'm Toby Lane. Remember, you offered me a job not too long ago? I'd like to come to work for you now."

Mr. Ambrose didn't look happy, but he shook Toby's hand. "Yes, I remember you, Toby, and I do need some extra carpenters. You've gained a reputation for being hard to work with, but I'll give you a chance."

"I appreciate it if you take me on. I won't be any trouble if you don't have women bossing me around," Toby said as he laughed.

Ambrose did not laugh. "Son, whoever asks you to do something, you do it. Do you understand?"

"Yes sir, I will. What do you have going on at the moment? Where can I help you?" Toby asked.

"Right now, we're doing some renovations down in the skyboxes at the stadium. Some of them haven't been refurbished in years. The team is out of town for the next two weeks, so we have some time. Some of the boxes have cracked windows, loose countertops, peeling paint—stuff like that. I'll send you down there with one other man, and you do whatever needs to be done," Ambrose said.

"I'll be happy to do that. Sounds like an interesting job. I've never been up in any of them skyboxes. They must be fancy if they're where the bigwigs sit." Toby thought he might like to hang around at the stadium; he might see Coach Astin and could learn his routine too.

Chapter 66

Toby enjoyed working in the stadium skyboxes. It was fun to imagine watching a game up there with all that food and alcohol. Yes, it would be a great place to watch the games. He enjoyed the guy he was working with, too. Jerry Hogan had gone to the same high school, and they had known each other. Jerry also worked part-time as stadium security during some of the games and was able to show Toby all around the place. Jerry wasn't crazy about the coach either, so they spent time complaining about the point spreads the coach had blown.

Jerry liked to bet on the games, too, and they were picking their teams for the next week when Toby noticed Coach Astin walking on the playing field with a group of people. Some were holding pads and giving instructions, and one of them had a big camera. How lucky could he get? There was the famous coach, strolling around on his football field doing a commercial or something. With that pretty face of his, he did an awful lot of that kind of thing. Toby couldn't help himself. All of a sudden, he raised his fist, pointed his forefinger, raised his thumb, pointed at the coach, and said, "POW, POW."

"What ya doin', man? I said I wasn't crazy about the coach, but I don't want to shoot him," Jerry said.

"Well, Jerry, you and I might be different. I really hate the man," Toby said as he raised his fist and repeated his pretend shot, "POW, POW."

"You're crazy," Jerry said, a puzzled look on his face as he walked off.

It was quitting time, and Toby was ready to drive back out to the Astins' condo to wait and see if he could catch Mrs. Astin going somewhere. He hadn't been able to follow her anywhere yet. She always had that guard with her. But he wasn't giving up.

Toby got off at 3:30 and immediately drove to the condo. There was Mrs. Astin, getting in her car with some big bags of something. He went down the street to wait for her to pull out. The guard was following her. Once again, Toby couldn't believe his luck.

Chapter 67

November 1996

The eighth game of the season went well, and the team looked better. The backup players were working hard. Kendall was relieved and felt more confident than she had in several days. Thankfully, she was busy filling her life with activity, and one day she had an idea. During the next week while Duke was busy getting ready for game nine, Kendall called Mary Denton, the director of the Spouse Abuse Center.

"Mary, would it be possible for me to visit again? I know you don't want people going in and out. I'll be careful. I have some gifts for everyone. Hopefully, it will cheer them up and I would enjoy it, too." She held her breath, waiting for an answer.

The director hesitated a moment and said, "I know it would be wonderful for the women and children and would probably make them happy."

"I've gone to the university bookstore and bought sweatshirts and T-shirts for everyone. You know, I've kept in touch by phone but haven't seen them in a while. I especially want to see Margie and her girls," Kendall said.

Mary finally allowed her to go with a promise that she would be extra careful. Kendall was sure that no one would suspect anything. The guard at the Astin house left around 3:30 and the new one had just arrived. Kendall told him she had an appointment at a doctor's office downtown, and he could follow her. She would zip right in and out. It would only take about an hour.

She gathered up two big bags and threw them in the back of the car, taking no notice of the truck following her and her guard at a distance. She was thinking how much fun the kids would have. She had added some footballs and basketballs—soft ones they could play with inside. There were pompoms, too. Lots of team spirit.

Once she'd parked, she waved to her guard and walked into Dr. Faraday's office, confident all was well.

"Surprise, surprise," she said cheerfully as she entered the living area. "Come over here, kids. I have some goodies for you."

The children crowded around her. "Miss Kendall, how do I look?" Lisbeth grinned as she struck a pose in a sweatshirt that went almost to her knees.

"Perfect. You look great. Here, Jane Ann and Carrie. These are some T-shirts and sweatshirts for you, too. All of you kids—each of you take one."

The girls grabbed the pompoms and started shaking them. "Look, we're cheerleaders," Lisbeth said with a grin as she began to dance around the room.

One little boy, who had been so quiet when Kendall stayed at the center, grabbed a Nerf football and started tossing it to one of the other little boys. After a few minutes, he came up to Kendall and whispered in her ear, "Miss Kendall, tell your husband I will be a quarterback for him someday."

Kendall smiled and said, "Of course I will. He'll be so happy to hear about you. And I'm sure he'll be glad to have you at quarterback."

"Thank you," Margie said. "This has been so much fun. The kids think it's Christmas." She gave Kendall a hug.

Kendall stayed an hour or so, catching up with all the women. When she left the building, she was grateful for such a wonderful visit with everyone. She knew it meant more to her than it did to any of them. Lost in thought about her visit, once again she didn't see the truck parked a little way down the street.

Chapter 68

Toby sat in his truck a long time after Mrs. Astin and her guard drove away. He had to decide what to do. He thought Margie and the girls were probably in that building. He had looked for them everywhere. This was his first lead. Why else would the woman take big bags of things inside and come out empty handed? The building had a sign out front saying "Doctor J. C. Faraday." He didn't know what that meant, but he had to check it out. He needed a plan.

After Toby sat there for about an hour, he drove off toward J. B. Carter's supply shed. He knew where Carter kept dynamite. They'd used it to blow up granite when they cut a steep driveway in the lake development. Since Toby had quit so abruptly, he'd never returned the shed key to Carter. He would go in tonight and get a box of dynamite sticks and put them in the back of his truck. Tomorrow, he'd go about his regular workday and then drive back to that building in the late afternoon, see what he could find out. He felt glad to have a plan.

The next afternoon, Toby walked into the office of Dr. J. C. Faraday. A nurse sat behind a glass window. The name plate on her desk identified her as Gloria Potts. She was rather imposing and seemed like the type you wouldn't want to cross. Toby felt uncomfortable as he scanned the room. He saw only one closed door to the left. No one else was in the waiting room. The nurse slid back the window and said, "Hello, may I help you?"

Toby hesitated a few seconds and then said as politely as he could manage, "Yes, Miss Potts, I believe my wife and daughters are here. Can I see them?"

"Did she have an appointment with Dr. Faraday this afternoon?" the nurse said calmly.

"I don't know nothing about an appointment. I just know my wife is here," Toby insisted. "Her name's Margie Lane."

Nurse Potts began looking through an appointment book and said, "Sir, I'm sorry, but I don't show that she has an appointment today."

Toby was getting impatient. "Listen, lady, as I said, I'm pretty sure my wife is here and I want to see her."

Gloria Potts remained calm. But she didn't like this smart-ass white dude at all. Knowing he was going to be trouble, she flipped the switch that turned on an intercom system in Sara's office upstairs. Now Sara would be able to hear everything that was transpiring downstairs.

"What was her name again? And why do you think she's here?" Nurse Potts said casually.

Toby was getting mad and raised his voice, as if Potts were stupid, deaf, or both. "Margie Lane. I saw Mrs. Astin, the coach's wife—you know who I'm talking about. She came in here yesterday afternoon with some big bags, and she stayed about an hour and left without the bags. My wife has disappeared, and that Astin woman helped her. I know she did. Can't think of no one else that did. She was bringing stuff to my wife. Now let me see her."

Still maintaining her calm, the nurse said, "Well, Mrs. Astin did have an appointment yesterday afternoon with Dr. Faraday. It was lengthy because she did some X-rays. They also chatted for a while. Dr. Faraday is very friendly with her patients."

"Woman, I've had it with you. Let me see this Dr. Faraday right now," Toby demanded.

"I'm sorry," the nurse said, her voice growing stern. "Dr. Faraday is with a patient. Would you like to sit down and wait?"

At that point, Toby rushed over and tried to open the door to the left, but it was locked. "Let me in! You hear me? Let me in."

Gloria Potts was finally getting irritated. "Sir, you can't go in there. I'm going to have to ask you to leave."

Now Toby was shouting. "Hell no, I'm not gonna leave until I see my wife. And if you don't let me see her, I've got some dynamite in my truck and I'll blow this place up! I'm serious—now tell Margie to come out!"

At this point, Gloria Potts stood and reached in her big purse and took out a Colt .45. Her demeanor changed completely as she said, "Listen, dude, get your fat ass out this minute. My husband's a policeman, and he's taught me how to use this gun. You say you're gonna blow us up with dynamite; I'm gonna blow you up with this! You're threatening us. That's a crime. I'm calling the police." Gun in one hand, she picked up the phone, never looking away from him. Toby lunged for it through the window, but she stepped back out of his reach and instructed someone named Sara to call the police.

Gloria was now expertly holding the weapon with two hands, pointing it straight at Toby. He could tell she knew how to use it and wouldn't hesitate. "I'm leaving, I'm leaving," he yelled. "But now I know where she is, and I'll be back. You hear me, woman? Tell Margie I'll be back. She has my baby girls here, too. She can't do this to me. Yes, I'll be back."

Toby rushed out of the building, jumped into his truck, and almost hit a car as he barreled out of the parking lot.

Hearing the revving motor and squalling tires, Margie barely parted the blinds and saw Toby's truck. She sobbed, wondering how he managed to find them. He'll try to kill us all, she thought.

Toby was speeding down the road when he passed two police cars going in the opposite direction. His hands were shaking. He had to think straight. What should he do now? He hadn't given his own name, but they knew he was Margie Lane's husband. The police would know who he was and where he lived. He couldn't go back to the farmhouse. The police would be after him. He had to disappear for a while. He'd have to go back to Grandpa's cabin in North Carolina, and there was no time to spare.

Toby headed straight for the freeway and turned north. He couldn't waste a second. He hadn't washed the truck in weeks, and he'd driven through mud last night going to Carter's. Maybe the color of the truck was hidden by all the muck. Maybe the authorities wouldn't be able to read his tag. He was trying to think of everything. Don't stop, he told himself. He had a full tank of gas. He could make it a long way before he had to get supplies. Yes, he'd just go to the cabin in the woods and think of a plan. He had to calm down and figure out what to do next. He had to be smart. He couldn't make any mistakes.

At least he knew Margie was in that building. It had to be the Spouse Abuse Center that bitch had talked about on TV. Why else would the nurse have a weapon—and a .45, no less? It all made sense to him now. For the time being he had to vanish, but he would return with a plan. Margie, that Astin woman, and her husband couldn't get away with tricking him. They would have to pay.

Chapter 69

Kendall and Margie were on the phone together, both of them sobbing. "I should never have come back out to the center. I'm sorry I endangered everybody," Kendall said.

"No, it's not your fault. I should've told you a long time ago that I thought Toby might be the man who threatened your life. I don't know what has happened to him. He's so mean now; all he thinks about is harming people. He hasn't always been like that. I'm so sorry." Margie's words tumbled out, heavy with tears.

"You have nothing to do with this. Don't blame yourself. If anybody has any blame to carry, it's me. I thought visiting the center would make me feel better. It was selfish of me. I was told not to come, and I talked the director into letting me visit. It was so careless, and now I've put everyone at risk," Kendall insisted.

This time it was Margie who took charge of the conversation. "Mrs. Astin, I mean Kendall—can't get used to calling you that—the police have been here. Our guard downstairs—Gloria Potts—is married to one of the officers. He's the only officer in that group who knows this is the center. Gloria told them a man threatened a doctor's office. We're still protecting our identity. Toby is just guessing. She never said I was here. Extra guards are being placed outside. You already have a bodyguard. We need to calm down. Both of us. Will you promise me you'll quit blaming yourself? Remember, you've already done so much for me and all the women here."

After listening to Margie, Kendall began to pull herself together. "Margie, you are handling this better than I am. I'm proud of you. You've gotten a lot stronger since you came to the center. I'll try to quit blaming myself. Thank you so much." The two of them promised to stay in touch only by phone in the future.

Margie appreciated what Kendall said to her. She had gotten stronger since arriving at the center. She was pleased with her ability to get control of herself and think clearly. But she knew she would never be at peace as long as Toby was somewhere out there plotting against her and the girls.

Chapter 70

Kendall was thankful the football team was out of town the next weekend. She didn't want to meet and greet people at the game, much less sit through all four quarters. She knew she'd have been even more nervous than usual, especially after someone tried to run them off the road and then her visit to the center went so badly. She was having a hard time staying positive. She really needed to get away. Carter had suggested that she drive to a wholesale nursery and look at plants for landscaping. That sounded great to her. She was thinking about going when Dr. Jansson's wife, Glenda, called. When Kendall invited her along to the nursery, Glenda said she would love to ride with her. It was about an hour and a half drive, and they could listen to the game on the car radio. Kendall enjoyed being with Glenda and looked forward to a fun day and forgetting her worries for a while.

They started driving at about 11:00, with her bodyguard following at a safe distance. Kendall laughed about the entourage of guards she and Duke had acquired. "It's really crazy," she told Glenda, "but there's always something happening. The police insist on keeping the guards. They're our Secret Service." She couldn't tell Glenda anything about the Spouse Abuse Center and the threat from Toby. At least today she didn't resent the bodyguard as much as usual; she didn't know what Toby might try next.

"It's just outrageous," Glenda said. "Axel and I hate it for you. I know it's a burden—all the threats you two have gotten. I've never seen anything like it anywhere."

"Oh, football is so important to these people. Emotions run high. And then there's the gambling. But let's talk about other things today."

Kendall was telling Glenda all about the house when she realized it was time for the game to start. "I guess we'll listen to the game a little bit before we get to the nursery," she said as she turned on the radio. It was an early game, and the team had just kicked off. They were playing a strong Tennessee team, but Duke felt that his guys were ready. On the first possession, though, the quarterback threw a pass from the twenty-yard line and it was intercepted. Tennessee scored. On the next possession, the Bears' young running back fumbled the ball, which the other team promptly picked up, scoring three plays later. The score was already 14-0 in the first few minutes of play.

"This isn't good. I say we turn off the radio. What do you say, Glenda?" Kendall asked, thinking she couldn't stomach listening to this today.

"I certainly agree with you. Let's talk about something else," Glenda responded.

Kendall was thinking maybe this was the loss they'd been fearing. They'd won all the other games this season, so it was bound to happen eventually. But she knew this would set off the fans, especially the gamblers, who had money on the team to win. She thought about all the heartbreak that would follow a loss as they pulled into the nursery.

"Welcome to our home and nursery," a rugged, athletic-looking man said as they stepped out of the car. "I'm Joe Collins, and this is my wife Tina. We're so pleased that you've chosen us to help with your landscaping. I understand you want to use native plants. You've come to the right place. Those are the ones we love." Joe gestured as he led them into the nursery.

"Yes, I would love to use rhododendrons and wild azaleas. I'm thinking about mountain laurel, too," Kendall said, immediately liking this man and appreciating his expertise.

"Come this way. I have lots to show you," Joe said as they began to walk through endless rows of lush green plants.

After an hour or so, Tina invited them to take a break. "Ladies, Joe will wear you out. He gets so enthusiastic about his plants. I've prepared a picnic for us. There's a wooden table overlooking a lovely mountain view. Come on over and get off your feet for a while."

Kendall was enjoying the day so much that she forgot about the game. By the time they had been at the nursery for several hours, she realized they had better start for home. Joe and Tina promised to visit the Astins' new home and make a detailed landscape plan. Kendall and

Glenda thanked the couple for their hospitality and waved goodbye as they drove away.

"Well, I guess I'll turn on the radio and get the bad news. The game should be over by now," Kendall said as she flipped the switch. There was a postgame show on the air already, and Duke was talking about how proud he was of the team and what a great win it had been. They soon learned that the final score was 52-14.

"Oh, my goodness, they won," exclaimed Glenda. "Aren't you sorry now that we didn't listen to the whole game? You missed it."

Kendall laughed. "No, I'm not sorry at all. They won, and I didn't have to sit through it. On the radio or in person, it would've been stressful to watch them catch up and get ahead. I was having a wonderful day, thinking about something else. I wouldn't change a thing. 'A win is a win,' however you get it, and Duke will tell me all about it later." Yes, she felt much better and loved their day away from football.

Chapter 71

The team got home late. It was almost midnight when Duke walked in the door and spotted her waiting up on the couch. He walked over and gave her a hug. "Well, how did you like that game today? It was really fun!"

She laughed and told him the story of how she'd turned off the radio after the two touchdowns early in the game. She admitted that she'd missed the whole game but told him it hadn't bothered her at all. "You'll have to tell me all about it."

"Kendall, I'm glad you didn't listen. It would've been tough in the beginning—stressful as you say—but then we came back like gang-busters. I was so proud of the team's spirit and determination," Duke said, and he described one great play after another.

Kendall enjoyed his excitement. "I think I like hearing about the games from you better than watching them. I love how much you love it," she said earnestly.

"But I have to tell you the most moving thing that happened at halftime. By then the score was already 35-14 in our favor. But I go in the locker room and there stands Mac Andrews, our offensive line coach. He's sobbing. I mean, really sobbing. I put my hand on his shoulder and ask him what's wrong. He looks up with tears in his eyes and says, 'Coach, we've got a real football team. A real football team.' He was sobbing for joy! I think we were all feeling it. We've worked so hard through so much adversity, but we've come through it with a real team—a real good team," Duke said, tears in his eyes, too.

Kendall was happy and relieved. Some of the tension had drained out of her. Some of the anger was gone, too, but not all of it. This shouldn't be so hard. But nonetheless, the team had done it. They'd come to a good place. She was thinking how strange it was to be so sad one day and so happy the next. But she wouldn't think about that now. This was a happy day, and they would enjoy every moment.

Chapter 72

There was great anticipation when the team played their tenth game of the season. They were on a roll. Kendall's family came from Atlanta—Daddy, Mama, her brother Randy, and Randy's wife Sue. David and Vickie were there as always. The Bears were playing a Fort Worth, Texas, team with a lot of young, inexperienced players. Duke had his players ready, and they never got behind in the game. The team was playing with confidence, making no mistakes. The Texas team couldn't do anything well—they fumbled, threw interceptions, and dropped balls. Kendall began to feel a little sorry for them. Duke's team had been through those bad spells before, and they were hard to overcome. But, of course, she didn't feel too bad for them. She was able to relax more than usual at the game and was even able to eat some of the food. She laughed and told the group that this was her favorite kind of football game. Why couldn't they all be like this one?

They celebrated when the game ended, 52-7. While they were still sitting in the box together, Kendall decided to take the opportunity to say some things she had been wanting to say.

"I want to say thank you to you guys. You get me through these games. Just your being here. David making small talk. The laughter is therapeutic. But I worry about what Duke and I put you through. Daddy, have you quit reading the newspaper—especially the sports section like I asked?"

"Kendall, you know I can't quit reading the newspapers. I have to read the paper and know what's going on. I've always read the paper cover to cover. I must admit that sometimes I get a little upset reading the sports page, but I have to read it," her father insisted.

"Daddy, it isn't good for your health. I worry about you and Mama," Kendall said.

"Oh, Kendall, it's fun for us to open the paper and see what mischief you and Duke are getting into. It keeps our lives from being boring," David said in his clever way, with a smile on his face.

"That's right, you and Duke certainly don't live boring lives," said Kendall's father. "But I will say this: your mother and I have decided not to come to the game next week. At our age, we can only handle so much excitement."

"Well, let's go home, have some wine, eat, laugh, and celebrate this game and not worry about next week," Kendall said, relieved to know her folks wouldn't be at the last game.

As they left the stadium walking to their car, she heard all the cheering. Some of the people recognized her and said nice things. Of course, the team was now 10-0—why wouldn't they be happy? They were yelling about next week's game. She didn't want to think about it yet. She knew it would be a huge game for the school and the conference. Duke's guys would play their archrival, a good, strong Clemson team that had lost one game on a contested call, sure they had gotten robbed. They would be chomping at the bit to win the game, too. But Duke's team would go in 10-0 playing for the conference championship. Then there would be a big bowl game and possibly even the national championship. All in Duke's first year! It was unbelievable.

Kendall shook her head, willing herself to forget about it for now. Enjoy today, she told herself. They had to take the good when they had it and really savor the feeling. Heaven knows, they'd had enough bad in this season. Other folks weren't aware of all the stress they had experienced, and she certainly wasn't going to tell her parents. For today, they would simply be happy.

Chapter 73

The next week, Billy Bob and Roland sat down for one of their regular lunches at the club. As usual, Billy Bob was there first, getting started on his vodka and cranberry juice before his friend arrived.

As Roland walked to the table he said, "Sorry I'm a little late today. Where's Tommy Lee? I thought he'd be here before me."

"Oh, we've lost Tommy Lee for the week. Some of his old teammates are in town for the game. They're gonna make a week of reminiscing about the old days. Anyway, I'm tired of hearing him brag about the eighty-yard run in the Cotton Bowl. Also, Tommy Lee has completely sold out; he loves this new team." Billy Bob shook his head and took a sip of his drink.

"Not me," Roland answered quickly. "Not me and not my kid. J.J. rants and raves about that coach every day. It's all he can talk about. Doesn't go to class hardly at all. All of a sudden, he's gotten out his old band instruments and plays loud music all the time. You know, the drums and his trombone. Some days he has his old buddies over—his old band friends—and they're running me out of the house. I swear, he's acting crazy. I don't know what to do with him. I think I'm just gonna go to Vegas this weekend. I've been feeling a little tired—playing too much golf, I guess. You know me, when things get rough with that kid, I have to leave—let him work it out. It'll get me away from the noise at home, and I don't want to see that game anyway. I'm afraid that coach might win again."

"I don't blame you for wanting to get away. But J.J. is just being a kid. Don't worry. You know that coach told J.J. he wasn't good enough and he didn't like it. Of course, I appreciate other folks that don't like the coach. There are fewer and fewer every day." Billy Bob gulped down his drink and signaled the waiter for another. "Yeah, I like other folks that feel the way I do. I hate the damn coach."

"Well, what do you have on your mind to do today? Have you come up with any new ways to harass the guy this week?" Roland asked.

Billy Bob knew he couldn't say anything about Antonio's man. He hadn't heard a word since the meeting in Charlotte. But he liked it that way. He was a little nervous about the whole thing, but not nervous enough to call it off. Antonio had assured him there was no way anyone would ever know about his involvement. He hesitated for a moment and then cleared his throat, smiled, and said, "Actually, I do have something in the works, but I can't talk about it. You'll just have to wait and see when it happens."

Roland was surprised that Billy Bob wasn't telling him everything. But Roland would leave it at that. He had other things to think about, like what was wrong with J.J. He knew he hadn't been the best dad, and at this point he didn't know how to change. He and J.J. had never communicated very well. Maybe he needed to have a talk with the kid.

Chapter 74

Toby drove late into the night and arrived at the cabin after picking up some essentials at a truck stop—beer, liquor, cigarettes, and canned food. He had already calmed down a lot, and being here would make it easier. He had to figure out what he was going to do.

It was gorgeous in the woods at this time of the year. Leaves had been falling for a month or so now and were piled high. He liked walking through the dry leaves and hearing the twigs snap wherever he stepped. He would carry his hunting rifle and enjoy shooting some game, which he'd cook on the spit outside. It was cool enough at night that he could build a fire in the old fireplace and watch it die down late into the evening. He could drink and smoke, and nobody would bother him. He never saw another human being. Nobody telling him what to do. He loved that about Grandpa's cabin. It was the only place where he could really think.

He thought about Margie and the girls a lot. He loved them and missed seeing them. He knew he'd made a mess of his life. He had to apologize to Margie and try to make things right again. He wasn't like his father, was he? He hoped he wasn't, but the idea of it began to weigh on him. His daddy had always made growing up miserable for Toby. Is that what he was doing to his girls now? He had to fix things. He would go back and try. He would make things better. Of course, he had to find a way to talk to Margie, convince her that he'd changed. He also knew he had to do something about his drinking. But not tonight, he thought, grabbing a beer. That would come later.

The old radio was his only contact with the outside world. It was scratchy at best, but he could hear a few games of some North Carolina or Tennessee teams. He got enough sports news to know that Coach Astin was winning big. After Toby stayed at the cabin a couple of weeks, he finally decided on a plan. The championship game for the conference would be played in the last week of the season. Everybody would be going wild thinking and talking about that game. They would forget about him by then. He would slip back into town right before the game. Jerry, the carpenter who worked with him in the skyboxes, also did part-time security at the stadium. Jerry would help him get up to the boxes. Toby decided he would watch the game from up there with the fat cats. He now knew every inch of that stadium, and he was ready to carry out his plan.

PART 4

THE FINAL GAME

November 1996

Chapter 75

It seemed like everybody in the country wanted to go to this championship game between the Clemson Tigers and the Benton Bears. Billy Bob was getting calls with folks asking for tickets right and left. He was irritated. First, he hated it when people asked him for tickets, but more than that, he hated to hear them talk about how great Coach Astin was. He didn't want to talk to them anymore and had told his secretary to tell them no tickets were available. But when he got a call from Antonio in Chicago, he grabbed the phone.

"Antonio, why are you calling me?" Billy Bob asked nervously. "I thought I wasn't going to hear from you."

"Relax, relax," Antonio said quickly. "I was just wondering…our guy wants to go to the game. Can you get him an all-access pass?"

"Are you out of your mind? What's goin' on, man? I thought whatever happened would be an accident and I wouldn't know anything about it." Billy Bob tried to keep his voice down so his secretary wouldn't hear.

"I know. I know. Let me just say he's working on it. There's been one attempt that didn't work out. But nobody knows anything about it. Just stay calm. We'll find another way," Antonio assured him.

"Stop. Don't tell me anything. I don't want to know. I want to be able to plead innocence, no matter what."

"Relax," Antonio said again, laughing. "Trust me, this isn't a big deal. Our man just likes to roam around. He never stays in one seat. He'll be watching everything—the coach, his wife, the stadium layout. He just wants to observe. If truth be known, I think he just wants to go to the game."

"I can't believe it. There's nothing funny about any of this." Billy Bob took a deep breath, reining himself in. "Look, I'll get him the pass, but I don't want to know anything about him. No name. Not his whereabouts. Nothing. Do you understand?"

"He'll use a fake name. You won't see him. Everything will be fine."

"Talk to my secretary. She's the one who handles ticket requests. Just say you need an all-access pass for a friend, and she'll work it out. But I don't want to know anything about this. You and me haven't talked today. Do you understand?" Billy Bob hollered. "This conversation never happened."

Chapter 76

When Roland got home, J.J. was on the sofa tossing a football up in the air. Roland had always had trouble communicating with his son. In fact, Roland had trouble talking to most folks. He chose his words carefully as he cleared his throat. "Hey, J.J. I'm glad you're home. I've been wanting to talk to you." After a long pause Roland continued. "I don't know how to say this. But I'm worried. You haven't been going to class. You seem depressed. Are you okay?"

J.J. jumped off the sofa and stared at Roland. "No, I'm not okay. My life is ruined. That coach ruined my life when he said I wasn't good enough to be on the team," J.J. blurted. "You've always said I wasn't good enough either. You've never encouraged me or approved of me. It seems to me the only time you have approved was when I did something bad. You know, like when I tried to get Elijah to let up and hurt the team or when I threw a rock through the coach's window. Is that the only time you like me—when I do something for you?"

"No, son, that's not true. I always like you. I know I don't say it often, but I love you. I just don't know how to be a good father. I'm sorry. And listen, that coach hasn't ruined your life. You have so much going for you. Your whole life is ahead of you. Go back to class, get your education, get married, and have a good family life—all the things I didn't do."

"That's a strange way for you to talk, Dad. What's come over you?" J.J. said with anger in his eyes. "You've always wanted me to stay out of your way. You've said I could do what I wanted to do. All you asked is that I be tough like you—learn to shoot the gun, go hunting, or play golf. You've never cared if I went to class. So what's up with you today? You aiming for father of the year? Good luck, asshole!"

"I know, son. I know. I haven't been a good father or role model. But I do care about what you do." Searching for something to say,

Roland offered, "I tell you what, why don't you take the skybox and have some friends go to the game with you? You've enjoyed that in the past. That'll cheer you up and put you in a better mood. I don't want to go to the game. I'm going to take a relaxing trip to Vegas."

"Yeah, yeah, you always take off for Vegas when things get tough. Whenever I've needed you in my life you've been gone," J.J. grumbled. "But sure, I'll take the box for the game. I was going to ask you about it anyway. But I want to sit in the stands with my friends for the first two quarters or so. I'll go up to the skybox at the end of the game. You know, watch all the celebrating after the big win and see the coach walk off the field with his arms in the air, waving to his fans. That's when I'd like to be upstairs for the fun."

Roland was pleased to see a spark in J.J. for a change. But he didn't know what to say about his son's anger. "Whatever you want," he told him. "I just want you to be your old self. Don't worry. Have some fun." Roland was sweating profusely now. He didn't know this man child who was stomping his ego with glee.

J.J. looked at his father with a gleam in his eyes. "Oh, I'm going to have some fun. Don't *you* worry. You'll be impressed with me. Damned impressed, you jerk!"

Chapter 77

The final game of the season between Clemson and Benton was a security nightmare for Chief Patterson. Last games were always like that, but this year would be worse. There wouldn't be an empty seat in the stadium of eighty thousand. More fans who couldn't get tickets would mill around in the parking lots. Tailgate parties would start as early as Thursday night before the game, with RVs sprinkled all over the place.

Alcohol would start flowing Thursday and continue into the morning of game day, so that by kickoff half the folks in the stadium would be drunk. But at this game, the crowd would be almost equally divided between the two rival teams, unruly, calling each other names, taunting each other, and breaking into fights all over. Yes, this was going to be a rough game to manage and keep the peace.

Thank goodness, every law enforcement officer in South Carolina wanted to be there. Patterson had no trouble lining up help. Campus security was ready, as they were at any game. But today the entire city police department was also enlisted, along with men from neighboring towns. State troopers would protect the governor, lieutenant governor, senators, and other special guests. State troopers always served on game day to escort the team buses to the stadium and to protect the coach as he got off the bus, entered the locker room, and walked on and off the field. With the threats Astin had gotten, the state troopers were especially appreciated today.

Patterson also had officers strolling the parking lots before the game, when the partying was at its height. Those same officers would come in and walk around in the stands during the game, watching for anything unusual. When the game started, officers would circle the playing field to keep fans from running out there during or after the game. As crazy as it seemed, someone had once streaked across the field, a kid who was drunk as a skunk and naked as a jaybird. It was always a challenge to keep the kids off the field after a big win. Sometimes, no matter what they did, the riotous fans would manage to break through the barriers. Patterson had heard of one school that used hoses to spray the fans, but he couldn't imagine himself allowing that. It was too cruel. He just hoped he had enough extra men to hold them back.

What made this year so extraordinary was the fact he had been protecting this coach and his wife since the day they arrived on campus. He had assigned bodyguards to both of them for the whole season. In previous years, it had never occurred to him that he would need to protect the coach's wife. The idea of it was absurd. He really liked them and was sick about the whole mess. But it was the reality this year. So one of his best men was stationed outside Mrs. Astin's box to make sure nothing happened there either.

Patterson hoped he had covered all his bases. He had his second in command, James Anderson, keeping watch from command central up in the press box. Patterson planned to be down on the sidelines, but they would all be connected on the radio—a closed circuit with all the officers on walkie-talkies. Everyone was instructed to be alert and report anything unusual. If trouble arose, they would be on top of it. At least, that was Patterson's plan. He just prayed that he had thought of everything. He didn't want something unexpected to happen today. The usual trouble was bad enough.

Chapter 78

Before he left for the airport, Roland drank his morning tea. Coffee was bad for his nerves, but tea calmed him. He threw an egg into a blender with protein powder and a banana to make the smoothie that had been his breakfast for years. His diet had kept him fit all these years. Why change anything now?

J.J. had left early for the game, saying he had to carry something to one of his friends. Roland was thinking about J.J.'s anger and sullenness when the phone rang. It was the young pilot, Jack Dawson, who often flew Roland's plane for him. "Mr. Rigby, glad you haven't left for the airport yet. We have a mechanical issue. The guy said something about a landing gear. It's no big deal, but they have to get a part. It'll take a couple hours. Sorry about that. Why don't you just sit tight, and I'll call when it's fixed. I'll come pick you up, too. No reason for you to fight the game traffic in town today, which you know will be awful."

"I'm in no hurry. And thanks, I'll take you up on the offer of a ride. You're right that traffic will be bad," Roland said. He was enjoying just sitting this morning. He didn't mind the delay the way he normally would. He guessed he really was getting older. He sure didn't have the energy he used to have. He was tired a lot of the time, and his doctor had told him to slow down. He knew he had pancreatic cancer, but he didn't plan to tell a soul. He didn't want any pity, and he was taking care of it and doing everything he could.

J.J. was still on his mind, too. He had acted strange after their conversation, but at least he was intent on going to the game and seemed excited about it. It was good to see him going out to do something instead of lying around the house. Roland picked up the phone and tried to call his ex-wife Jesse. Maybe he could get her to call J.J. He knew she hadn't talked to her son in a long time. If he had been a poor father, Jesse had been a worse mother. He got her answering machine.

Thinking she was probably still asleep as usual, he left her a message suggesting that she call her son, who was having a tough time. He knew she probably wouldn't call, but he had tried.

Roland read the paper. It wasn't a big newspaper, and the most exciting news of the day was the big game, which filled the sports section. After skimming the headlines, he started watching the goldfinches at the bird feeder outside the kitchen window. He enjoyed watching them. He remembered when J.J. was a kid and the two of them had filled the feeder together and watched the birds, trying to identify them. They never mentioned the birds much anymore.

Sitting there looking out at the lush grass in the backyard, Roland thought of the years he and J.J. had thrown the football back and forth, back and forth for hours. The kid never tired of throwing the football with him. Sometimes they rolled in the grass together laughing. But it hadn't happened very often because he was gone so much when J.J. was little. Maybe that was when they began to lose contact. Roland's life had always taken him away from everyone. First there was Vietnam. Then there were his many years working for the government. He had been an agent for the CIA, but he could never tell anyone. His profession had made him secretive and hard. Now here he was with no one in his life. He sat there for a long time, thinking about his life and what it meant. The phone rang again, shattering the silence.

"Mr. Rigby, we've got the plane ready. I'll pick you up shortly," Jack said.

"Is it time? Two hours have flown by. Yes, I'll be ready to go," Roland said. He hung up and went to get his bag.

The ride to the airport took longer than usual. The game had already started, but there were still people in town—media trucks, caterers, stragglers who tried to get tickets and couldn't. The private airport was out of town and the drive took about forty minutes. When they arrived and pulled up to the plane, Roland slowly climbed the steps into the Citation jet he leased with two buddies. There was a pilot, a copilot, and an attendant. He sat down and stretched his legs, thinking how much he enjoyed the plush, comfortable leather seats. For some reason he couldn't explain, he asked the attendant to tell the pilot to wait a few minutes. Roland sat there staring ahead for ten minutes or so as the crew members looked at one another, not knowing what to do.

Finally, Roland said, "Men, I appreciate you getting the jet ready to go and waiting on me. You will be compensated for your time. But I'm not going to Vegas today. Jack, take me back to the stadium and drop me off. I want to see my son. We'll have some good father-son time."

Chapter 79

When the game started, Patterson began to stroll up and down the sidelines behind the home team, looking around for anything unusual. He enjoyed football but wasn't nearly as fanatic as the folks around here. He hadn't grown up in this part of the country where football was so important. He had grown up in Indiana where basketball was the sport. He wasn't a real student of football, but he appreciated what sports did for kids—how they learned responsibility and unselfishness. During the year, he had gotten to know Coach Astin and admired the way he interacted with his players. Astin wanted the best for them as student athletes, not just players. Patterson could tell the players liked and respected their coach, too. Astin wasn't too friendly with them. He had achieved that wonderful mixture of being able to laugh with them and then, when it was necessary, get down to business.

Patterson had been on the sidelines for several games this season and enjoyed seeing the action from this perspective. As far as watching plays develop, the sidelines were the worst place to watch a football game. But seeing the looks on the faces of the players and coaches made the drama come alive. Today, the kids were giving every ounce of energy they had to run, catch, and block. He couldn't help but admire both teams. They were playing so damn hard. He was enjoying the game and had quit worrying so much.

The game went back and forth. Denny Durham was unbelievable, leading the defense with one spectacular tackle after another. Patterson thought he must be setting a record for number of tackles. Both teams were having trouble scoring. And the young players that people had gotten to know only this year—no. 20, no. 16, no. 80—were playing their hearts out on offense. Patterson still got their names mixed up, but he would know their names after today's game. He was thinking he would have to watch a replay of the game when he could really concentrate.

It was a real defensive battle, and the score was only 6-6 at half time. Both teams had to settle for field goals. The second half wasn't much different, but Clemson finally scored a touchdown early in the fourth quarter. Then, with only seconds left on the clock, Astin took his team to the five-yard line and the fullback scored a touchdown. They kicked the extra point, and the game was tied 13-13. What a battle! Patterson thought it would be fair for the game to end in a tie. But such thinking was blasphemous to the hometown folks. Of course, he wanted the Bears to win, but he couldn't help admiring the play of both teams. What a magnificent game. Now they would have to go into overtime. There were those new rules about not letting a game end in a tie. He thought overtime would start on the twenty-five-yard line. But he wasn't sure about all the new rules.

At the end of a similar game one time, Patterson had heard someone start to criticize the losing side. Then a great coach said, "Don't criticize either side. There was so much glory on the field today on the part of both teams." Patterson thought about that quote—the glory on the field—as the clock wound down to zero.

In overtime, Benton won the coin toss and elected to play defense. Clemson got the ball first on the twenty-five-yard line. To everyone's amazement, their quarterback immediately threw a touchdown pass. This player had struggled during regulation, but now he made it look easy. After their kicker put the ball through the uprights for the extra point, the Bears got their chance. It wasn't as easy for them when they got the ball, but the players were determined. They managed to grind out a first down running the ball, and then one of the young backs was able to break away and score. The crowd went wild. Most people probably thought Astin would just have them kick the extra point to tie the game again. But then the fans realized he'd decided to go for two points to win the game. Sometimes Astin would gamble like this, making the game that much more exciting.

It was as if the whole stadium froze. There was complete silence and then a huge roar. The sound was deafening. Patterson couldn't see what had happened. Players were standing in his line of sight. All he knew is that something was very wrong. Then he saw the look on the faces of those closest to Coach Astin. One of Patterson's officers came running frantically toward him. "Chief, you've got to come over here. Astin is down, Astin is down, he's been shot." All Patterson could think now was no, no, not on my watch. Dear God, no, don't let this be happening.

Chapter 80

When Patterson pushed players and coaches aside, he saw Coach Astin facedown on the turf in a pool of blood. The image would stay with him the rest of his life. It was so horrific that it would keep him awake and give him recurring nightmares. It was only a brief glance; he looked away quickly. He wouldn't say it, but he felt sure Astin was dead. At the present moment, however, Patterson had to take care of business. Take command immediately.

The team doctor had already called for a stretcher, and the ambulance was pulling onto the field. Patterson asked people to move back. When Doctor James saw Chief Patterson, he started pointing to the press area and skyboxes behind the home team benches. He was shouting, "The bullet came from up there. It hit him in the back of the head. Look up there, up there."

Patterson left the officer nearest him in charge on the field and ran toward the elevators up to the skyboxes. He called upstairs and told Anderson, "Don't let anyone leave the press area or skyboxes. Astin has been shot, and it came from up there." A few people around him heard what he said and yelled, "Someone was shot. Someone was shot." Half of them started running for the exits, and the other half ran toward the field to see what was happening. The early celebrating turned into something else. Some fans just stood and stared at the ambulance. Fans in other parts of the stadium were still cheering because their team had won, and other fans stood stunned, disappointed that they had lost. Some began pointing toward the ambulance. They were yelling, "What's happened? What's going on?" Patterson had to push folks out of the way. He needed to get to the elevators fast.

He made it to one of the elevators just as the door was opening. "No one gets off this elevator," he ordered. "You're going back up with me." As he squeezed into the elevator, he saw two of his officers behind him. "Stop the people getting off those elevators from the skyboxes and come upstairs with them. No one leaves."

When the elevator reached the top, Patterson got off giving instructions. "Everyone that was in this area on the press level and the skyboxes must be detained. Get everyone's name, how we can reach them later, ask if they saw anything or anyone suspicious." He was trying to think of everything he should do, as people asked him one question after another. "What happened? Why are you holding us? We did nothing." It was a chaotic scene.

He felt like he was herding cattle. Finally, he was able to bring a semblance of order. "Quiet, quiet. You must calm down. I will tell you what's happening. But you must calm down. Back up. You're not leaving until we've talked to each one of you. You might as well calm down."

First Patterson instructed his officers to start organizing the people into smaller groups around tables or in corners. Separate them as much as possible. Then ask them where they were sitting, who they were sitting with, whether they'd seen or heard anything unusual. And not to let anyone leave without being questioned.

Patterson then stood on a table and gave the audience the bare facts. "At the end of the game, someone fired a weapon from somewhere in this area, either the press area or the skyboxes. Someone on the sidelines was hit. He is being taken to the hospital in the ambulance now. I don't know the condition of the person. Every one of you will be questioned before you leave. If we can do this in an orderly fashion, we'll get out of here before too long. If not, we may be here all night."

At that point, someone shouted, "Chief, who was shot? Who was shot?"

Patterson looked somber and then said, "Coach Astin."

A huge gasp went up from the group. All the women and some of the men began to cry. Others just stood stunned. One of those standing nearby and looking shocked was Billy Bob Craven.

Chapter 81

Billy Bob was panic-stricken. His mind raced as he thought, what have I done? It was as if it dawned on him for the first time that he had done something terrible. He'd wanted to get rid of Astin, but did he really want this? Everyone was so upset. The women were crying. Many of the men were hanging their heads. He only saw a few who seemed OK. Was he the only person who really hated this man? Maybe he'd made a big mistake. Now Patterson was going to question everyone. Antonio had assured him he wouldn't be tied to anything. He had to calm down. Did he look guilty? He was trying to get control of himself when a young officer walked over to him.

"Sir, please give me your name and where you were sitting," the officer said.

Billy Bob's first response was to ask the kid why he didn't know who he was. After all, he had practically paid for the construction of this whole stadium. But under the circumstances, he thought he shouldn't respond that way. "I'm Billy Bob Craven. You know, my family owns Craven Construction. We built this stadium."

The young officer seemed unimpressed, "I see. Sir, where were you sitting today?"

Billy Bob couldn't help feeling frustrated with this man as he answered, "In my skybox, of course, where I always sit for games."

"Who was sitting with you?" the officer asked, his expression unchanged.

"My God, there were so many. I'm not sure who all was in my box. It's pretty big," Billy Bob answered.

"Please sit down and make a list. Also tell us anything unusual that you saw. Sit right here, sir," the young officer said as he pulled out a chair.

Billy Bob was about to blow a gasket. Antonio had told him there was no way anyone would know about his involvement. And now here he was, being asked all these questions. He was beginning to sweat profusely. Did he look as guilty as he felt? He sure hoped not. He had to answer these damn questions and then go call Antonio. Maybe he should talk to his lawyer, too. Am I in trouble? he asked himself. Then he answered his own question. Hell no, there's no way I'm involved in this unfortunate incident.

Chapter 82

Once Patterson got the situation under control, he realized that he hadn't spoken to Kendall Astin yet. He dreaded seeing her and wasn't sure what to say when he knocked on the door to her box. David Flynn quietly opened the door. Patterson walked in and saw Kendall sitting and staring out toward the sky over the top of the stadium. Her friend Vickie was sitting with her, holding her hand.

"Mrs. Astin, I am so sorry. I admired your husband. I don't know what to say. There are no words," Patterson said softly.

Kendall just sat there in silence. In fact, all four of them were quiet for what seemed like a long time.

Finally, Patterson spoke again. "I want you to know what we're doing. We believe the bullet came from up here somewhere. Everyone has been detained that was in the press area or here in the skyboxes. We're questioning them all to see if they saw anything unusual. We may be here quite a while. But we won't leave until we find something that tells us who did this. I just want you to know that we had maximum security today. I thought I had all the bases covered. I don't know how this could have happened. I'm so sorry. I want you to know that we will find who did this. We will work day and night until we do." Patterson knew he was talking too quickly now. But he felt he had to say something, fill the space somehow.

Kendall finally spoke. "It's not your fault. One of those people did it."

Patterson wasn't sure what she was talking about, but he knew it wasn't the time to question her. "I'm going to give you extra protection to escort you home. And I'll come see you tomorrow. Are these people going to stay with you?" He gestured at David, who nodded and said they wouldn't leave her alone.

Kendall then spoke again. "I want to go to the hospital. Where did they take him?"

"Of course, of course. I'll have my men escort you. Come with me, and I'll take you out to your car." Patterson offered his arm, and Kendall rose slowly and took it. David opened the door, and they walked into the crowd outside. At the sight of Kendall, everything went silent as everyone stared at her. She kept her eyes straight ahead, and they walked slowly. She didn't say a word, but her mind was racing. She wondered if the killer was still there. She detached herself as if she were looking down on the crowd. Yes, the shooter might still be trapped up here. She felt like she was in a movie, like this wasn't really happening to her. It couldn't be real. Could it?

Chapter 83

As David drove her to the hospital, with Vickie sitting in the back seat, her hand on Kendall's shoulder, Kendall was remembering the last night she'd spent with Duke. It was Thursday night before the game. They'd sat before the fire, eating their dinner and talking. They'd always loved those nights together. They had great conversations, laughing and reminiscing about old days. But that night they'd also done something they often did when they faced tough situations. It was almost like a game. They discussed the best case and worst case of what could happen. Somehow it eased the tension.

"Worst case would be that we lose the game Saturday and then lose whatever bowl game we have," Duke had said. "We've still had a great first year, winning ten games. And then we get to move into our new home. Even with recruiting, you and I will have more time together." He squeezed her hand and smiled, the firelight flickering in his eyes. "I want to remind you that I'm excited about the new house. Again, I'm sorry I haven't been more attentive through the years, but I will get better."

"I'm going to hold you to that promise!" Kendall had said, squeezing his hand back. "But remember, best case would be that we win Saturday, then win our bowl game, and then win the National Championship in your first year. After that big win, we get to move into our new home, and you'll really be a hero and I'll never see you again." She laughed.

"No, no, I don't want that hero talk. That's not what's important in life. At the end of the day, it's your relationships with those you love."

When they'd finished eating, Duke had taken her hand and led her to bed, wrapping his strong arms around her. "I'm so sorry about what I've put you through this year. I never dreamed that my job would cause you so much grief. I don't want to live this way. I want us to be happy. I love you with all my heart, just like I have from the first time I saw you." He kissed her gently, and she melted into his embrace.

Safe and protected from the world, they expressed their love as they had so many times. But for some reason, it meant more to her that night than ever. She would never forget it. She had wept in gratitude for the love they shared.

But now she would never see him alive again. They would have no more great conversations by the fire. No more nights of love. No new life in their new home. No new beginning. She couldn't bear to think about that now. It turned out that they hadn't known what the worst case would be. The worst thing that could have happened had just happened. Someone had shot and killed Duke. Not only had they destroyed his life; they had destroyed hers as well.

When Kendall entered the operating room, two doctors and three nurses in white scrubs looked at her solemnly. They were gathered around a table where Duke's body was laid out before them. A white sheet covered his body and another one was draped over his head. One doctor cautioned her not to remove the sheet covering his face. That was no problem for Kendall. She wanted to remember his beautiful face the way it had always been. She took his hand and held it. She then leaned over and put her head on his chest. She told him again how much she loved him and always would. She felt his strength and goodness even in death. She also vowed to him that they would find who did this and see justice done. She wept quietly and took several deep breaths. Reluctant to leave Duke and unable to move, she stood with her head bowed for several minutes. Then she laid her hands on his chest one more time and said goodbye. One thing she had learned that night would never leave her: there is evil in the world, and it can strike at any time. She would fight that evil for the rest of her life.

Chapter 84

Patterson and his men had been working for an hour or so when one of them said, "Chief, we have someone that you should interview. She's worked here at the stadium for years. Her name is Juanita Cochran."

"Yes, Juanita, what did you see that was strange?" Patterson asked.

"Well, sir, one of the boxes that I service with food and beverages stayed locked the whole day. Only one person came in early this morning. He locked the door when he left and didn't come back until the second half. I'm sure of this because it was so unusual," she said.

"Let's take a look inside that box. Can you unlock it?"

"Yes sir, I have a master key we use for cleaning. I can open it for you." She led them toward the box.

When they opened the door, the box was dark, the lights off. They flipped on the lights and saw that only a few bar stools were out of place. The food was untouched. Some of the high stools had been moved around, but that was all. Patterson asked some of his men to begin searching the box carefully. "Go over this place with a fine-tooth comb. Get down on your hands and knees, go over every inch. We might just find something in here." He turned to Juanita. "Now tell me exactly what you saw early this morning."

"Well, I get here several hours before the game. It was very early. I don't remember what time exactly. I didn't see any strangers. I just saw Mr. J.J. come in with some kind of strange case. Mr. J.J. has been coming here with his daddy since he was a kid. I know him well. I asked him what was in the case, and he said it was a musical instrument. I think he said trombone—something about bringing it for a friend. I didn't think anything of it because it was Mr. J.J. I asked him who he was bringing up to the box today and he didn't answer. When I saw him leaving before the game, he said he would be back but to keep the door closed and locked. He was planning something special. I smiled and said I bet he was bringing up that pretty brunette he liked so much. I asked if it was just going to be her. He said, 'No, but it'll be something special.' That's all he said."

She stood thinking for a minute and then added, "I remember that I got very busy, and I never saw anybody go in that box. But I did see Mr. J.J. leave right at the end of the game. He was carrying that music case with him."

At that moment, one of the men said, "I found something, Chief." He was holding up a shell casing on the end of a pen. "We didn't see it the first go-round. Then we started over and looked again. There was this loose baseboard under the counter. I hadn't noticed it the first time. Right there tucked in the opening I saw something. I pulled back the board and there was this shell casing. It must have bounced and rolled over against that board. Funny thing, when I pulled the board back a little, there were these little toy soldiers and—what do you call 'em— matchbox cars...you know, that kids play with. We might have never found that shell casing. We were mighty lucky, but here it is."

Patterson stood there looking at the shell casing and said, "Bingo! I knew we would find something. Good effort by all. Whoever did this wasn't very smart. Must have been in a hurry. An expert would never leave the shell casing. This will have fingerprints. Let's get our people in here and search for fingerprints on these chairs, the doorknob, and everywhere else. We'll get this casing off to the state crime lab right away." He turned back to Juanita. "Who owns this box?"

Juanita didn't hesitate. "Why, Mr. Roland Rigby. You know him, I'm sure. J.J. is his son. If Mr. Rigby is out of town, he lets his son J.J. use this box. Yes sir, Mr. J.J. has been coming to the box forever, but I have to say he wasn't acting like himself today. I don't know what it was exactly, but he wasn't the J.J. I've always known. He was somebody else today."

Chapter 85

Billy Bob Craven finally got home three hours after the game was over. He was exhausted and having what he thought might be a heart attack. His heart was pounding, he was sweating, and he could barely breathe. He went straight to the liquor cabinet to fix a stiff vodka. Forget the healthy cranberry juice this time. He would have just a splash of tonic along with the vodka. He gulped down his drink and then called Antonio using the special number he had been given. There was no answer, but he left a lengthy message.

"My God, I didn't think the guy would do it on national television. Now they're questioning me. You said there was no way I would be involved. Why didn't you tell me how he was going to do it? This isn't good. I said I wanted to get rid of the coach but not like this. It was too public. It's bad publicity for the program. How are we going to get a good coach now? Come here and get shot! For heaven's sake, this wasn't the way to do it. Call me tonight. Call me tonight, Antonio. I think I might be having a heart attack. I'm very upset. Yes, I think I might be having a heart attack!" Billy Bob ranted on for several more minutes and finally ended the call.

He was walking in circles trying to think what to do. He'd never wanted anything like this. Suddenly he thought of Janice, his sweet wife who had loved him so much. She would be so disappointed in him. He felt like she knew about the evil thing he had done. Tears filled his eyes as he said out loud, "Janice, I didn't mean for this to happen. I wasn't supposed to be involved. What have I done? I didn't think this out. Janice, I got to ask for forgiveness."

He was lost in remorse when the phone rang, and he grabbed it and heard Antonio's serious voice on the other line. "Billy Bob, I got your call. I said I would do you a favor because you're my friend. What did you think I was going to do?"

"Man, I don't know. But you said I wouldn't be involved. I was detained after the game and questioned. I was questioned! I might not have handled it well. I tried but I was upset. You know what I mean. I don't think I had realized the horror of it. On national television—what was your man thinking? It's not good publicity for the program. How are we going to get a good coach now?" Billy Bob kept talking as fast as he could. "I think I'm going to have a heart attack. A heart attack and die!"

Antonio listened to Billy Bob rattle on. He was almost laughing at this guy. What a wimp, he thought. I'll think long and hard before I offer to help this man again. He wished he could end Billy Bob's suffering, but he couldn't—not all the way from Chicago. "I'm sorry Billy Bob, but I haven't talked to my man. I don't know what happened."

Billy Bob couldn't believe it. "How could you not know? Don't you keep tabs on these things?"

Antonio answered calmly, "My man doesn't call me every day. He has to be very careful. I'll let you know when I hear from him. Sorry, my friend."

Antonio hung up the phone and Billy Bob was left to fret, wring his hands, and drink vodka. He kept muttering, "This is bad. This is very bad. What am I going to do? No, I wasn't involved. I know nothing about any of this!"

Chapter 86

Toby had gone out hunting one more time and enjoyed the beautiful day alone in the woods. It was windy, though, the dry leaves falling and piling up all around the cabin. He thought he should rake them away from the house sometime. He remembered the fire ranger had told Grandpa that it wasn't good to have the leaves around the cabin walls. He would take care of that the next time he came down. He needed to leave tomorrow morning to get back for the big game.

He made a fire in the fireplace and opened a can of beans to go with the leftover rabbit he had cooked. He started drinking beer with shots, thinking again how much he enjoyed it here where nobody told him what to do. He would come back as soon as he could. But he had to take care of business back home. First, he had to find Margie and the girls. He would apologize and promise to start over. And then there were all the people he wanted to punish. Yes, some folks needed to be punished. The more he thought about Margie, and the Astins, the more he drank. After a couple hours of drinking, he began to doze off. The cigarette he was holding dropped on a pile of old newspapers. The fire in the fireplace was still sending out an occasional spark onto the old wood floor, and the combination of the two ignited the newspapers. The fire grew, soon reaching the old curtains on the windows and the old rag rug on the floor. It didn't take long for part of the blaze to reach the box of dynamite Toby had brought into the house for safekeeping. BOOM! A huge explosion splintered the walls and roof of the cabin, shooting fragments into the sky. Massive flames of fire showered sparks onto the dry leaves and then the trees. In moments, the surrounding forest was caught in sheets of fire. Old trees burned quickly, and the old cabin was gone in seconds. Toby never knew what had happened.

The fire and smoke were visible for miles. Forest rangers were soon fighting one of the worst fires they had ever seen. The volunteer firemen from Andrews, Murphy, and Bryson City arrived almost immediately. It was dark already, but they fought through the night and the next day. Finally, after building fire walls and having planes fly over with water from several lakes and retardant material, they were able to bring the fire under control. Investigators determined it had come from an old cabin, and the only thing that told them who was there was the charred remains of an old truck with a rusty license plate. The trunk was registered to a man named Toby Lane. They would have to reach out to next of kin. That's how Margie learned she didn't have to fear Toby anymore. Even so, she thought it was sad how his life had ended.

Chapter 87

J.J. made it home, thinking that things hadn't gone as perfectly as he'd planned, but at least the mission was accomplished. He'd been shaken, more nervous than he thought he'd be. He was a little fuzzy about the details of what had happened, but he'd done what he was supposed to do. He had quickly left the box, gone to the exit, and walked down the ramps. Hadn't waited for the elevator to come. Hadn't talked to anyone. No one had asked him about the case. Nobody saw him; everyone in the stadium had their eyes on the field, trying to understand what was happening. But he knew. One shot had taken out the coach.

J.J. thought about what he would do next. He looked at the case with the rifle inside and figured he'd just put the rifle back in the gun case that displayed all the rifles. But then he decided to take it down to the basement. He would hide it somewhere down there. He didn't know why; he just thought that was a better idea. He looked around in the basement and settled for sliding the case under an old cabinet that held garden supplies. It was dark and dusty. He and his father never went down there anymore.

Speaking of his father, the pilot had dropped Roland off at the stadium late in the fourth quarter. After the game, J.J. had driven them home in his Mustang. Roland, who didn't feel well, had gone upstairs to lie down. Now J.J. sat by himself, staring at the trophy cases and gun racks. He stared at them for a long time. There were a few of his sports awards, but most of the trophies were for his father's golf and hunting. His father always got most of the awards in the family.

After a while, he turned on the TV, wondering if the news had hit the airwaves yet. He didn't have to wonder long. It was breaking news all over the place—on all the networks and on CNN. He couldn't believe it. He hadn't really considered all the publicity, but it was great. Everyone in the country was marveling at what had happened. One perfect shot. They had already announced that the coach was dead. J.J. didn't feel sad for him; the man deserved to die.

He was so wound up that he sat in front of the TV late into the night. His mind kept jumping from one thing to another. He kept marveling at the success. He drank one beer after another until finally he fell asleep thinking about the unbelievable events of the day.

Chapter 88

Patterson's mind was racing. Late Saturday night when he and his team left the stadium, he was thinking about what would happen in the coming days. He couldn't believe their good fortune of finding the shell casing. He knew where the crime had originated and who had been at the scene. Everything was pointing to this J.J. kid. Patterson knew he had to think carefully and not go about this the wrong way. The kid's father was a powerful man, and he would bring out all the stops. No mistake could be made. J.J. didn't know he was a suspect, and that was good. But in case he tried to leave town, Patterson decided to have one of his men stationed down the street from the Rigby home in an unmarked car.

On Sunday, the town was in a daze. No one could make any sense of the horrific crime. It was almost as if everyone was sleeping off a bad hangover. It was unbelievable what had happened. The whole country was saying the same thing. By Monday morning when Patterson arrived at the police station, phones were ringing and folks were rushing in and out. The mayor, the governor, worried mamas of players—they were all calling. Every TV network in the country wanted an interview. The publicity was bad, and everyone wanted this crime solved immediately. The chief needed to stay focused and not let all these interruptions get to him. He had to concentrate on his job, and that wouldn't be easy in this chaos.

He immediately sent one of his men to deliver the shell casing to the state crime lab. He asked for special treatment. He needed a swift response on fingerprints. Because of the unusual circumstances, he thought they would be quick. Patterson then had his assistant contact all the news media and ask for anyone who saw or heard anything unusual to get in touch with his office immediately. A special number was given, and the calls started coming in. He knew most of them would be useless, but every now and then something helpful might show up.

Patterson then went to see Judge Manford Stevens and asked for his signature on a search warrant and an arrest warrant. He explained to the judge what he knew and that he was looking for a weapon in the home of Roland Rigby. The judge was shocked but immediately signed the warrants.

The officer tailing J.J. reported back to Patterson on Monday afternoon. Time was passing, but the suspect hadn't tried to leave town. The administration at the university had decided to hold classes as usual. They knew the students would be distracted but maybe a semblance of normalcy would help. J.J. had gotten up and gone to class. The officer, who was dressed as a student, sat in the back of the class and watched the kid doze off as soon as the professor started lecturing. The officer reported that after the class, J.J. had followed a girl across campus and started whispering something to her.

Patterson listened to his officer's report and couldn't help but think how stupid this kid was. He was careless and probably believed no one suspected him of anything. He was probably anxious to tell someone, too. That happened often in high-profile crimes like this one. Maybe that's what he was telling the girl. But more than anything, Patterson thought about how sad it was that this young man had just ruined his future. He would probably be in prison for most of his life.

"Kid must really be sick, but who knows?" Patterson said to the reporting officer. "Keep an eye on him. It's getting late, and I have an appointment to go out to visit with Coach Astin's wife." He hung up, grabbed his hat, and walked out of the office.

Chapter 89

Kendall sat by the condo window, looking down toward the lake as the sun began to go down. She loved watching the sunsets at the lake, but today her attention was drawn to one tree. She stared at the gingko tree with its gorgeous yellow, fan-shaped leaves. She had always loved those trees, but now this one held a special fascination for her. The trees were not indigenous to the United States; she'd heard they were native to China. She thought someone must have planted it years ago by the old house that once sat on this property. She'd heard the trees could live for a thousand years, resisting disease, drought, and storms. Could that possibly be true? How could that be? Why would they be allowed to live so long while humans had such short lives and were susceptible to so much danger? She was lost in thought when she heard someone ringing the doorbell.

David went to the door. He and Vickie had stayed with Kendall constantly, and her parents had arrived from Atlanta. The weather was cooler, and David had built a fire in the fireplace. Patterson noticed the huge flower arrangements on all the tables. He could immediately smell the flowers. His first thought was that it looked like a florist shop, but then he changed his mind; it was more like a funeral home with a somber atmosphere.

"Come in. I know you're here to see Kendall. But she hasn't had much to say since Saturday night," David said. "It's been quiet around here. We're all at a loss for words."

"I know you're all having a hard time, and I don't want to interrupt," Patterson offered. "But I did want to come by and speak with Mrs. Astin briefly."

"Go on over and sit in that chair beside her. She's not doing well. We haven't been able to get her to eat anything. She seems to be in a stupor. We're all really concerned." David motioned toward the window.

When Patterson saw Kendall up close, he was stunned. He had never seen her look like this. She had always dressed professionally in a dress or suit, hair in place and makeup done. Here she was in jeans, an old UCLA sweatshirt, no makeup, and hair pulled back in a rubber band. She was still a lovely woman, but she was changed. It was as if she didn't care at all about her appearance or what was going on around her. He sat down and waited for her to speak first. Several minutes passed before Kendall even seemed to notice him.

"Sorry, I was lost in thought," she said. "Isn't that a beautiful tree? It's a gingko. I'm watching and waiting for its leaves to fall. Did you know that they drop all their leaves with the first frost? The leaves rain down suddenly. It's getting colder. We might have the first frost soon. Isn't that interesting?"

Patterson hesitated, not knowing how to continue. "Yes, it is," he finally agreed, "but I'm afraid I don't know much about trees. It is beautiful, though." He paused and then said, "I'm here to let you know what's happening and see if there have been any other threats."

Kendall jerked her head around and looked at him sternly. "Why would there be threats now? Someone out there accomplished what they've wanted to do since we got here. They were successful. I wonder how they feel today. For months I was agitated and going crazy. I was horrified by the threats, the rock in the window, the car trying to drive us off the road. Now I'm numb, and I'm angry."

She was agitated, and her voice began to rise. "Yes, I'm angry. Now I know I was correct all along. Check all the calls. We must find out who did this. We must find out quickly. Let me help you. I'm a lawyer. I know a lot of people in law enforcement. We must find out who did this and send him away for life. I will have no peace until then. I'm so angry, and I can't live like this."

"Kendall, please calm down," her father said as he put his hand on her shoulder.

"No, I will not calm down. I am so angry. Who would do this to a good man like Duke? It makes no sense. I will have no peace until we know who did this horrible thing." Her words tumbled out, and her voice kept getting louder. "I will have no peace until we know! I may never have any peace the rest of my life. I am so angry."

Patterson was hoping she would listen as he said, "Mrs. Astin, thank you for your offer of help, but we have an army of people working on this case. I can't tell you what we've found, but we have some good leads already. I believe we'll have some answers very soon, and I'll let you know the minute we have anything."

Kendall said no more, just stared at him as if to say he had better do his job and do it quickly. Patterson turned to go, and David walked him to the door. "Everyone in this house is suffering," David said quietly. "But Kendall really has us worried. We don't know what to say to help her, but we have a friend who is a counselor coming to talk to her. Of course, we'll stay with her. Keep in touch and let us know as soon as you have news."

Patterson left with a greater sense of urgency. For the sake of everyone in this community, but especially for this woman, he had to get this crime solved as quickly as possible.

Chapter 90

The next day Kendall was back at the window, watching the tree, when there was a gentle knock on the front door. Her mother opened it to a beautiful young woman with three little girls.

"I don't want to bother anybody, but I'm a friend of Kendall's and I wanted to come by and see her. My girls have a bouquet of flowers for her," Margie said as her youngest daughter Carrie held out a bunch of flowers for Kendall's mother to admire.

"Those are lovely flowers, dear. I'm sure Kendall will be glad to see you," Mrs. Harris said as she invited them in.

When Margie saw Kendall, she ran over to her and put her arms around her, and the little girls did the same. The two women broke into tears as the children squeezed hard.

"I'm so sorry. I'm so sorry," Margie said over and over. "I don't know what to say except I'm sorry. The coach was such a wonderful man, and I know how much you loved him. It was so wrong what happened."

Kendall kept holding Margie and saying, "Thank you. Thank you." Then it seemed to dawn on her that Margie was actually standing before her in the condo. "But what are you doing here? You're supposed to be in the Spouse Abuse Center. You must be careful."

"No, that's what I came to tell you. Toby is dead." Margie's tears came again. "It was so sudden. When I heard the news, I had the strangest feelings come over me. It was a combination of relief and sadness. I began to cry thinking about the man Toby could have been without his addictions—to alcohol, to gambling, and to getting revenge. They destroyed him. He could have been a wonderful husband and father to the girls. I seem to be grieving what could have been."

Kendall held Margie in her arms. "I know what you're talking about. I've been thinking of what Duke's future could have been."

The two women were silent for several moments, and then Margie wiped her eyes and said, "But I wanted you to know I'm finally safe. I left the center today and came straight here to see you. You're the one who saved my life. Never forget that. I don't know what would have happened to me and the girls if you hadn't taken me to the center. You saved us."

Kendall nodded, not trusting herself to speak.

"But I also wanted you to know that Toby wasn't the shooter," Margie continued. "When I heard what happened, I was terrified that Toby did it. You know all he could think about was punishing me, and you, and Coach Astin. Then late yesterday afternoon I got a call notifying me that Toby had died in a fire in North Carolina. I had been calling my mother occasionally to let her know we were fine. The authorities had hunted her down trying to find me. There was a horrible forest fire, and Toby was in his grandpa's old cabin in North Carolina. Knowing him and his drinking, he was probably the one who started the fire. It's sad that his life ended the way it did. But he had turned into someone who was cruel. He lost his way."

Margie paused, and then Carrie held up the flowers and said, "Miss Kendall, we brought you some pretty flowers to cheer you up."

Kendall looked up at Margie and smiled. It was the first time she had smiled since Saturday. She kept smiling, tears rolling down her cheeks, as she whispered, "Thank you, thank you for these beautiful flowers. I am so happy to see you all."

Margie stayed for a bit, visiting with Kendall's family while the girls ate some cookies Mrs. Harris gave them. Kendall seemed to enjoy telling her family the story of Margie's bravery. Everyone was sad to see Margie and the girls leave. But they needed to get to Margie's mother and father, who were anxious to see them. Kendall invited them to come back and told them they were a great help to her. Margie promised to return soon. As they stood at the front door, Kendall smiled and hugged them all. She thought to herself that she would stay close to them, and they would help her survive. They would all survive together.

Chapter 91

Just as Patterson had hoped, things were moving fast. The state crime lab confirmed what the officers suspected: J.J. Rigby's fingerprints were on the shell casing, the doorknob, and some of the high stool backs. The year before, J.J. had been fingerprinted for a DUI. With the signed warrants they needed, Patterson and several of his best officers headed to the Rigby residence to search for the weapon. When they arrived unannounced, J.J. answered the door. Patterson immediately noticed the uneasy look on J.J.'s face. All J.J. could mumble was, "Come in."

"Hello, I'm Chief Patterson of the city police department. These are some of my officers. We're here to perform a search of your rifles. We have a search warrant signed by Manford Stevens." As Patterson spoke, Roland Rigby walked up behind his son.

"What is going on here?" Roland barked. "What are you doing in my home?"

"Sir, we are investigating the murder of Jonathan Wayne Astin, and we have evidence that suggests your son may have been involved," Patterson answered.

"Are you out of your mind? I'm sure my son had nothing to do with it."

"We have reason to believe otherwise," Patterson said, his eyes on the gun case in a prominent position on the right-hand wall of the den. There were five rifles displayed, but the end slot was missing a rifle. He instructed one of his officers to begin removing the rifles from the case and asked the others to search the entire house, upstairs and downstairs. He didn't have to tell them to do a thorough search. They were trained to look in every closet and under every piece of furniture. It would take a while, but that didn't matter. Time was on his side now.

"You can't take those rifles," Roland yelled. "Some of them are expensive. You don't have the right to take them."

"Yes, we do. This warrant allows us to look in your residence for the murder weapon. We will be looking to match one of these rifles to a shell casing we found in your skybox at the stadium. As you may or may not know, we can do that," Patterson informed him, thinking Roland was suddenly looking a little gray.

"My God, what are you talking about? This can't be true. I'm calling my attorney right this minute," Roland said as he left the room.

There were a lot of guns in the house, both rifles and handguns. There was another rifle case in the back hall, and Patterson's men retrieved six more rifles. The number of handguns was somewhat surprising. Patterson was wondering why in the world a person would need so many handguns, when one officer opened the basement door and went down the steps. J.J. watched him go and began to get agitated.

"Man, you can't do that. Nobody goes down there," J.J. said. He was wringing his hands and mumbling to himself, "No, no. You can't go down there." Patterson couldn't help but think that he looked like a guilty kid who had been caught doing something bad—a very dumb kid at that.

It didn't take long before the officer came back upstairs. "Hey, Chief, found this down in the basement. It was under a cabinet in some kind of case. It's a Remington deer rifle with a scope and one of those expensive silencers. I think this is what we're looking for."

One of Patterson's men had been making a careful list of the rifles they had collected. Once he added the rifle from the basement, he handed the list to Patterson.

"Roland Rigby, this is an inventory of the weapons we will take for testing. They will be returned to you in seventy-two hours," Patterson said. Then he turned to J.J. "J.J. Rigby, we are arresting you for the murder of Jonathan Wayne Astin." He read him his Miranda rights and escorted him to a police car outside.

Roland Rigby was furious. Yes, he would see what his lawyer could do. These cops couldn't come into his house and take all his rifles and arrest his son. What right did they have to do this to Roland Rigby?

Chapter 92

After J.J. was locked up, Patterson went back to his office and found that he had some important messages. Several people had called the hotline with meaningful information. At the end of the game, a man working an exit gate said J.J. Rigby had walked out at a fast clip carrying a case of some kind. He knew him from years back when he was a kid and came to the games with his daddy, Roland Rigby. A couple of football players, distraught over their coach's death, reported outrageous things J.J. had said after Coach told him he wouldn't be on the football team. One reported that J.J. said he wanted to kill Coach Astin. A young woman called and said she wanted to meet briefly and was on her way over after class. Patterson was thinking she would probably arrive soon when there was a knock on his office door. One of the female officers appeared and said, "Chief, I think you should see this young lady and hear what she has to say."

The young woman walked in carrying several books and looking a bit nervous. "Sir, my name is Marilyn Pope. I'm a freshman at the university. I have to tell you something. I heard the message that was sent out asking for information. This is crazy, but this boy I've known for years—I went to high school with him at the academy—he wanted to tell me something a few days ago. He followed me out of our first period class and walked across campus with me. He was whispering in my ear. He does that all the time—drives me crazy. Half the time I don't even listen to him. But that day he said it was very important and that I couldn't tell another person. I can't believe it, but he said he had shot Coach Astin. I usually don't pay attention to his bizarre stuff. But it was like he wanted to brag about it. It freaked me out. He had this weird look on his face. Maybe he was saying it to impress me or something. He scared me. I just looked at him and told him he was nuts. He smiled this strange smile. I couldn't sleep last night and decided I should tell you. What should I do? I'm scared."

"Marilyn, you did the right thing to tell me. But you don't have to be scared because we just arrested him," Patterson said.

"Oh my God, you arrested J.J.! You think he really did it? I was thinking you all would believe I was crazy coming here to tell you this."

Patterson smiled. "Oh, you did the right thing. I know it was frightening for you, but it also took some courage to come here."

"I just couldn't believe this boy I've known for years and even dated in high school would do something like this. I quit dating him our senior year when he started having these weird moods and was always talking about guns. He loved to hunt and shoot animals. He talked about watching them die. Ugh, he was creepy! But he's been trying to get me to date him again. Gosh, I'm glad I didn't."

"I would say you have good instincts and picked up on some things other folks didn't. Fortunately, we do have some evidence now. I can't discuss it with you at this point, but we hope to carry him to trial before too long," Patterson explained.

"Wow, this is happening so fast. It's hard for me to take it in. I'm sure a lot of other folks will be shocked, too. Gosh, J.J. Rigby has been arrested for shooting Coach Astin on the sidelines of a game on national TV. What could be crazier? It's still hard to believe."

"Yes, and you will likely be asked to testify at his trial at some point. Are you willing to do that? Your testimony will influence a jury, I would think."

"Yes, I am," Marilyn said with conviction. "I loved our coach, and this was such a horrible crime. J.J. must have lost his mind or something. But if he did it, he should go to prison."

"You are a brave young woman. Please leave your contact info here with us. This is going to move quickly. We thank you for coming in," Patterson said as he rose to shake her hand. "Obviously, J.J. thought he would impress you, but he misjudged you."

"You can say that again. J.J. has lost his mind! To think he could impress me by telling me he shot the coach. He is an idiot and a creep!" Marilyn was still mumbling to herself as she walked out the door.

Chapter 93

Patterson left some of his men questioning J.J. and drove out to see Mrs. Astin. He had told her he would report any new developments. He wanted her to hear about the arrest from him rather than on TV. When Kendall's father led him into the room, Patterson saw Dr. and Mrs. Jansson sitting and talking with Kendall.

Axel Jansson immediately rose and greeted him. "Chief Patterson, it's nice to see you. We'll leave now and let you visit with Kendall."

"No. I'm actually glad you're here. It will save me a trip to your office later. I came to tell you that we have made an arrest for the murder of Coach Astin."

There were anxious looks around the room. It was as if they were all holding their breath when Patterson said, "It will be difficult for you to believe. It has been for me. But we have arrested a student and former walk-on football player who goes by J.J. His full name is Jason James Rigby. Dr. Jansson, I'm sure you know Roland Rigby, the wealthy contributor to the university. Well, J.J. is his only son, obviously a troubled young man."

"Yes, I know Roland Rigby," Dr. Jansson said. "But I don't know his son. You're right—this is hard to believe."

Kendall didn't move and only looked down at the floor. The news was obviously a shock to her, but she stayed silent. Patterson decided to keep talking. "After the game, we did a search of the skyboxes and found a shell casing in Roland Rigby's box. It was locked during the game, but J.J. was seen leaving it at the end of the game carrying a musical instrument case large enough to hold a rifle. He's been going to that box most of his life and is a familiar face for people who work at the stadium. We believe he positioned himself in the back of the box and used a deer rifle with a scope and silencer. The kid is known for being a good marksman. We have reports that he was upset when he wasn't allowed to stay on the team. Players heard him saying hateful things about the coach—one even heard him say he wanted to kill coach. But they didn't think he was serious. Folks hear people say stuff like that all the time and think they're just blowing off steam. He hasn't been examined by a psychologist yet. I don't know if you would call him a sociopath or not, but he doesn't seem to feel any remorse. This is a horrible situation, and I hate to be the one bringing you this news, but I promised I would keep you posted." Patterson focused on Kendall, who was still sitting motionless.

After what seemed like several minutes, Kendall finally said, "You are correct. This is hard to believe. But the whole thing has seemed surreal to me. I keep thinking it's a dream. I'm having to acknowledge that it's real. To hear that a player, even a former player, did this breaks my heart. Duke always wanted the best for his players and worked so hard to let them know that he cared for them. I can't imagine how a player would so misunderstand him."

"Oh, they knew how he cared," insisted Dr. Jansson. "If you could hear what the players have been saying, it would warm your heart. I know you're not watching or reading the news, nor should you at this time. But the players are being interviewed and saying the most amazing things. Duke won their respect and love so quickly. This season was a testament to the bond he created with them. The fans are saying great things, too. In a short year, Duke won the masses over. I know there was a vocal group at first who made threats and said they didn't want him. But they were drowned out."

"I don't believe all those evil people went away," Kendall said calmly. "I think the vast majority was won over by Duke. But some of those people would never support Duke. I don't know, but I imagine this young man heard a lot of hate talk. In his fragile state of mind, he wasn't able to process it all. He probably believed he was doing a good thing. I don't know for sure, but I do know that words are powerful. I just can't believe he didn't hear someone encouraging him over and over that he was supposed to shoot Duke."

Kendall sat quietly again and then said, "I've been so angry. I've been frantic to know who shot Duke. That anger has consumed me. It's still there now, but it's not the same. Now I'm feeling anger mixed with profound sadness. So many lives have been affected. Duke's life was cut off in its prime. This young man has also destroyed his life. All the players and coaches have gone through such a trauma. I'm going to have to figure out how to go on with my life, too. Yes, I am profoundly sad today about the loss—the loss to us all."

"None of us will be the same after this," Dr. Jansson acknowledged, "but I believe you will survive and do something great with your life. I have no doubt of that."

"I wish I could share that confidence, but thank you for your kindness and caring," Kendall said as she looked out the window, her eyes landing on the gingko tree. "I must live one day at a time and try to figure it all out. For some reason, I don't feel that this is over. It's not as simple as this. I know for sure it isn't going to be easy to put my life back together."

After a few quiet moments, Patterson got up to leave, saying he needed to get back to the office. Suddenly Kendall motioned him and the Janssons toward the window. "Come here and look out the window at that big, bare gingko tree. I got up early this morning and the wind was blowing. Did you realize we had our first frost last night? Gusts of wind were howling, and the yellow leaves were flying everywhere. It was exciting, and I got to see it. The gingko did drop all its leaves at once—it was glorious. They will come back year after year for heaven knows how many years. For some reason, that gave me joy and I wanted you all to know," Kendall said as she smiled.

PART 5

THE TRIAL

May 1997

Chapter 94

During the next few months, Kendall shut herself off from the outside world. She didn't want to read or hear the news reports about the arrest and trial of J.J. Rigby. She couldn't bring herself to go to any of the court proceedings. District Attorney Derrick Henderson, known as the best prosecutor in the state, was to present the evidence against J.J. She was confident he would do a masterful job. Her brother Randy and her friend David, both lawyers, would be in the courtroom every day, keeping her posted on what was happening. She just didn't believe she could sit through the description of events, the pictures, and the testimonies. She didn't want to be photographed or asked for interviews by reporters. It was all she could do to get through each day with this profound sadness. She didn't want to replay it all in her mind, didn't want to hear people making excuses for why this young man shot her husband.

By the middle of May, the trial had been going on for weeks and everything was pointing toward a guilty verdict for J.J. But on Friday afternoon of the fourth week, David and Randy rushed in to tell Kendall what had happened in the trial that day. They were excited. "I don't know what's going on," David said, breathless. "It looked like they were about to wrap everything up and send it to the jury when the judge called for a recess until next Monday, saying the defense team was calling another witness. What could be said that hasn't already been said? Reporters were running out of the room to file their stories. Everyone in the courtroom was wondering who would have any new information this late in the trial. It was chaos. They've been so thorough, it doesn't make sense."

"Yeah, Kendall," Randy agreed. "David and I have sat through this whole trial. No matter what the high-powered lawyers try to say in defense of this young man, the evidence is clear, with his fingerprints on the shell casing and witnesses who saw him leaving the stadium carrying something that could hold a rifle. That rifle in the home matched the shell casing. I think they've interviewed just about everyone who was at the stadium that day, from ticket takers to elevator operators to students. I have no idea what anyone could say to save the kid."

"It won't change anything. Duke is still dead," Kendall said. "But I've thought all along that there was more to this crime than a young man being upset about Duke cutting him from the team. We got so many threats from what seemed to be different sources. How could it just be this one kid? At any rate, I guess we'll have to wait until Monday like everyone else and see what happens."

Kendall was in the condo by the window where she had sat for months. When David and Randy left, she turned and looked out at the gingko tree. It wasn't bare anymore but covered with tender new leaves. The cycle of life had started again. She longed to feel that renewal in her own life. Maybe someday, she could have joy again.

Chapter 95

Monday morning the courtroom was packed. It was the eleventh hour of the trial. Everything was almost wrapped up, but now the defense had a secret witness. It seemed to be by design that they withheld the person until now. No one knew what was going to happen when the judge called the court to order.

"Your honor, the defense calls Roland Rigby to the stand," announced Scott Mathison, the lead defense attorney. A gasp went up from the people in the courtroom. No one expected the wealthy war hero and father of J.J. to take the stand. Supposedly, he had been out of town the day of the game. Roland Rigby had always been a man of few words, and he had seemed reluctant to answer questions. The defense had not called him earlier. What had changed their mind? What could he possibly add that they didn't already know?

"Mr. Rigby," Mathison began, "I understand that you have additional information that you would like to give to the court. I will just let you tell the court what that information is. Proceed, please."

Roland cleared his throat and twisted in his seat before he finally began to talk. "I didn't believe this trial would go the way it has. I thought my lawyers would be able to clear my son quickly. I see now that's not going to happen. I can't sit and watch my son be convicted of a crime he didn't commit."

Roland paused for a few seconds, adjusted his collar, shifted his weight, and looked out at the crowd. "Most people thought I went to Las Vegas and missed the game. I did go to the airport and got on the plane but decided to get off at the last minute. My pilot brought me back and dropped me off at the stadium late in the game. I wanted to try to connect with my son, who had been having some problems."

Roland paused and Mathison asked him, "Mr. Rigby, what time was it in the game?"

"It was very late. The two teams had tied and gone into overtime. I dashed up the elevator and walked to my box. Strangely, it was locked but I had a key. No one seemed to notice me. Everyone had their eyes glued to the field. When I opened the door, everything was dark inside. It was mid-November and already pretty dark outside. The lights were off. I had to adjust to the light and was reaching for the switch when my son said, 'No, don't turn on the lights.' Then I saw that J.J. had a rifle that he was aiming at the field. I immediately said, 'What the hell are you doing?' My son answered that he was going to shoot Coach Astin," Roland explained calmly.

People in the courtroom were surprised by his nonchalance. "My son was shaking and sweating profusely," Roland continued. "I knew he wouldn't be able to aim the gun and shoot a moving target. I figured if he fired, he would shoot someone but not the coach. I told him that. I also said he was going to ruin his life and I couldn't let him do that."

Roland paused and Mathison asked, "What did you do next, Mr. Rigby?"

With a blank expression on his face, Roland looked out at the courtroom and said, "My son was determined. He even pointed the rifle at me and told me to stand back. I was trained in hand-to-hand combat. I grabbed the gun and shoved him down. I'm still strong. He had a breakdown or something—he was sobbing. J.J. kept saying, 'Coach has to die; he ruined my life.' Something came over me. I still have flashbacks sometimes. I felt like I was back in Nam."

The courtroom was quiet. There was an awkward silence. Roland seemed to have drifted off, and then he said, "Once it was over, I jerked J.J. up and stared him in the eyes. He was shaken. As I put the gun in the case, I told him to leave immediately and walk down the ramps. I told him I would look for the shell casing and then follow him. He was to pull his Mustang up to the gate and pick me up. I knew we had to get out quickly without attracting attention. Then I shoved him out the door. Unfortunately, I couldn't find the shell casing. I figured if I couldn't find it, neither could anybody else. Obviously, I was wrong about that. But everyone had their eyes glued to the field and we're regulars around here, so no one noticed us leaving." The matter-of-fact expression never left Roland's face.

"Wait a minute, Mr. Rigby. You've lost your train of thought. You didn't tell us what happened when you grabbed the rifle," Mathison said.

Everyone was watching Roland's face. After a pause, he began to talk again. "What I did destroyed my life. I couldn't let my son make the same mistake. You see, I was partly responsible already. J.J. heard nothing but talk of how to get rid of Coach Astin. He had been asked to do certain things like throw rocks through his window. You all probably remember that. No one ever knew who did that, but it was J.J. But he was just doing what we told him to do. It was what I wanted him to do, so he thought he had to do it."

Roland paused again and Mathison asked, "You keep saying 'what we asked him to do.' Who else was involved?"

"I am taking responsibility for what I did. I will let the others come forward on their own. There were those of us who knew that Astin was the wrong coach for this university, and we were determined to get rid of him. I did what I did to save my son. He was determined to go through with this crime, thinking it would please me, and I had to stop him. You see, I had done it so many times that something happened to me. It was like I was back in a war. I had to shoot the enemy to save my comrade. I really don't know what came over me, but the deed was done."

Mathison stood quietly and then said, "Sir, you are rambling. What are you saying?"

Roland looked straight at Mathison and said, "I was a sniper in Vietnam, and I worked for the CIA for years. I've shot a lot of people. I know how to do it. My son could never do it. Do with me what you will. But my son is innocent. I'm the one who shot Astin."

Chapter 96

The courtroom erupted at Roland Rigby's confession. The judge pounded his gavel, trying to restore order. Prosecutor Derrick Henderson jumped up, objecting, "He's just trying to save his son. He's crazy." Henderson and Mathison both went up to confer with the judge, who finally decided to proceed. Both sides gave closing arguments. Henderson argued that Roland was making a desperate attempt to save his son and that nothing had changed—J.J. was guilty. Mathison argued that only someone with military training as a sniper would be able to make the shot that killed Coach Astin—J.J. was not guilty. The prosecution argued that only J.J.'s prints were on the shell casing, but the defense said that even though he loaded the rifle, he didn't fire it. The arguments were made forcefully, and then the jury was sent out to decide if J.J. should be convicted.

The case drew national attention. Folks everywhere argued about what they thought. Emotions ran high, arguments went unsettled—it was endless. The jury had the same problems because they stayed and argued for three days. Finally, they sent a note to the judge that they could not agree. The judge gave them the Allen charge—a charge to a deadlocked jury to make a further effort to reach a verdict—and sent them back in to talk some more.

Finally, the word was given that the jury was returning. David and Randy had been waiting like everybody else and rushed in to hear the decision. The jury of twelve—seven men and five women—walked slowly back into the room. Everyone was anxious when they finally appeared. Had they reached a decision? The courtroom fell quiet as the fore person rose and said, "Your honor, we cannot reach a unanimous decision."

The courtroom burst into chatter, with everyone letting out their opinion to whoever was within earshot. Reporters hurried around outside, and TV broadcasters jumped into airing their stories immediately. David and Randy made a quick exit to go tell Kendall. They knew she would want to hear the verdict from them and not the media.

When they reached the condo, Kendall was sitting looking out the window as she always did. David was the first to speak. "Kendall, I don't know what to make of the verdict. They have a hung jury. After all those days of deliberation, they couldn't agree. It's a mistrial. I believe the prosecution will call for a new trial."

Randy chimed in, "I agree. When Roland started saying 'we,' I think folks started thinking that there are things we don't know. Who else was involved? Was there other criminal activity? Sounds like to me there might be other influential people in this town that are mighty nervous right now."

"I believe you're correct," David said. "There might have been more than one scheme or dirty trick."

Kendall finally looked at them. "It really doesn't matter to me which one killed Duke. One of them did. I'm glad the wider picture is coming to light. This could go on for a long time and we may never know the truth. But I know one thing—I'm going to try to move on. I'm so tired of thinking about who killed Duke. None of this is going to bring him back. If I don't let go of it, it's going to eat me up. I will let the 'long arm of justice' settle the issue."

Randy took her hand in his. "I'm so glad to hear you say that. I've been worried about you sitting here by this window constantly. Yes, you can and must move on with your life."

Kendall smiled at her brother and her friend. "I just have to keep going with life. I can't give up. I want to have some joy again. And I want to do something meaningful—something that will commemorate Duke's legacy but also something I can do in my name. I know that's what Duke would want me to do, too." Kendall brushed at a tear on her cheek. "I don't know what it will be, but I must begin the search."

Chapter 97

Billy Bob was in the law office of Thomas Benson first thing Tuesday morning, and he was frantic. He was sweating, and his hands shook as he said, "I couldn't wait to see you. I have to talk to you right this minute. What in the world happened to Roland Rigby yesterday? Has he gone mad—all this stuff about being a sniper and a member of the CIA? I've known him all my life and he's never said a word about being some hotshot sniper! He's just trying to save his son. My God, what is wrong with him? And he has everyone wondering who 'we' could be. Everyone knows we're good friends and have lunch together every day."

"Calm down, Billy Bob. Sit down and let's talk about your situation. If you haven't done anything, what are you so upset about?" Benson asked.

Billy Bob wrung his hands and looked at Benson with terrified eyes. "I am hiring you immediately. Now do we have attorney-client privilege?"

"Of course we do. I've worked for you for years. Now tell me why you're upset."

Billy Bob began to tell him about the lunches at the club and how he had spewed hatred of Coach Astin to anyone who would listen. He reluctantly told him about getting folks to make threatening calls, and then he stopped talking and sat for a few minutes, like he was trying to figure out his next words. Finally, he started telling Benson about Antonio. "There's this guy from Chicago who's been coming to the games and sitting in my box for years. I'm not sure exactly what he does, but he's a tough guy. At any rate, I was telling him how much I hated the coach and wanted to get rid of him. He said he had this guy. I didn't know exactly what he was talking about, you know. But he said he would help me." Billy Bob looked sheepishly at Benson, who was holding his head in his hands.

"What in the world are you talking about when you say, 'get rid of the coach'? Who was his guy, a hired hit man? My God, Billy Bob, do you realize what you're saying?" Benson's tone was pleading, as if he hoped he'd heard wrong.

Billy Bob looked at the floor and said, "Nothing ever happened. I never met the man. I wasn't involved. I don't even know the man's name."

Benson gave Billy Bob a troubled look and asked, "Is this Antonio the same guy that has the new casino in North Carolina—the one with all kinds of connections to gambling, which is illegal in our state? Are you involved with him?"

Billy Bob met Benson's eyes and said, "Yes, my company built that casino, and we've done a few other projects together."

Benson didn't hesitate. "Billy Bob, you're in trouble. You will need all the help you can get. By the way, have you read the morning paper?"

Billy Bob shook his head, and Benson said, "There's an article written by that young sportswriter, Jay Stewart. You know Laura Mae Hurley, the widow of a dean at the university, she called him last night and told him a story about overhearing a conversation at the club where you have lunch every day. She hadn't known what to do about it, but with all the news about Roland yesterday, she was inspired to call the newspaper. It seems she was at a table close by and heard you, Tommy Lee, and Roland talking about giving some player $14,000 in a paper bag. You shushed Tommy Lee and told him 'It was illegal as hell.' Is that correct? Because if it is, there will be an NCAA investigation about cheating at the university and you will be in the middle of it."

Billy Bob sank down in his chair and looked like he might faint. He took out his handkerchief and wiped his brow as he said, "Well, the shit has really hit the fan now."

PART 6

RENEWAL

May 1997

Chapter 98

Moving on with her life was a lot harder for Kendall than she thought it would be. She had hoped that after the jury reached a verdict, she would feel better. Even though it wasn't definitive, and no one was sure who pulled the trigger, somehow that didn't matter to her. She had made up her mind to move on, but it was easier said than done.

Spring had always been her favorite season and she had hoped it would lift her spirits. The trees were green with leaves and flowers bloomed. But Kendall still found herself sitting by the window, looking out at the lake for hours at a time. She didn't want to teach at the university anymore. She didn't want to stay here at the condo. She had sold the dream house she and Duke had built, but where could she go? She was lost in thought one day late in May when the phone rang.

"Hello, Kendall, this is Sally Caravati," the caller announced. "I hope you're doing well today. I thought I would come by and see you. I have something for you."

In a rare move for the time, Duke had put Sally in a job traditionally given to men—Director of Football Operations. She was responsible for making travel arrangements for the team—hotels, planes, buses, etc.—and keeping the schedule for practices. It was a big job, but she had done it beautifully. Kendall liked her very much and told her she looked forward to seeing her.

The next morning, Sally arrived carrying a big box. "I'm so glad to see you," Kendall said as she greeted her at the door. "Wow, what a big box. Put it on the table. It must be heavy. Then have a seat. I have coffee made. Would you like some?"

"I would love a cup," Sally said as she sat down. For a couple of minutes, she was quiet, and then she began hesitantly, "I've been thinking about you. I haven't known what to do or say. This has been hard on everyone in the office. We've all walked around in a daze for much of the time. I guess you know Mac Andrews is acting as interim head coach. He's doing a good job. But everyone misses Duke so much."

"Yes, I miss him every day and probably always will. Having folks like you visit helps me. Thanks for coming," Kendall said, sensing that Sally was at a loss for words.

Sally smoothed her skirt and sat up straight. "I've really been wanting to do something to let you know how we all loved Duke. You know me, I'm not much of a talker. I'm a doer, an organizer, and I've been working for weeks now compiling something for you. That's why I'm here today. Everyone has been helpful and has wanted to participate." She opened the big box and pulled out two large three-ring binders. She instructed Kendall to open the first one.

The notebook was heavy, and Kendall put it on her lap and slowly opened it. It was full of letters from all the players and members of the football staff. Each one was enclosed in a plastic cover with an individual headshot.

Sally quickly said, "I knew the headshot would help you identify who each player was. You didn't know them as well as we all do, because you didn't see them daily. But they all wanted to express to you what Duke meant to their lives. I thought it would be very meaningful to you. We even have letters from President Jansson and his wife Glenda and some faculty who wanted to be included. The letters are a beautiful tribute to Duke, and I think you'll enjoy reading them."

Kendall couldn't hold back tears as she turned through some of the pages. "I am so touched. You put an awful lot of work into this project. It's just wonderful. I don't know what to say except I'm grateful. I can't wait to start reading them," she said, knowing it would take hours and maybe even days to read them all.

She began to stroke the pages gently and said, "I am sincerely moved. Please thank everyone for me. I know that reading these letters will help me. Thank you so much."

Sally said she needed to get back to the office, so they hugged good-bye. When she left, Kendall sat down and started reading. Tears rolled down her cheeks because the letters were so beautiful. They were not all the same but very individual. Some of the players expressed themselves in the simplest terms, as if they weren't sure how to say what they wanted to express. She understood that. They missed Coach. He had taught them about life. He had wanted them to get a good education and do the right things. He cared about them. He was a wonderful man. He was like a father to them. Many of them said, "I loved Coach."

Other letters were lengthy and precise, as if the writers had been thinking about what to say for a long time. President Jansson wrote an eloquent tribute appropriate for a eulogy, listing all the things Duke had done for the university in a short time. Kendall would treasure it. Some professors' letters were similar. Elaborate or short, they all moved her. She read into the evening and couldn't stop. Then she came to Elijah Ray Johnson's letter. He had written:

> Dear Mrs. Astin,
> I don't say much to most folks, but I could talk to Coach Astin. He wanted to know what my dream for my life was. He was interested in me as a person, not just because I could play football. I hadn't had that before except from my mama. I told him I wanted to play in the NFL a few years, buy my mama a house, and then coach ball like he had. I want to help young men be better men. I want to live my life like he lived his. I will always teach young men what he taught me. Be honest, work hard, take care of your people, and help young men be better men. I loved Coach Astin and will always remember him.
> Sincerely,
> Elijah Ray Johnson

Elijah's words made her pause. They were so easy to understand. She sat and thought for a while. These letters had come at the perfect time. They had given her an idea. She knew something she could do for Duke. She would start a foundation in his name. She would give an award each year for the college player who exemplified his values. It would go to a player finishing his college career who was outstanding as an athlete and student. But she would add another component. The player would also aspire to be a coach and make "young men better," as Elijah put it. She thought about how she had opposed Duke going into coaching from the very beginning. They had fought about it often. But it meant so much to him. She knew now that she had been wrong. This is what would make him happy. Duke would be thrilled to know a player like Elijah wanted to live his life the way Duke had lived his. There could not be a better legacy for Duke.

Kendall didn't know all the details yet. She would have to raise money, form a board, and decide how to make the award. There would be a certain amount of work to get it set up as a nonprofit and get donations. The only thing she knew for sure was who the first winner would be—Elijah Ray Johnson. The award would be called the Duke Trophy. Yes, that was a good idea, and she was finally excited about something. It was an excellent way to preserve Duke's legacy. She was surprised when she thought that maybe the nonprofit could even help troubled young men like J.J. Rigby before they destroyed their lives and the lives of others around them. I don't know if I am approaching forgiveness, she thought, but maybe it's a good start.

Chapter 99

June 1997

Kendall was surprised about another decision and the positive image it had left in her mind. Even though she loved the house she had built for a life with Duke, she knew she didn't want to live in it without him. Back in the winter, she had put the lake house on the market. On a cold day in March, Betty Friedman, the real estate agent who had originally shown her the lot, tapped gently on the condo door.

"Kendall, so good to see you. I hope you're having a good day. I'm so sorry to bother you. I know you usually don't do this, but I have a young professor from the university, with a beautiful young family, who wants to look at your house. I think you will like them. Would you mind giving them a tour?" She turned and gestured behind her, where the family was standing by their car in the driveway.

"Betty, it's good to see you," Kendall said, somewhat annoyed at first. But then she saw the children—a boy and a girl—who were looking at her eagerly. "Sure, I'll be glad to show you around."

The family stepped up to her door, and the young man held out his hand.

"Thank you so much," he said. "My name is Brent Andrews, and I teach in the English department at the university. This is my wife, Jamie, and our children, Stephanie and Michael. As you can see, we have another child on the way, and we've outgrown our home. When I recently made tenure, we decided now was the time to put down some roots. We were out driving with Betty and fell in love with the setting of the house you built. The kids started begging to see it, so here we are. Please forgive the intrusion."

"I'm glad you like the house and where it is. I'll tell you all about it," Kendall said as she grabbed her jacket. The finished house more than met Kendall's expectations. It was perfect.

As soon as they arrived at the house, she began to tell them every detail of the construction. "I wanted the house to look like it nestles in the trees. With the board and batten siding and the cedar shake roof, it looks like it should be in the woods. It's built around the great room that I copied from a ski lodge in Wyoming. I love the old beams in the cathedral ceiling. I wanted a big kitchen where everyone could gather. The cabinets are custom made and have an antique finish to look like old furniture." As she talked, she could see that Brent and Jamie appreciated the attention to detail and the care she had put into the planning. Even Stephanie and Michael were glued to her every word. It was obvious that the whole family loved the house.

When they had finished the tour, the children wanted to go outside and play.

"Mama, please, may we go down to the lake? It's so beautiful," Michael called to his mother.

"Okay, but watch out for your sister. Don't let her get too close to the water," Jamie instructed him.

Kendall loved seeing the children laughing and having so much fun. The parents were fascinated by every aspect of the house. "I love that office/library with all the bookshelves. I desperately need those," Brent said.

"And the fireplace with the blue and white tiles. Blue is my favorite color. I plan to decorate everything in blue and white," Jamie said enthusiastically. "It is simply wonderful."

"Honey, we can't get too excited. I love it, too. But it'll be a stretch for us to get the loan," Brent said with a nervous laugh.

At the end of the day, Kendall knew they were the family who was supposed to live in the house she had built with so much care. It was meant to have children growing up in it. She was pleased when the Andrews family purchased the house and promised they would send pictures of the children as they grew. It had taken a couple of months before all the details were worked out to close the sale. Somehow, Kendall managed not to look back or second-guess her decision to lower the price a little so that this young family could get the mortgage. Yes, the sale of the house to this beautiful young family was a happy memory for her.

Even though the sale had gone better than she could have dreamed, she still didn't know where she wanted to live or exactly how to go about creating the foundation in Duke's honor or what else she might want to do with her life. She seemed to be at a stalemate. Thankfully, her parents had been staying with her for weeks at a time, and their conversations helped her.

The three of them sat on the deck one beautiful summer evening, and Kendall said, "I can't tell you how much I appreciate you two being here. I can't bear to be alone. This view of the lake, the night sounds of crickets and tree frogs, the sun going down—this has sustained me as much as anything. I've sat for months just looking out the window. I've got to do something, but I don't know what."

"I'm glad we're here, too," her mother said. "Somehow it helps us all to be together. We're all grieving. It's part of the process, but you'll figure out what you want to do, I'm sure."

"I'll tell you what has helped me—those visits from Margie and those precious little girls," Kendall's father said.

"I love seeing the way you two light up when the girls are around," Kendall said. "They're almost like the grandchildren you never had. I have come to love them so much, too."

"That Lisbeth reminds me of you—so smart and determined to take care of everyone. She is beginning to speak up. She says the most amazing things sometimes." Her father shook his head and laughed.

"I'm not sure I want to wish my mouth on anyone," Kendall said. "But it does make you think she'll be able to take care of herself no matter what."

"Exactly," her father said emphatically. "That's what I'm talking about. I remember my father saying, 'You've got to have a little vinegar,' and you certainly have it. Remember all the things you've done—taking off for California to change the world, becoming a lawyer and taking on so many causes. Sometimes I was exhausted trying to deal with you, but I was always proud. You have what some folks in the South call gumption, and you have it in spades. That's the reason I know you're going to come through this and do something wonderful with your life. Remember what you're passionate about and go after it. And remember your mother and I love you very much."

"Oh, Daddy, thank you. I needed to hear you say those things. I'm trying to remember who I am; I've got to move on. Must find my vinegar," Kendall said as she smiled and squeezed her father's hand.

"You're getting better, and so is Margie. She has a good head on her shoulders. I have really enjoyed our long talks, and she's decided she would like to go into accounting. Isn't that great?"

"You've finally got someone to nurture in your field. I didn't want to do it, but now at least Margie will."

"Yes, and I can help her with a scholarship at GSU that we have set up to help students with financial needs. I believe she will do well," her father said.

"Margie told me today that she's selling the house Toby built to one of his cousins. It's full of bad memories. She and the girls are starting over the same way I am. We're going to have to reinvent our lies after horrific loss. The long conversations we have are comforting. To have someone else to talk to and say exactly how I feel has been such a relief. We can help each other."

All during the night, Kendall thought of the conversation with her parents. Ideas started pouring into her head. It was almost as if she woke up from a long sleep. The next morning when Margie pulled her Explorer into the driveway, Kendall opened the door immediately and greeted them all with hugs. "Margie, leave the girls in the kitchen with Mama. She's baking cookies. Come out on the deck with me. I want to talk to you," Kendall said enthusiastically.

"Okay, I'm all ears. I haven't seen you this excited ever," Margie said as she followed Kendall outside.

"Yes, I'm beginning to get some ideas—a lot of ideas. Remember how I want to start a foundation in Duke's name, and how planning it has helped me not think about my sadness as much? Now I have something else I want to start, and the planning will help us both."

"That's great." Margie tried to say something else, but Kendall was talking too fast.

"For the first time, I'm excited about something I want to do. You know I've had an offer to go back to Atlanta and teach in the law school at Emory University. I'll do that and enjoy it, I'm sure. But that isn't what I'm so excited about. I want to start a nonprofit foundation for women, too. I've become so involved in the epidemic of abuse in our country. This organization will help women through the trauma. But it will also assist them with job training and building self-confidence. And I know exactly who I want to help me—you." Kendall couldn't contain her excitement.

"Gosh, I don't know that I'm qualified for something like that. I don't have a degree yet. Why would you want me?" Margie asked.

"You will know what they're going through; you experienced it. And you will have your degree before too long. You can move to Atlanta with me and get the girls in a good school. When you graduate, you can be my business partner and keep the books. I'm horrible with numbers and remember that you actually enjoy them."

"I do have a little money from the sale of our house—not much, but it will help," Margie said cautiously.

"Margie, whatever you need, I'll make sure you have it. Mama and Daddy have even said we can stay in their big empty house until we figure things out. There's plenty of room. They love you and the girls. We can take our time deciding where to live."

Margie had tears in her eyes. "This is all so wonderful. I know the girls will love it."

"I'll also help you with the girls' education. You've helped me begin to come out of this ordeal. I know I've helped you, too. We are good for each other. You and I have been through unspeakable sadness, but we are survivors. What do you think about that? Yes, I believe for the first time that I'm seeing a way forward for us," Kendall said as she gave Margie a hug. "I can see a meaningful life ahead for us two survivors."

Margie smiled and said, "Okay, we'll move with you to Atlanta. It's a big step for the girls and me. But we'll go with you. Wow, my head is swimming. So much all at once. What made you come up with all these ideas so quickly?"

"I found my vinegar," Kendall said with a laugh. "I'll explain that later. But now I have another surprise for you. It's going to do you, the girls, and me so much good. I have one more important thing to do for Duke. We are going to Hawaii!"

Chapter 100

July 1997

"Look at the clouds! They're so puffy. Like white cotton candy," Lisbeth exclaimed as she pointed out the window for her sisters to look. The three of them kept giggling. They had never been on an airplane, and everything was exciting.

"Mama, this is so much fun. Now will you read *The Little Mermaid* one more time?" Carrie asked.

"We've already read it three times," Margie said. "Don't you ever get tired of hearing about Ariel? And anyway, here comes your dinner. Pull your trays down."

"Oh boy. That looks good. Mama, if I eat all my beans, do I get to eat that whole brownie?" Carrie asked.

"Sure, but then you all have to get some rest. You need your energy to play in the ocean tomorrow," Margie reminded them.

"Before we go to sleep, will you tell us the story of Duke and Hawaii again, like a bedtime story?" Jane Ann asked Kendall.

"Sure, I will," Kendall said, smiling. She had come up with this idea of how to introduce the girls to Hawaii and the story of Duke. She wanted them to know him and love him, too.

The girls quickly ate their meals and turned to Kendall.

"Okay, girls, put those little pillows behind your heads and get comfortable. You must be very still and quiet for me to tell you this story," Kendall began as she tucked a blanket around Carrie.

"There was this little boy named Duke who had dark brown, wavy hair and grew up in Honolulu. That's a city on the island of Oahu, way out in the Pacific Ocean. It's in the state of Hawaii about 3,600 miles from the United States.

"Duke's mother was a beautiful woman named Maya who wore flowers in her hair and colorful long dresses called muumuus. His father John was in the US Navy, and he taught his son all about sports, playing with him whenever he could. Duke was a happy child, and everyone loved him very much. He was tanned by the sun. He was very strong and energetic like you are. Every day he would get up and run to play a game—baseball, basketball, or football. But the thing he loved to do most was go to the ocean. When he was very young, he would run into the waves, splashing water and laughing. When he got older, he learned to ride a surfboard and go out beyond where the waves were breaking." The girls began to nod off, but Kendall kept talking until they fell into a deep sleep. They slept for much of the nine-hour flight from Atlanta to Honolulu.

Kendall took it all in like a breath of fresh air. Something had been lifted off her chest and she could breathe again. Looking at Margie, she could see that she was enjoying everything the same way. Kendall hadn't been this happy since the days before Duke died.

When they finally landed after their long flight, Kendall told the girls there would be a surprise for them. As they stepped off the airplane, they heard ukuleles playing Hawaiian music and saw Duke's childhood friend, Sonny Lum, approaching with leis covering his arm. Dressed in surfing shorts and a silk flowered shirt, he greeted them with hugs. "Aloha, aloha, welcome to Hawaii."

The fragrance of orchids brought back the memory of Kendall's first trip to Honolulu with Duke on their honeymoon. Sonny had met them then, too. With tears in her eyes, she hugged him hard and said, "I can't tell you how happy I am to see you."

Turning to the girls, she said, "This charming man is your surprise. He's going to be our guide while we're on the island. He will show you all the wonderful things and tell you magical stories. He was Duke's best friend and is so much like him." Looking at Sonny, Kendall found that her heart was pounding. She hadn't anticipated how his resemblance to Duke would touch her so deeply. This beautiful, lovely human being was more like Duke than anyone in the world.

Sonny and Duke had grown up together and shared a love for sports and, of course, surfing. Sonny wasn't as tall as Duke, but he had the same muscular, athletic build. Sonny's ancestors had always lived in the islands, and he was full of island lore. He excitedly told stories of ancient Hawaii and almost danced when he acted them out. But his most outstanding feature was his beautiful smile. He was the personification of what Hawaiians call the "aloha spirit." Kendall had loved him from the first time she met him.

Sonny immediately leaned down to talk to the girls at eye level. "Did you know that Hawaii was created by Pele, who is the goddess of volcanoes, fire, and lightning?" The girls looked on in rapt attention, instantly fascinated.

"Do you mean like a princess?" Carrie asked, wide-eyed.

"Oh, she's more than a princess," Sonny said as he walked toward the car, holding Carrie's hand. "I will tell you stories this week about her and how she created the islands."

Kendall smiled as she watched Sonny, thinking of how Duke would have been the same way with the girls, telling stories and making them laugh.

"Sonny, you are so kind to pick us up. I know you're busy with your restaurant," Kendall said as they climbed into his convertible. Kendall sat in the front seat as Sonny drove. In the back, Margie held Carrie in her lap, with Jane Ann and Lisbeth squeezed in beside her.

"Kendall, you know I would do anything for you. I've taken the week off to devote to you and your friends and family. We're going to celebrate Duke's life in a beautiful way. You will love it!" Sonny said with excitement. "Duke was my best friend and a great man. So many here loved him and were proud of him. Yes, we're going to give him a great island celebration."

"I can't thank you enough. It means so much," Kendall said.

"I know you're tired now, and I'm going to take you to your hotel to rest and get settled. But I've taken care of everything. Duke was part of a very tight group growing up; we called ourselves the bruddahs—you know, brothers who loved to surf. We will return his ashes to the sea the Hawaiian way. You will see. We have it all planned," Sonny said with a smile.

Kendall had talked to Sonny several times in the last few months. She had told him that she was planning to bring Duke's ashes back to

Hawaii and sprinkle them in the ocean that he loved. She wanted to visit his family and share the experience with them. That was all she had said, and he had asked if he could take over the planning. Of course, she was happy to let him help. She trusted him completely.

The girls had never been in a convertible before and burst into laughter. They loved the wind blowing their hair, and they threw their arms up to feel the warm breeze that embraced them all. Like most days in Hawaii, it was beautiful and sunny. Sonny drove them to the Kahala Hilton on Waikiki and helped them get into the hotel.

"Okay, my new friends, I want you to get a good night's sleep," Sonny said as he got on one knee to talk to the girls. "Tomorrow morning I'm going to take you to visit Duke's parents. You will love them—beautiful people. Then I will drive you all over the island and tell you the history of Hawaii and how our ancestors came here in boats from far away."

"Yippee, we know about Duke and his parents. I'm going to give them big hugs," Carrie said, waving to Sonny as he drove away.

By the time they arrived at their rooms, the girls had heard too much about the ocean to wait another minute. "Please, please, let's go to the beach," Jane Ann said as she started unpacking her bathing suit. Carrie and Lisbeth did the same. Margie and Kendall agreed, knowing they had no choice.

It was a glorious late afternoon with a light, warm breeze. The sun was beginning to go down over the ocean, turning the sky a pale pink. "Look at the sun. It's a giant beach ball about to drop in the ocean," Lisbeth said, laughing. "It's so pretty!"

"Oh, yes, it's wonderful. Everything is perfect," Kendall said as she and Margie sat down in the sand. The girls took off running, squealing and laughing with delight. It was such a joy to see them experience the ocean for the first time. Hearing the girls' giggles was a tonic to their spirits as they sat watching them splashing and throwing water on one another. It was a beautiful way to end their first day in Hawaii.

Chapter 101

The next morning, Sonny drove them to Duke's childhood home, and as soon as they arrived the girls jumped out and ran to hug Maya and John. "We know all about your son Duke and how he loved Hawaii. We knew you would have a flower in your hair," Carrie said to Maya.

"Oh, I'm so glad to hear that. How did you know I wore a hibiscus in my hair?" Maya asked.

"Oh, Miss Kendall told us all about you," Carrie said.

"Well, I'm so glad she did. Please come in. I have a wonderful breakfast for you. Do you like mangos and pineapples?" Maya asked as she took Carrie's hand.

"I've never had a mango," Carrie said as Maya led her to see her mango tree in the yard.

"Come and sit outside on the lanai and enjoy the warm morning," John said. He pulled out chairs around a wooden table piled with fruit, sweet breads, and an egg casserole with a big arrangement of purple queen protea in the middle. "Maya has worked hard to put out a spread for you this morning. I hope you're hungry. It's a special day to have you visiting, and we love meeting these beautiful young girls. Margie, I know you're proud of them."

Margie nodded her approval. "Oh, yes, I'm proud. And this is a trip of a lifetime for all of us. We are so happy to be here with you."

"We're honored to have you. Girls, I'll finish showing you all the plants after we eat," Maya said as she brought Carrie back to the table. "Tell us what you've done so far."

"We went to the beach last night," Carrie said, jumping up and down. "It was fun. The sun was going down and we played in the water until it was getting dark. But we're going back this afternoon."

"That's great," John said. "Your excitement reminds me of Duke when he was little. He got excited about everything but especially the ocean."

"We know he loved the ocean," Jane Ann said with a big grin, "and so do we. We're just like him."

"I believe you are, little lady," John said.

After a wonderful meal, the girls started running around in the garden. "I love the bananas. Mama, did you see the bananas?" Lisbeth called out. "And you're not going to believe the Bird of Paradise flower. It really looks like a bird with a long beak. Come see it." She waved at Kendall and her mother to come see.

"Yes, it's fascinating." Kendall smiled at Maya. "I think you can see that the girls love your garden."

"I love it, too. It has meant more than it ever has in this last year. I don't know what I would have done without it. There's something about digging in the soil and seeing something grow—some beautiful thing—that gives me some relief. Do you understand?" she asked Kendall, tears filling her eyes.

"Yes, I do. Seeing these innocent little girls begin to find some joy in their lives has been a similar blessing for me. Find the beauty in life wherever you can," Kendall said as she gave Maya a hug. "This has been a wonderful visit. Thank you for the scrumptious breakfast. Come on girls, let's get going. You'll see John and Maya later in the week."

The visit with Duke's parents was bittersweet. Kendall hadn't seen John and Maya since the funeral. It wasn't surprising that they seemed to have aged since Duke's death. But she could see that their spirits were lifted by the girls.

"We have loved having you visit us. Please come back often," Maya said as she gave each of them a hug.

"Oh, we'll be back. This is my family now," Kendall said as she hopped into Sonny's car. "And thank you again for the delicious meal. See you on Saturday."

The week flew by with visits to all the tourist sites—Pearl Harbor, Waimea, Diamond Head, and rides everywhere in the convertible. The girls couldn't get enough of the beach, so they spent many hours enjoying the sun and surf. By Saturday afternoon at the end of the week, everyone was excited to see what Sonny had planned. He had been very secretive about it all, assuring Kendall that everything was going to be wonderful.

When they arrived at Queen's Surf, a favorite surfing spot on Waikiki, they saw a crowd beginning to gather on the beach. John and Maya were already there, looking regal in their traditional Hawaiian dress. Maya was as beautiful as ever in a long muumuu. John wore a colorful shirt but stood ramrod straight, despite being over eighty years old. They proudly introduced Kendall to more aunts, uncles, and cousins than she could ever remember. She was soon greeted by Duke's friends from Punahou—Brad and Elise, Kai and Malia, Tom and Dian, May Ling and Matt. Of course, there was Sonny and his lovely wife Anna and their four children. Then she was meeting the surfing brothers—the bruddahs—the tight-knit group that had spent so many days on this beach surfing as kids. She was overwhelmed. It warmed her heart.

More and more people came onto the beach. Sonny said he didn't know them all. They had come from all over the islands. He then explained to Kendall that this Hawaiian celebration was also done for Duke Kahanamoku when he died in 1968. Sonny said, "I know that nothing would make our Duke happier than to have the same ceremony his hero had when he left this earth."

"Sonny, I can't believe this outpouring of people. I never expected anything like this. It's just wonderful," Kendall said.

At that moment, a murmur went through the crowd. Some people clapped as the popular singer Israel Kamakawiwo'ole was escorted onto the beach, carrying his ukulele. He was an enormous man of Polynesian descent who had the most soothing, beautiful voice. He greeted everyone warmly and finally came up to Kendall. "I am so happy to meet you and to sing at this celebration of Duke's life. It is my honor. I loved him and was proud of him, as were so many in Hawaii." He then sat on a small stage in the center of the beach and began to sing his famous medley, "Somewhere Over the Rainbow" and "What a Wonderful World." It was more than Kendall could take in, and tears spilled down her cheeks.

A Methodist minister who had served at a church that Duke's family attended began a brief eulogy. He recounted some wonderful stories of Duke in his youth. "Duke was such a daredevil. He had no fear. And such curiosity. How many of you remember him when he was just a little tike, climbing a huge Jacaranda tree to see the purple blooms up close? Of course, then he could not get down." Everyone laughed at Duke's boyish pranks.

After the minister read several beautiful verses in the Bible, he ended with the Twenty-third Psalm. His words, "though I walk through the valley of the shadow of death, I will fear no evil," spoke to Kendall. She had feared evil, and it had hurt her; it had taken away her joy in life. But it wouldn't rule her anymore, not while she could re-member beauty and love.

The minister closed in prayer, and Sonny directed those who were participating to get in canoes or on surfboards and follow him into the ocean. He took the canister containing Duke's ashes from Kendall and carried it for her as they got into a canoe. Duke's parents joined her in the canoe with Sonny, and Margie and the girls got in another one nearby. Sonny knew exactly where to go as he paddled them through a channel between the reefs. Looking down, Kendall caught glimpses of fish and turtles swimming underwater. It was magical. They went out beyond the breaking waves. When they finally stopped, Kendall real-ized how many people had followed. Canoes and surfboards formed a large circle around them.

Sonny told her it was time to sprinkle Duke's ashes and say good-bye. Kendall whispered, "I love you and am bringing you back to the ocean you loved so much. I'll be fine. I'm going to let go of my anger and live again." Then she gently took the lid off the canister and began sprinkling his ashes in the ocean. She realized that everyone else was dropping orchids in the water. The ashes and orchids floated gently on the surface, surrounded by people who loved Duke. It was a moment Kendall would always treasure.

When they got back to the shore, the sun was going down and runners were lighting torches around the beach. Sonny had arranged for his restaurant to serve traditional Hawaiian food at a luau. Long tables draped with bright tablecloths were covered with trays piled high with pineapple, papaya, mango, and a medley of vegetables. A man in a grass skirt and yellow shirt trimmed pork from a large bone. A woman served beverages in flute-shaped glasses with little umbrellas for decoration. It was a true feast—nothing was lacking. Israel began strumming his ukulele again, and everyone enjoyed a wonderful time.

That evening, Kendall felt so much gratitude for those lovely people. She had seen so much evil in the previous year that she had almost forgotten about the goodness in the world. She knew right then that, for however many years she had on this earth, she would build her life around the good people and not let the evil have control over her ever again.

—THE END—

Acknowledgments

When I picked up a legal pad in Hawaii many years ago, I had no idea what would happen to the pages I wrote. If the COVID-19 pandemic had not marooned us all in 2020, this book may have never seen the light of day. I am a historian and had a lot to learn about writing fiction. Fortunately, I had encouragement and support from many who were willing to share their expertise. I am grateful for them all.

Some gave expert advice on topics about which I knew very little. Retired Atlanta Police Sergeant Charles Mack helped me with criminal procedure and weapons. Nate Kelsey, who ran security for the Atlanta Braves for nine years and is now Assistant Director of Public Safety and Security at Mercedes Benz Stadium in Atlanta, briefed me on large stadium security. Pete Wellborn, a lawyer, give advice on football rules and legal issues. All three of these men are good friends and played football for my husband at Georgia Tech. Bob Hunter, also a lawyer, did not play football for my husband. He is a Canadian/American who played hockey, but he became our son-in-law over twenty years ago and was willing to give legal advice as well.

I had a brigade of family members who wanted to read my book. Dr. Bo Axel Wilhelm Carlsson and his wife Glenda read it and were thrilled to be the model couple for my Swedish university president and his wife. Gloria Payne, a retired nurse, is enthusiastic about so much in life but especially about reading good stories. Glenda and Gloria are my first cousins and "sisters." My daughter, Dr. Kristin Hunter, who teaches English, politely made suggestions of some things I might do to improve the book. My daughter-in-law, Kelly Curry, was an early reader and encourager from day one. My brother and his wife, Ron and Pam Newton, were also supportive readers. All were sincere and helpful with their comments.

Susan Wellborn, a Georgia Tech engineer who also works as an overqualified assistant for my husband Bill, read this book and was supportive in numerous ways. Friends Carroll and Martha Sterne showed interest from the beginning, read it, and made meaningful suggestions.

Ann Hite, Georgia writer of the masterful Black Mountain series, read my book and became my creative writing teacher. I have laughingly said that I wrote a novel and then took a course to learn how to do it. She reminded me to use my "fiction brain" instead of my "nonfiction brain," to show instead of tell. I am indebted to her for her expertise, her patience, and her cheerful insight.

Ron Greer, a pastoral counselor, author, and close friend, patiently read my book several times. His contribution was of paramount importance. He helped me understand and better explain emotions that accompany great suffering.

Since I wrote my biography of a Civil War heroine, *Suffer and Grow Strong*, five years ago, my publicist Kathie Bennett, President of Magic Time Literary Publicity, has been pushing me to write another book, never dreaming it would be a murder mystery. Nonetheless, she has been an enthusiastic reader. I appreciate her tireless encouragement and good cheer.

I am indebted to Cassandra King Conroy and her late husband Pat for their gracious support of *Suffer and Grow Strong*. Cassandra, an avid fan of football, has read this new book and again offered support. Her words in celebration of it mean more than she will ever know. I am grateful yet again.

I have had nothing but positive experiences with Mary Beth Kosowski, Marsha Luttrell, Allen Wallace, and others at Mercer University Press. After reading my first draft of this novel, MUP Director Marc Jolley was not shy about telling me that I had some things to learn about writing fiction. I had to admit he was correct. Now, after many rewrites, I can say that I am thankful for his guidance, candor, and courage to tell the truth. And despite his honesty, we remain good friends today.

I give my love and gratitude for their constant support to our daughter Kristin Hunter, her husband Bob, and their daughters Evelyn and Claire; and to our son Billy, his wife Kelly, and their five sons—

Alex, Elliot, Brett, Jack, and Jamie. As a mother and grandmother, I am truly blessed.

My husband Bill answered my questions about football, proofread for errors, and encouraged me daily during the long months of COVID-19. He was by my side throughout the long process of writing and re-writing, giving me encouragement and support all along. I give my love and thanks to him always.

Finally, to my readers, who enthusiastically read my book *Suffer and Grow Strong* and made me think I could do it again, THANK YOU.